RETURN

TO

ME

RETURN

TO

ME

by Justina Chen

LITTLE, BROWN AND COMPANY

New York   Boston

Little, Brown and Company

Hachette Book Group
237 Park Avenue, New York, NY 10017
Visit our website at lb-teens.com

Little, Brown and Company is a division of Hachette Book Group, Inc.
The Little, Brown name and logo are trademarks of Hachette Book Group, Inc.

The publisher is not responsible for websites (or their content)
that are not owned by the publisher.

First Paperback Edition: July 2014
First published in hardcover in January 2013 by Little, Brown and Company

Library of Congress Cataloging-in-Publication Data

Chen, Justina.
    Return to me / by Justina Chen. — 1st ed.
        p. cm.
    Summary: Always following her parents' wishes and ignoring her psychic inner voice takes eighteen-year-old Rebecca Muir from her beloved cottage and boyfriend on Puget Sound to New York City, where revelations about herself and her family help her find a path to becoming the architect she wants to be.
    ISBN 978-0-316-10255-1 (hc)—ISBN 978-0-316-10258-2 (pb)
    [1. Self-actualization (Psychology)—Fiction.   2. Architecture—Fiction.   3. Family problems—Fiction.   4. Moving, Household—Fiction.   5. Clairvoyance—Fiction.   6. Love—Fiction.]   I. Title.
    PZ7.C4181583Ret 2013
    [Fic]—dc23   2012001549

10 9 8 7 6 5 4 3 2 1

RRD-C

Printed in the United States of America

For Baba,
Dr. Robert T. N. Chen,
my father,
who is rooted in
Integrity and all that is
Right and True.

And for Tyler and Sofia,
believe in Love.
I do.

Part One

For the most part things never get built the way
they were drawn.
—*Maya Lin, artist and architect*

Chapter One

I f you believed my so-called psychic of a grandmother, she predicted that I would almost die. Her eerie, creepy forewarning made no difference at all. I was seven. I still jumped into the murky lake. I still dropped to its mossy bottom. I still almost drowned. Moments before Dad saved me, my arms had become blurry fronds far, far in front of me, as if I had already faded into a ghost.

Ever since that brush with death, I've hated fairy tales where spindles could be murder weapons, a bride could be killed for opening a locked door, and women in my family supposedly could see the future. What good was a sixth sense if life itself could derail your best-laid plans? Like after spring break in my senior year. That's when I almost drowned again—only this time, in disbelief.

"We're moving with you," Mom had announced without

looking up from her massive, post-vacation to-do list at the kitchen table.

"You mean moving me, right?" I gulped, breathing hard as I tried desperately to safeguard my future.

Why bother? Once Mom made up her mind, not one miracle or oracle could change it.

Case in point: her answer, "No, *we're* moving, too." She tucked a strand of flat-ironed hair back into its designated spot behind her ear, then drew an emphatic tick on her list. No doubt Mom was checking off yet another item: Destroy daughter's college experience.

"You can't come with me to Columbia!"

"Rebecca Kaye Muir, this move is great for your dad's career." Mom's voice had shot over mine, bullet to bull's-eye, in a tone designed to quell any teenage uprising. Her blue-eyed glare included my younger brother, Reid. He had dared to groan when it registered that Dad was quitting what must be every boy's dream job: head honcho of a new game company. For about three weeks, Reid and I limped around our house like the living dead, my brother too listless to read a single one of his fantasy novels, and me too disappointed to enjoy the final laid-back weeks of high school.

None of this alarmed or deterred Mom, though. Life according to my mother's accounting followed a simple principle: A bigger opportunity was a better opportunity. And Dad's deliciously high-powered job offer represented a welcome end to his start-up-business nonsense.

So now, two days before my family exodus for the East

Coast, my dad and I were enjoying one final campout in my treehouse. Our once-a-summer tradition had begun when we moved to Lewis Island, a twenty-minute ferry ride from Seattle. The only change in our fifteen-year tradition had been to swap our old, dark tent for a newly built treehouse when I turned ten.

I woke this morning to Dad waving the remains of our half-eaten bag of Cheetos under my nose. "Breakfast?" he asked, crunching a cheese curl noisily in my ear.

"Thanks," I said, and grabbed one, even though I wasn't particularly hungry. Only then did I gaze up into the cloud-filled skylight. Last night, stargazing was as much an act of futility as imagining some semblance of independence at college in two months. It was all too easy to picture my mom "dropping in" for a visit because she was "in the neighborhood." Before I knew it, she'd be color-coding my future roommate's binders and rearranging my closet into ready-made outfits. The overcast night sky had flattened into a slate of mourning-dove gray. I rolled onto my side to face Dad. "I'm going to miss this place."

"Trust me, you'll be so busy at college, you won't even think twice about any of this," he said, waving one arm as if to brush away my treehouse, my home, and my life as I had always known it.

Ninety-nine percent of the time, I agreed with Dad, but on the topic of my treehouse, we disagreed. It probably sounds stupid, but we hadn't even moved and I was already homesick for this tiny nest that housed all my architecture books and sketchbooks. The bunting I had sewn and strung above the windows with my favorite paint swatches. The photos of me flanked by all my male cousins and uncles. And best of all, the models I'd constructed at the summer camp I attended two years ago through the architecture school at the University of Washington—the birdhouse, artist studio, and modern shack. These were the projects that made me fall in love hard and fast with architecture the same way I fell for Jackson.

Jackson.

My heart contracted at the thought of breaking up with him in a few hours. Like everyone says, long-distance relationships are impossible, especially in college. Still, I couldn't even think about ending it with Jackson without tearing up.

Not now. Not yet.

I cleared my throat to ward off the threat of tears and managed a wry smile for my father. "No offense, but I would have been more excited if I was going to college by myself."

"None taken." Dad smiled indulgently at me, his gentle brown eyes crinkling at the corners. Other than a few strands of gray along his temples, at forty-five he looked virtually the same as the broad-shouldered high school football star he'd been. Days ago, Mom had removed the photos of Dad's good old days from his man-cave office and mummified them in biodegradable newsprint for the cross-country move. My treehouse was one of the last rooms to be dismantled today, according to her well-executed moving plan. Dad continued, "I totally understand that a fresh start is something we all need at one point or another. But you know how your mom gets."

We both rolled our eyes, then grinned at each other even as irritation burned my throat. Dad was right; it'd take an apocalyptic disaster to change a single detail once Mom had charted his new corporate career, my college decision, our family move.

"At least I talked your mom into moving to New Jersey instead of New York. That'll give you some breathing room, right?" Dad said, crumpling the empty bag of Cheetos before tossing it carelessly onto the floor from the warmth of his sleeping bag.

"You have no idea how much I appreciate that," I said fervently, only now eating my cheese curl.

The clock my grandpa George had given me when I was recuperating from my near drowning ticked loudly in the silence that followed my crunching. As I listened to the faint drumbeat of time, I recalled how one of the fairy houses I had woven from twigs had blown off Grandpa's houseboat deck and into the lake. Dad alone was with me, and he had said, "Just let it go."

But I had jumped into the murky green water, so completely focused on rescuing my creation that I forgot I couldn't swim, forgot my grandmother's prediction.

"Dad!" I had screamed before I drifted downward. He reached me fast, diving into the deep to grab me.

An idea began to form now, and Dad was once again the one I sought to rescue me. I sat up in my sleeping bag. There just might be a way to salvage the beginning of my college experience. Dad had rented a temporary apartment in Manhattan two months ago to start his job while Reid and I finished school here. That apartment was going to be empty, conveniently and blissfully empty. Why not live in Dad's apartment in

New York rather than in our New Jersey house until freshman orientation?

"Hey, Dad," I said, throwing off my sleeping bag, "could I crash in your apartment before school starts, since you'll be with Mom and Reid anyway?"

"Well, you know how your mom gets when people change her plans." Dad's voice was hushed as though Mom could overhear what we were discussing, even though she was back in the main house and well out of earshot. "Her and her lists."

That quiet, confidential tone reminded me of how it had always been: Dad and me, conspiring against Mom. Dad allowing me to leap off a whirling merry-go-round even though I had fallen from it the day before. Dad buying me an enormous ice cream cone a half hour before dinner. And like a refrain in our duet of rebellion, Dad would say with a puckish grin, *Just don't tell Mom.*

"Yeah," I said, even as I felt the sting of disappointment. "Mom and her lists."

"Look, New Jersey won't be so bad for a few weeks." He grabbed the iPhone that he had left by his pillow, to check a chiming alarm. "In fact, while I'm thinking about it, there's an architect there that Uncle Adam's been using for a couple of his new development projects. I'll bet you could still score a great summer internship with him—Sam Stone."

"Sam Stone?" My voice went squeaky with enthusiasm. Shadowing an architect famous for his mammoth, cutting-edge corporate campuses—the kind Dad's family built, the kind I wrote about designing in my college applications—was nothing short of an oasis in this desert of a summer. "Really?"

Dad laughed. "Sound good?"

"Sounds awesome," I said, grinning back at him.

"Great! I'll set you up."

I had no doubt that Dad would follow through. After all, when he moved to Manhattan without us, he had promised, "I'll be flying back every other weekend, even if it's hard for me." Dad climbed out of his sleeping bag and stretched so strenuously, I actually heard his spine crack. He winced and rubbed his lower back. "I'm getting old."

"Come on. You're going to be one of the youngest dads at college."

"College." He shook his head while ambling to the door. "I can't believe I've got a kid in college." Bending down, he hoisted his duffel bag easily onto his shoulder and wedged his hand into the front pocket of his now-wrinkled chinos. "Okay, kiddo, gotta catch my flight."

"Wait, you're leaving?" I said, surprised. "I thought you were flying out with us tomorrow night."

Dad rubbed the stubble on his cheeks with the back of his hand. "I've got a ton of work. And since your mom's got this under control, I thought I'd take an earlier flight home and get ready for you guys."

Home? Since when did New York become home to Dad? Still, he was right. Mom had this move—just as she had all our vacations and summer programs and school schedules—graphed out in nice, neat schedules of deadlines and deliverables. No wonder Dad had already escaped to Manhattan. The same freeing effect of living three thousand miles away from my mother was why I'd chosen Columbia over UW, my decision made in March, before I met Jackson.

We passed the moving truck dominating the driveway and made our way to Dad's rental car out in the street, miraculously without attracting Mom's attention. A week from today, our belongings would be trucked to the other side of the country. Thanks to Mom's efficiency, Dad's car had been shipped eight weeks ago so that he had transportation upon arrival. Now Dad slid into the rental and rolled down the window. "Hey, your college experience is still going to be great."

"How can you say that?"

Dad adjusted the rearview mirror. "I'll tell you what: Why don't I use miles to fly Jackson out for a visit after school starts?"

"What?" I blinked at him, uncomprehending. "I thought you said long-distance relationships are impossible to maintain."

He held up both hands defensively. "Hey, all I'm saying now is . . . they *are* hard. But you never know."

Astonished, I wanted to ask Dad to repeat this unexpected manna of parental approval. Before, on the topic of Jackson, my parents had serenaded me with all the reasons to break up, harmonizing perfectly with Dad's melodic "A little freedom in college is a good thing" and Mom's drumbeat about "Jackson's lack of plans" and "Look where that lackadaisical attitude landed your grandpa George."

"Dad, I was going to break up with Jackson today."

"Think about what'll make you happy. That's all that really matters."

Dad and I smiled at each other, back in sync as coconspirators. Right as I was about to thank Dad for his offer, I heard a hard, racking, shuddering wail. A wheezing intake of breath so pained, it sounded as if a woman was suffocating. I recognized this prickling down my neck, this deep-gut knowing, even if I had refused to acknowledge it in years.

"What's up?" Dad asked, concerned.

As always, I gritted my teeth against the gathering vision— now I saw a wood door, gnarled and knotted; now I felt the old-growth fir, worn smooth like resignation. I forced a placid smile. "Nothing," I lied brightly, even as I commanded myself to stop dreaming the way I have at these first telltale signs of a premonition, squelching them the way I'd learned to these last eleven years. But before I could spit out hasty sentences, spoken fast and loud to drown that whispered voice, there it was: *Do not move to New Jersey.*

I swallowed hard, nauseated from battling this overwhelming sense of foreboding.

As though Dad guessed I was having a vision, he said, "See you in two days," then reversed out of the driveway, all haste and hurry now. Visions, miracles, predictions—none of these Dad believed. Not against-the-odds company turnarounds and certainly not near-death experiences, not even when the paramedics told him after my close call in the lake, "It's a miracle that your daughter's still alive."

Even though my stomach was roiling and a cold sweat

beaded my forehead, I sprinted after my father. Gravel kicked up on my calves, pinpricks of pain. Urgency I couldn't explain propelled me forward. "Dad, wait!"

But Dad's car roared away. All that remained was a tuft of putrid smoke from his exhaust, then silence. The same silence in my hospital room that followed Grandma Stesha's accusation aimed at my father: "How could you let Reb swim after I warned you that she would drown?" The same silence after I admitted to my parents, "I dreamed it, too." The same silence after Dad abruptly left that antiseptic room with a disgusted snort. As the door clicked shut behind him, my mother glared at my grandmother, blaming her.

"Reb!" I could practically feel Mom's frustration mount from inside our soon-to-be-emptied house. "Where are you?"

Dad had the right idea. If Mom wanted this move, she could orchestrate the entire project down to how boxes were packed, the way they were labeled, the treehouse she was about to strip, the lives she disrupted. I pressed my hand hard to my chest to imprison every wail, every doubt, and every premonition deep inside me.

Unexpectedly, as though in answer to my *SOS-save-me-from-my-mother* plea, I heard a familiar rumble down the road.

Jackson.

Chapter Two

Sometimes I felt like I was dating two guys: Jackson and his car. I'm serious. The 1965 Mustang, a gift from Jackson's parents for his seventeenth birthday, doubled as a nice bribe to sweeten the move to Seattle in the beginning of his junior year. When he drove, we went one speed: sexy. If I closed my eyes when I was riding shotgun, I could smell the prairie grass of Jackson's Iowa even though we never ventured much farther than Vancouver to the north and Portland to the south. Three hours either way was our bubbled universe, and that bubble was about to burst the next day.

I looked away from the window and back at Jackson, who was staring at me intensely. That smoldering instant reminded me of my first good look at him four months ago, in March. There we were, on our separate spring breaks, sharing the same air space in a hotel lobby. There he was, barrel-chested and wide-shouldered, more sturdy than stocky, and his legs . . . The words *highly defined* barely described his muscle-man quads and calves. And here we were, together ever since.

"You're quiet," Jackson said, placing one hand atop mine as we idled at the stop sign at my neighborhood crossroad.

The conversation I'd been dodging for weeks stirred between us like a caged animal slamming against the metal slats for its freedom. I heard Mom now, chiming with annoying clockwork that it was time to break up. But Dad's voice—the voice of inspirational business speeches that could rally game developers who'd been coding around the clock for weeks—lured me with the tantalizing thought that long-distance love could be worth the work and worth the wait. So why not try?

Before Jackson shifted the car back into gear, he looked at me hard, as though searching for something that had already gone missing. I still wasn't used to his attention. Boys rarely spared me a flyby glance. After all, at five foot nothing with mousy brown hair, I wasn't anything special—unlike my best friends Shana, with criminally long legs, and Ginny, whose exotic looks had caught the fleeting attention of a casting agent when she was nine.

"So . . . I have something I want you to see, Rebel."

Rebel.

I swallowed and looked away from him so I wouldn't break into tears. Only Jackson used that nickname, as though it were his personal password to me. How he had known that I had never felt like my father's Rebecca or everyone else's Reb, I could never quite understand. Even if that nickname belonged to a wild girl who did whatever she pleased, I secretly reveled every time Jackson used it.

Damn it, why had I chosen Columbia when UW was right here, a stone's throw to Viewridge Prep, where Jackson was enrolled for another year?

"Trust me?" asked Jackson, his warm hand settling on my thigh as I curled on my side in the passenger seat, leaning toward him.

All I could do was nod. Yes, I trusted him. Yes, let's hurtle straight past these next endless months, straight past Manhattan. Yes, aim for the future, and never, never, never stop.

Finally, after driving through the dense, green heart of Lewis Island, navigating down winding streets I'd never seen before and, frankly, never needed to see, Jackson parked on the side of the potholed road. He killed the engine, then pushed his door open. Cold air surged inside, a tangible reminder that while the rest of the country sweltered, summer had yet to come to Seattle.

"It's freezing out there," I said. "Polar bears would protest."

He leaned toward me, eyebrows cocked up: *For real?* Then he said, "You're going to have to toughen up if you want to survive the East Coast winters with me, Rebel."

Forget the "Rebel." It was the "with me" that warmed me now and made me seriously consider what Dad had offered: his tacit approval if I chose to stay with Jackson over Mom's wishes.

That "with me" convinced me to open the door and follow him outside. The wind rushed me, furious, and I staggered back.

"Okay, cold," I gasped.

Jackson was rounding the hood of the car, already sliding out of his leather jacket. "You aren't going to last five minutes in winter."

"No," I said when he handed me his coat. "I don't want you to be cold, too."

"I'm a guy. I never get cold."

"Tell that to Shackleton."

"You're a nut," he said, and tugged me to his chest, wrapping his jacket around me like wings. I burrowed in, inhaled deeply, and smelled sweet saltiness. Call me odd, but deodorant is overrated on Jackson. After a long bike ride, he smells like a guy who can take on the world. I stood on my tiptoes and kissed his neck and felt his question beneath my lips: "Did I tell you that I like my women smart?"

"Women?" I said, pulling back and stabbing my finger in his chest. "As in plural?" *Stab.* "As in a stable of women?" *Stab, stab.* "As in a plethora of women?"

"You must be warmer now," he said, rubbing his chest.

After days of rain, the air smelled clean and moist. The clouds parted, revealing the sun. The warmth felt good on my face.

"This," I said, stretching my arms sunward, "is almost better than being kissed."

"Oh, yeah?" he said, challenged the way I knew he'd be. He kissed me the way I wanted: long and lingering and very, very thorough. The sweet urgency of his lips, the slow stroke of his tongue along mine, made me wobble, unbalanced. That kiss-induced tippiness only made Jackson grin wickedly at me, confident that nothing bettered his kiss. He grabbed my hand and led me down a paved path, fringed on either side with purple-flowered vinca and feathery ferns.

"Close your eyes," Jackson said.

It was too much work to stay crabby after a kiss like that—even after a drive that had lasted an eternity during what I might add, yet again, was One of Our Last Hours Together.

Finally, he let me open my eyes at the edge of a small pond I never knew existed, lined with tall, striated reeds and nestled within a ring of trees. In the middle of the pond floated a tiny dock, sized for two people, complete with crank and steering wheel. Two ropes connected the dock to the shoreline, and Jackson began winching the dock toward us.

"What is this place?" I asked, my voice quiet, as though I knew this was a special space.

"A bird-watcher's sanctuary." He opened the gate and waved me aboard. "Your dock awaits."

"Are we allowed here?"

"Remember? It's better to ask for forgiveness than permission. Anyway, my dad's listing it on Monday. So think of it as us providing some quality control to maintain my dad's carefully cultivated reputation as the leading waterfront real estate agent in the Pacific Northwest." Jackson lifted his eyebrows. "So, my badass girlfriend, what do you say?"

"You had me at *badass*," I said before I sashayed onto the

dock, glancing over my shoulder with the sultriest look I could muster.

Mission accomplished. Jackson cleared his throat. I gave silent thanks to Shana for making Ginny and me practice a billion expressions and struts for her photo shoots.

Jackson navigated us to the center of the pond, and once there, I gasped because I finally understood why he had brought me here—not to see this dock or admire the birds. Hidden among the trees was a tiny house, all wood and windows and built upon stilts.

"This is so you," he said, standing behind me with his arms wrapped around me.

"It's what a treehouse wants to be when it grows up," I said, leaning against him.

"I still don't see why you want to build corporate offices."

I sighed. We'd had this conversation countless times before. No matter how often I tried to explain that commercial work was a lot more financially prudent than residential work and that Dad's family was expecting me to be the resident architect in their real estate development business, I knew Jackson wouldn't understand. He was forever pointing out that Dad hadn't worked at the family firm since he was in business school.

So now I gestured to the pint-size house and said, "I've got to see it."

"First, we should talk," Jackson countered.

Just like that, I forgot about the house; such was the power of those three dreaded words: *We should talk*. If you have good news, do you preface it with "We should talk"? No. You say,

"Guess what?" Or, "You won't believe this!" *We should talk* is what doctors say when they're about to break it to you that you have a few months to live. It's what a boyfriend says when he's about to tell you that your romance had a shelf life that expired yesterday. But now I wasn't so sure anymore that I needed, or wanted, to break up.

"How can I talk? My teeth are chattering," I answered with a cheeky smile to buy time while I thought.

Jackson looked at me long and hard, as though he could hear me weigh the sure risks of staying together versus the unsure rewards of attempting and failing. Then he said, "Everybody says long-distance relationships are impossible. That it's totally stupid to try."

Wasn't that what Ginny and Shana—who both had a lot more experience in the Guy Department than I did, with their endless buffet of boys—had been telling me for the last month?

"But is it so stupid?" Jackson asked gruffly.

Here I was, alone at an unfamiliar crossroads in an unfamiliar neighborhood of a serious relationship. To the west was here, now, Seattle, the impossibilities of long distance. To the east was the future, New York, and being prudent and practical about my future plans, which had never included going off to college with a high school boyfriend. And through it all, like an aria of abandonment, I heard the crying again, the high-pitched heartbreak. On the verge of throwing up, I only managed to keep my arms at my sides instead of clenched over my stomach.

"What?" Jackson asked, watching me carefully, as if he sensed my crazy, conflicted emotions.

Part of me wanted to tell Jackson now about the inconsolable weeping, the inkling that something horrible would happen with this move. But tell him now and he would think I was an official nutcase. I'd be yet one more casualty of my family curse: Every woman on my mother's side has ended life alone, all spinsters. That is, except Mom. Case in point: Consider Grandpa George, the portrait of loyalty, who was there for every one of my performances and play-offs. Even he bolted when Grandma Stesha heeded her "calling" to lead tours of woo-woo weirdness to inexplicable rock formations and purported fairy circles around the world. Not even Mom faulted Grandpa for the divorce when she was about to set off for college.

But then there was Mom's overriding "why bother?" attitude about Jackson, a boy who didn't have a short list of colleges. The only college decision he had made was to refuse to consider the Naval Academy, which his dad was pushing him to attend. And even louder, I heard Grandma Stesha's conviction about our family curse: No man was capable of staying at our sides, not when generations of our women could predict their heart wounds, prophesy their futures, see through their lies.

So, as usual, I stamped on the sparks of my foreboding and spoke in a torrent of words, forcing them out so fast I staved off any vision: "I'm afraid it's not going to work out. I mean, it was hard enough to see you as it was—and this was with us living an hour from each other. So how're we going to keep close with three time zones and three thousand miles separating us? How?"

"Skype, text, IM. You name it, we'll try it."

I knew what he was suggesting—we buck conventional

wisdom and prove the improbable: Eighteen-year-old kids can fall in love, forever love. Jackson leaned down then to kiss me, a tender pledge: *I will be true.*

Resisting that was impossible. I threw my arms around Jackson and pressed close, my chest against his, missing him badly. His hand cupped my neck and he kissed me, imprinting his lips on mine.

Just then my phone chimed. Without looking at the screen, I knew it was Mom, with her impeccably timed interruption at the faintest hint of arousal, no different from the night of my first date with Jackson. I knew she was going to remind me that it was time to come home, time to step back into the antiseptic life she had orchestrated for me, which meant clearing our damned home of dust balls and clearing my life of Jackson. I ignored the phone and deepened our kiss, as if I could truly lose myself. It was Jackson who stepped away, breathing hard.

"Not yet," I moaned.

The phone chirped insistently. I sighed, irritated at my mom—even if, in some small way that I refused to inspect too carefully, I felt a tiny bit of relief at this reprieve from having the breakup talk with Jackson. Dad's unexpected approval had thrown my decision off kilter.

Jackson raked his fingers through his hair, looking frustrated before he managed a wry grin. He was always so Zen, my Jackson. For now he pulled me close, leaned his forehead against mine, and whispered, "Thanksgiving, and you'll be back. November isn't that long away, Rebel."

I nodded and leaned against him but didn't tell him about

the plane tickets Dad had offered. Jackson's fingers combed through my hair, making my scalp tingle with pleasure. The feeling almost made me want to grow my hair out, if it meant having his fingers for a few moments longer, that gentle downward pull, that melting along my spine.

Maybe I should tell Jackson, *Yes. Why not try?*

The phone rang again.

"Geez! What's her deal?" I groused, frustrated.

"Well, your mom was the one who asked me to come early so we could hang out together."

"Why?"

"It's a surprise. . . ."

So we climbed back into Jackson's car and drove home, my hand in his until he needed to shift the gear. Only then did Jackson move my hand to rest on his thigh, and squeeze me gently, as though he wanted me to feel him even as he let me go.

Chapter Three

As soon as Jackson pulled into my driveway, my two very best friends skipped down the front steps, waving at us. Six years ago, our mother-daughter book club was formed—Bookster Babes, so called because all our names were inspired by literature. Ginny for Virginia Woolf. Mine from the gothic novel *Rebecca*. And Shana from a torrid seventies romance novel, which the three of us surreptitiously read, graphic sex scenes and all. Now whenever Shana falls for a guy, Ginny and I tease her, "Yeah, but is he 'Ohhhhh, Ruark!'"

Over the last six years, we've held a Bed & Bookfest celebration, always at my home on Lewis Island, always once a season, always overnight. We have never skipped a single meeting. And apparently, we weren't going to miss this last one.

"Surprise," Jackson said, and leaned over to kiss me a

moment before my girlfriends yanked me out of his car. "I'll see you tomorrow."

"You don't have to drive me to the airport."

His look—*Are you crazy?*—melted me.

"Okay, Jackson, she's all ours now," announced Shana, sweeping her hair out of her eyes to mock-glower at him. He laughed, a sound that made me prematurely homesick for him. I was glad we'd have until tomorrow to say good-bye. Whether it was our final good-bye, my girlfriends wanted to know as soon as we stumbled through my treehouse door, leaving our moms in the main house until the evening book discussion.

"Hurry," said Shana, slinging her pink sleeping bag onto the floor. "We have got to talk."

"Not another talk," I groaned as I wedged my sleeping bag between hers and Ginny's. Then, following Shana's lead, I flopped onto my stomach.

"Oh, good." She brushed her long bangs out of her wide blue eyes to study me approvingly. "You broke it off with Jackson. What'd you say?"

"We didn't break it off exactly." I hid my face on my arms so I wouldn't see Shana and her five feet seven of long, lean disapproval. If left to her, Jackson would have been dispensed with weeks ago in a swift, clean text. Her formidable time-management skills were acquired not from juggling homework, like the rest of us, but from juggling boys. It wasn't unheard of for her to log a six-mile run early on Saturday morning with one boy, study with another at ten, and cap the day off with a late-night movie with a third. After her record five-boy day, Shana had called me up to complain: "That was exhausting. There's only so much flirting you can do before you realize you just can't have another tongue in your mouth."

"Shana! Gross!" I had protested.

But she was adamant. "It's true."

"Well, why not?" Shana demanded now. "It so does not make sense to stay together. You're going to meet a ton of guys in New York. And the minute you're gone, girls are going to pounce on him."

"Nice, Shana. Really nice." Ginny reached down from her perch on the window seat to squeeze my hand. Her glossy brown hair striated with light streaks fell over hazel eyes that tilted at the corners, and I could completely understand why my mom marveled over how beautiful mixed-race kids were whenever she saw Ginny.

"What? He goes to my high school, not yours. I see the way girls look at him. And she should know that they're so going to make their move." Shana pointed her finger at me before crawling into her sleeping bag. The pitfall of being so thin (not that I would know) is being perpetually cold. "Look, wouldn't you rather know?"

There it was, the question Grandma Stesha had put to my mom in my hospital room when I nearly drowned, and again two years ago before she left to launch her tour of fairy sites in Scotland: "But, Betsy darling. Isn't it better to know?"

Maybe I wanted to celebrate my inner ostrich and bury my head and forget how frightening it had been to know at seven that I might drown. Maybe I didn't want to know what was going to happen in the future any more than my mother did when she tucked me tight in the hospital bed after my near death. As though she didn't trust me to escape fate or tempt curse, she had ordered me, "Stop dreaming."

And so I did.

The story Shana was spinning now of Jackson cheating on me was my nightmare. The rare times the women in my family— Grandma Stesha and her three sisters, Mom and her two— gathered, the conversations were filled with stories lamenting their shared curse: Not a single one aside from my mother had a soul mate. That was not a future I wanted to inherit.

"Do you guys ever get the feeling . . . that something's not right?" I asked tentatively.

An uncomfortable frown flitted across Ginny's face, a look she wore the rare times I broached the topic of my maternal line's purported sixth sense. "You're just having moving jitters," she said, zipping her sleeping bag to her chin with one efficient tug. "That's all."

"You mean something not right, like, with Jackson?" Shana nodded sagely, as though I had finally seen the light. "I mean, you're only eighteen. You're starting college and, let's face it, that means it's fishing season. Besides, we're way too young to be this serious about anyone, even during college." She flipped onto her side, propping her chin on her hand. "It's not like you're going to marry him."

That echo of Mom was eerie: *You're way too young.* Irritation snaked up my skin. Why was everyone ringing my wedding bells when I hadn't even slept with Jackson?

I asked, "Why are you so sure I should break up with him?"

"Because first," Shana responded, now sitting up cocooned in her sleeping bag, "your mom might have gotten married because she was knocked up at twenty-four. But most people don't. And if they do, they grow out of each other. And, hello, you're going to college; Jackson's got another year left in high school. What are you going to talk about? Prom?"

Those remarks might have stung once, except for two things: Shana was right. There were my parents, superstars in their careers. Dad, a producer at his first game company in San Francisco, and Mom, a publicist at a start-up cell phone company in Seattle. All of that derailed with the two pink lines on the pregnancy test that was me. And second, Shana had given this rant for female independence a million times.

I stage-whispered to Ginny, "Watch out. She's about to invoke the head shave." Together, Ginny and I intoned: "We'll shave your head if you get married before you're thirty-five. Go see the world."

"Well, my parents are right. That's what we should do. See the world before we settle down." Shana grinned before whipping out her camera to take a candid shot of us. "But I plan to shoot the world."

Ever since her father gave Shana her first camera when she turned five, she'd vowed to make her living somehow with her photography, like her father wished he could but didn't dare. She couldn't understand his hesitation any more than mine to commit to the same kind of risky livelihood with treehouses. The last thing I wanted was to incite that particular monologue

25

now, so I stayed quiet while she lowered her camera to check the photograph. If I thought she'd forgotten her train of thought, I was wrong. Shana continued without looking up from her camera, "So tell him that you want to have an open relationship. That way, if you want to date other guys, you can."

"Other guys? I didn't even want to date Jackson, remember?" I said, flipping over to my back to stare at the moody sky.

Ginny smirked as she stood up, hands on her hips. "Uh, yeah, because you totally obsessed about that for two weeks." Her voice grew high as she swung her hips in time to each point: "I can't date The Boy! The Boy's a grade younger than me. The Boy lives an hour away. The Boy mountain bikes. Who the hell mountain bikes? I don't."

"I said that?"

Both of them nodded.

Shana actually threw her sleeping bag off, frustration overheating. "Come on, it's totally crazy to orient your entire life toward a guy who might be around for another month. Two, tops. Especially when he's come out and said that he won't go to a college just because it's near you. And—"

I interrupted, waving my arms at Shana. "Hello? I'm not orienting my life toward him. I'm starting college away from him. That's the whole point. Right, Ginny?"

Ginny shifted uneasily on the window seat. "Sometimes, to tell you the truth, I just wonder what the whole point of trying is, especially when it's hard. Look what happened to my parents. . . ."

A year after we formed the Bookster Babes, Ginny's father

had been diagnosed with late-stage prostate cancer. "Does everyone think kids are dumb?" Ginny had asked me the morning after one of our Bed & Bookfests while we were drawing. Her paper was covered with angry girls with grim lines for mouths; mine, with a series of Gothic treehouses. "I can hear what the doctors say about Dad."

"You should go home today. He's going to die soon," I had pronounced, speaking without realizing it until Ginny slashed an angry crayon line across my drawing. Even then, I barely recalled what I had intoned like an oracle, the words pouring out of me without thought.

"Take it back," she hissed.

But it was too late.

Two days afterward, as if my prophecy had cursed her father, he was dead. Ever since, I have been afraid of uttering aloud a single feeling, the slightest inkling, in case my visions were even more potent than my grandmother believed.

Ginny broke our silence now by plunking down a plate of thick brownies she'd snuck in without us noticing. "It's time for chocolate."

Of the three of us, only Ginny could cook a gourmet meal, but her baking went unrivaled. Not even the best bakeries around town could touch her pastries. Still, Dad thought she was wasting her life going to the Culinary Institute of America in the Hudson Valley rather than a "real" college: "That's called a retirement activity, not a retirement plan." I had to agree. Baking was as practical as me building treehouses for a living or staying with my high school boyfriend.

"Can you taste the coconut and curry?" Ginny asked with an eager expression.

I nodded my head, surprised at the heat and texture on my tongue. "Yeah."

The unexpected flavor of Ginny's brownie filled me with tearful yearnings. I didn't want to go. I didn't want to move. I didn't want to miss out on a single moment of life with my friends. It wasn't only Jackson who I didn't want to leave. I didn't want to say good-bye to my friends or my home, my sanctuary, my history. Lewis Island was everything I had ever known, the only place I'd ever lived.

The morning's anguished cry rang clear in my head. Part of me wanted to say something to my girlfriends; part of me wanted to know what was causing that animal wail. But I swatted away the real danger of probing too deeply and focused on the bittersweet dessert instead.

Chapter Four

Being the first girl in four generations of Muir men had its perks. Those lumberjacks who felled the ancient Northwest forests became Seattle's first real estate developers. They spawned an industry. They spawned a fortune. They spawned boys. So when Dad's father died fifteen years ago, he bequeathed the Lewis Island property into my parents' care under the condition that I inherit it on the day of my marriage. My dad told me later that my grandfather had his heart set on seeing me—his sole granddaughter—wed in this cottage, the one he had built as a weekend love nest for himself and my grandmother. Not a single person in the Muir family contested my inheritance or our move here immediately after my grandfather died.

The next morning when I awoke a few minutes before six, for one lazy second I considered rolling over, burrowing into my sleeping bag. But I wanted to say good-bye to my home in private. So I crept around my friends, grabbed my denim jacket off the door hook, and slid into my sneakers on the welcome mat outside.

As I set off for the beach, I cast a backward glance at my treehouse and swallowed hard. As frivolous as treehouses were, I loved this treasure box, barely visible in the forest unless you knew where to look. There was something whimsical and secretive about small spaces, however impractical they were. And this treehouse was my heart realized into four walls: snug, safe, and hidden.

Back when I was ten, my parents sold the very last of Mom's stock options from her job at Synergy to remodel the cottage. The architectural drawings enthralled me—long scrolls of paper detailing the front and back elevations of the house. Our architect, Peter Nakamura, wore a never-changing uniform of form-fitting black T-shirt and relaxed black jeans. His one accessory, the black Moleskine notebook he always carried. One morning after meeting with my parents, he had strolled to the coffee table where I was sketching my own architectural drawing of a treehouse. No sweet Snow White cottage, mine was a modern shack whose inspiration came from the eco-friendly houses in the book Peter had just published.

Peter folded his long body next to me on the floor and studied my drawings. "What do you like about this?"

"It's outside and magical."

My answer must have satisfied Peter, because he spoke to me like I was a colleague, his callused finger tracing the roofline.

"You know, if we changed the pitch of the roof, we could put in a bigger picture window so you'd really feel like you're outside." A few days later, Peter gave me my own Moleskine notebook and a paper scroll: my treehouse rendered as real architectural plans.

Drops of morning dew dampened my sneakers as I followed the grassy path toward the healing garden that Mom had been testing to surprise Ginny's dad for his convalescence, but never had the chance to plant in his yard. The closer I got to the beach, the more I could breathe. Weird, I know, since I'd almost drowned and swimming made me nervous.

At five foot one and typically dressed in jewel-toned polo shirts, Mom was a human hummingbird, flitting among her beloved plants and her myriad projects. So I was astonished to spot her lounging on the rickety, weather-faded bench facing the Puget Sound, a mug of tea in her hand, her knees tucked up under her chin.

"I'm going to miss this place," Mom said softly without looking up, almost as if she had been expecting me.

"Then why are you moving? I don't get it," I said, as annoyance swept away the calming effect of the water along with my intention to thank her for inviting the Bookster Babes over last night.

Only then did Mom wrench around toward me to respond hotly, "Because, Reb, family is made up of all the hundreds of daily moments. Not the big ta-da family trips to Italy. It's this." She gestured between us before widening her arms to encompass the beach, the property, my treehouse. "That's why we're moving, okay? Not just to be with you, but to be with your father. To support him."

Fine. I was going to leave her to her grouching, but instead I shot back, "Then how about you all move, and I stay here and go to UW?"

Mom guessed the role Jackson played in derailing me from wanting to attend one of the best undergraduate architectural programs in the country. She shook her head with so much vehemence that her naturally curly brown hair, flat-ironed into submission, whipped like a moon-shaped mezzaluna knife around her shoulders. "First of all," she lectured me yet again, "this is the time in your life to be totally selfish and focus on yourself. You've got this amazing opportunity where you get to invent yourself. And second, I didn't raise you to be that kind of girl who'd give up your dream to stay with a boy you just met."

Even though I'd never admit it to Mom, I hated the image of being That Kind of Girl, too, who would shunt aside her goals and shutter her ambitions for a guy. But I had to admit: The temptation shimmered enticingly. Columbia was an inconvenient eternity away from Jackson.

"I'm not putting away my dream. I can still study architecture here," I said, staring grimly at the receding tide.

"The graduate classes you could take at Columbia are way better than at UW," Mom countered, and set her mug between us. "Besides, your dad asked me to set up an informational interview for you with Sam Stone, and I already made the call. He wants to see you in a few days."

Even though the internship had been Dad's idea, now I

burned with irritation at Mom. Here she was again, intervening as always the moment she sensed me teetering off my preordained path dictated by her from my birth. That path included Columbia, where I'd crash as many graduate courses in architecture as I could to fast-track a master's degree. Then on to Muir & Sons Development, where I'd be the first and only girl in Dad's family ever to be employed.

"Dad told me it'd be okay to stay together with Jackson," I said over the shriek of a seagull out in the bay. As anger at my mom coalesced, so did my conviction that this might actually make sense. "He said some long-distance relationships are worth the work."

Mom stood so abruptly that the blanket fell from her lap. Instead of picking the mocha-brown cashmere blanket off the damp grass, she sidestepped it and headed for the gate to the beach. Beyond that rusting gate, a misshapen barrier of a log, gnarled and sea-soaked, lay across the slick boat ramp. That didn't deter Mom. She leaped over it to the rock-laden beach.

"Mom, what're you doing?" I asked, following her down to the exposed shore. The tide was lower than I had ever seen—so shallow, the receding water nearly beached the moored sailboats.

With unerring precision, Mom plucked a stone from the wet sand: a perfect circle, free of barnacles. When dry, the shocking fern green would dull to a mottled brown. Mom handed that Cinderella stone to me.

"Make a wish," she said.

"But it's yours."

"I found it for you."

What I wanted to wish for wasn't reprieve from my family's move; we were too far gone for that, with the house packed and our belongings journeying to New Jersey. What I wanted, needed, was reassurance that Jackson and I would work out. My heart contracted painfully, already missing him even though I knew he was driving me to the airport for our red-eye tonight. But just this once, I wished Mom would tap into the sixth sense Grandma Stesha insisted we both had and assure me I was doing the right thing with Jackson. Just once, I wanted her to tell me with absolute confidence, *Sweetheart, everything is going to work out fine.*

Who was I kidding? If I dismissed the notion of my having a sixth sense, Mom denied its existence in anyone altogether, most especially the family legend that we were descended from psychics and mystics. She practically derided Grandma Stesha's tours to sacred sites whenever anyone asked. In their dismissiveness of the unknown, my parents were united.

Ignoring me, crouched low to the sand, Mom sifted through the wet stones, rejecting one after another. Usually she was so mindful of the water, especially since my near drowning. But now, her back to the waves, she used both hands to shove aside a large, bulbous rock.

"Mom, geez, you're going to cut yourself," I said, alarmed at her frenetic searching, and held out the stone she had given me. "Here, take this one."

"No," she said almost angrily, "that's yours."

"Okay . . ." I said, shoving my wishing stone into the pocket of my denim jacket.

I wanted to leave but couldn't. *Stay.* Mom shoved aside another enormous rock. Both of us screamed when a sea snake, no longer than a foot, with a dangerous yellow stripe down its back, slithered out. Mom recoiled so abruptly, she lost her balance and fell atop the sharp rocks as a wave swept the snake away.

"Mom, you okay?"

The water crept to the shore, lapping at our feet, mine safe in my sneakers, Mom's exposed in her flip-flops. As the water drew back, I spotted the perfect wishing rock for her, egg-shaped and striated gray-green. Most importantly, a thin white line ran around the top third. That rare circlet, according to Grandma Stesha, was a good luck sign: a halo. I plunged my hand into the icy water to snag it for my mother.

Suddenly, against the soothing backdrop of the surf, I could hear the sobs again. The sound of inconsolable heartbreak. My heart raced in frantic beats. The premonition that something would go horribly wrong if we left here was almost unbearable. For the first time, I felt compelled to tell Mom about one of my feelings. Confess about the weeping I kept hearing. Ask for her interpretation because surely I was wrong.

Fiercely, Mom shook her head, a sharp, cutting movement, the same as the one at the hospital so many years ago: *Don't dream.* I could have been seven again, swamped with panic from my vision, needing to confide in someone. Only this time it was Mom who was leaving because of what I had seen, not Dad.

"Okay, let's go," she said sharply, turning her back on me, my premonition, and the beach.

"Mom, wait," I said, holding the wishing rock out to her.

"We've got a ton to do," she said, not seeing the stone offering, "and regardless of what your dad thinks, I can't do it all on my own."

I retracted my hand. "He would have stayed if you had just said something!"

Mom's lips pursed as if she were swallowing a mouthful of sour doubt. She marched to the bench, grabbed the blanket off the lawn, and swept up a clipboard I hadn't noticed. A paper lined with a long list of things yet to be done fluttered in the breeze, a white flag of defeat. "The movers are coming in fifteen minutes to pack your treehouse and bedroom. You need to make sure everything's ready for them. Pronto."

As Mom charged up the path with a last bark—"Come on, Reb! I mean it. You've got to pack!"—I drew back my arm and threw the egg stone I had found for her and wished her life would be as upended as mine was now.

With an unsettling feeling, I watched the wishing rock arc in the sky and trace an invisible rainbow. As it landed with an impotent thud back on the beach, guilt and worry engulfed me. Now I wanted to stay down where it was safe at the beach. Now I wanted to retract my wish. Now I wanted to insist that Mom backtrack, too, but she was lunging toward the endless tasks that would usher us to the future. It was too late to do anything but follow.

Hours of sweeping and mopping to prepare our house for rental did nothing to stop me from berating myself for that mean-spirited wish. Distracted, I ran the vacuum cleaner into the wall and smudged the meticulous beige with a dark mark. With an impatient sigh, I switched off the vacuum and was about to inspect the damage when, in the abrupt silence, I heard Jackson outside. When had he arrived?

I rushed to my bedroom window and leaned out, ready to call to him. Instead, transfixed, I watched him play with Reid. At ten, my brother was as burly as a middle schooler—precisely why all the coaches of peewee football were chasing him with the fervor of lovelorn NFL scouts.

"Okay, Reidster," said Jackson, drawing back his arm, "watch and weep as my fireball incinerates your temple."

"Not a chance, peon, because my arrow of destruction is going to obliterate your wimpy fireball," shot back Reid as his hands lifted to catch the football.

Just like that, I remembered my once-in-a-lifetime family biking trip in Italy, where I met and fell for Jackson. After a particularly long ride, Dad hibernated in the air-conditioned hotel room to catch up on work, but he wanted Reid to practice before football season started. That left Mom and me, which was a frightening prospect, since neither of us had ever touched pigskin. After watching our bumbling for a few moments, Jackson banished Mom and me from the hotel's clipped lawn. Watching him toss the ball with Reid back then, I knew with absolute certainty it would be a hop, skip, and a jump from merely liking to being smitten and falling in love with Jackson.

I flew down the carpeted stairs now, intending to spend as much time as I had left with him. Screw cleaning the cottage;

Mom could be her own Cinderella. I burst out the back door and onto the porch, where I stopped short.

The crying that haunted me yesterday restarted, building in pitch and intensity. I lowered myself onto the porch steps, fighting the compulsion to rock myself. At that moment, I would have done anything, said anything, to make that wailing in my head disappear.

"Hey, you," Jackson said, loping to my side.

I forced a placid smile even as my stomach roiled from my effort to ignore the crying that was growing increasingly sorrowful. Between Mom's order to stop dreaming, Dad's scornful denial of anything that hinted of premonitions, and Ginny's painful three-month silent treatment after I predicted that her father would die, I'd learned to stopper my sixth sense. I ignored the few visions I still had on rare occasions, afraid people would fire me from their lives. How different was that from Dad's terminating employees who didn't agree with his business vision?

A trickle of sweat that could have been a trail of tears slid down my cheek. Unlike other guys, Jackson didn't glance away awkwardly because I was upset. Instead, he stared at me tenderly, as if he couldn't believe I was real. The crying in my head became heartache, every tear a glass shard that pierced my resolve to break it off with Jackson. I didn't want to hurt as badly as that weeping, not now. So why not try? I turned from the panoramic view of the Puget Sound to Jackson's piercing eyes.

"So my dad said he'd fly you out for a visit," I said softly as a cool breeze brought the salty scent of the seawater to me. "October sound good?"

"What do you think?" he asked, grinning at me.

The weeping stopped. All I heard was our breath as we leaned into each other for a kiss, slow and sweet. Then, as if in benediction of my decision, Jackson's hand wrapped protectively around my hip, and with his forehead against mine, he drew me even closer.

Part Two

Form follows function—that has been
misunderstood. Form and function
should be one, joined in spiritual union.
—*Frank Lloyd Wright, architect*

Chapter Five

As soon as we cleared security at Newark Airport, Dad waved from the barricade, iPhone to his ear, and finished his conversation: "Okay, Mother, they're here. I got to go. Well, Adam's not always right, but if you want to buy that property, it's up to you. Okay, tomorrow. Yes, I'll call you tomorrow." With a long-suffering sigh, Dad hung up and pocketed his phone as though it were a distasteful secret he needed to tuck away. I had a sudden inkling of what my own life in college would be like in a few weeks. Like Dad, I could relocate across the country and still not be able to escape my mother's control.

Before I could commiserate, Dad hugged us each hard, then grabbed my messenger bag in one hand and slung Reid's backpack over his shoulder. He charged toward the baggage carousels. My phone chimed with Jackson's text: *Touched down safe? Hello. Bruised and not just from missing you.* Worried, I stopped abruptly in the middle of the corridor to text him back, asking what had happened. I hadn't realized Mom was trudging behind us until she stepped on my heels and sighed like I was in her way.

"Come on, Reb," Mom urged as though I were five and could get lost wandering from our pack. Scooting around me, she hiked her misshapen tote bag higher onto her shoulder; the sack bulged with emergency snacks and supplies, like antiseptic wipes to kill the germs lurking on the plane's folding trays.

"So, you kids excited to see our new house, or what?" Dad asked.

Baggage coursed down the chute and onto the carousel. As if this largesse of other people's possessions reminded Mom of what was still trucking across the country to us, she said, "We don't have furniture. Maybe we should spend a couple of nights in your apartment."

Dad shrugged. "Doesn't it make more sense to get the kids settled into the house as soon as possible?"

I rubbed my hands together, dry from the plane ride, uneasy because Mom was changing her well-armored plan and Dad was the one thwarting it. But why would he? He knew I wanted to be in New York. Now I wished I had landed anywhere but here. Wished I could jet forward six weeks, when freshman year would start and I could leave Mom and Dad to their house, furnished or not. Mom must have been watching out of her peripheral vision because she held out a small vial of lotion to me.

"Besides, one of the women at the moving company got air mattresses and sleeping bags for us," Dad said as he checked a message on his iPhone. "It's no big deal, Bits. It'll be just like camping in your treehouse, right, Rebecca?"

No matter how much I rubbed my hands together, I couldn't work in all the lotion, leaving my skin slippery, like I had dipped them in a vat of grease. Even though I was back to being the cheerleader, I couldn't muster the energy to agree with Dad that, yeah, sleeping on the ground was no biggie. So I simply nodded.

The tote bag slipped off her shoulder, but Mom didn't bother adjusting it, too busy scouting for our luggage even as she held out her hand to take the excess lotion from me.

The one sixth sense I might admit to having is my ability to feel space. For as long as I can remember, I could tell within a moment of entering a building—home, library, corporate campus—if the space worked or if it failed. The first time I felt true rightness was on Grandpa George's houseboat, bought a month before I nearly drowned. Even when I was seven, some internal tuning mechanism had declared this home pitch-perfect. That sense of rightness solidified the moment I spotted Grandpa's inviting window seat beneath the reclaimed wood stairs.

Our massive Georgian house in New Jersey, complete with faux Grecian columns, couldn't have differed more from Grandpa's charming houseboat, much less our quaint cottage on Lewis Island. A Street of Dreams house—that's how Peter, our architect, would have dubbed this mansion. An opulent show home built specifically for once-a-year luxury-house tours to show-case indoor waterfalls, twenty-thousand-bottle wine cellars, and theaters complete with red velvet curtains.

I stood in the cavernous foyer, shocked silent as I scanned the cold space. Even with every single stick of our furniture in it, this house would feel uninhabited and empty.

"I'm sure the house will be fine," Mom said, staring up at the overhead chandelier papered with dehydrated moths that had mistaken the hot lightbulb for home.

Though Mom's intention may have been to reassure, Dad flushed at her "fine," that damning descriptor of the Bland and Boring. I seethed at Mom even as I grinned toothily at Dad, determined to love our new home: "It's going to be awesome to have my own bathroom."

Dad swept his arm over Reid's shoulder. "Yeah, don't you kids think it'll be fun to live somewhere with enough space for once?"

"Heck, yeah!" I said, even if I wondered why Dad had gotten a place this mammoth when I would be living at college most of the time. Quickly, I read Jackson's new text explaining that his body was battered and bruised from a non-life-threatening spill. Aching to be with him, I replied: *Battered and bruised by parental bickering . . . and missing you.*

Still, Dad had it right. Six thousand square feet would provide us all with ample space away from Mom. Tired of the tension, I stepped away from my mother to close the front door, but not before I breathed in air so humid my lungs congested. I had the sudden image of being swallowed whole within the jaws of the mansion's wide front door. Even so, I forced myself to shut the door as Dad suggested, "Why don't you kids go explore?"

Reid scampered up the spiral staircase as if he were at summer camp, ferreting out the nooks and crannies before all the other kids. From upstairs, he shouted, "This is our own temple!"

Dad beamed and agreed, "The Temple of Muir."

Meanwhile, I turned another full, slow circle in this paean to modern architecture so vastly different from Mom's shabby chic and my Zen minimalist styles.

"It'll feel like home soon," Mom assured me, assuming I felt as out of place as she did.

"It's home already," I shot back, and bolted upstairs, wanting to escape in my sketchbook. As I reached the landing, a feeling of disquietude made me hesitate. I heard a sharp intake of breath, the breath that preceded wild sobbing.

Stop, stop, stop.

"Welcome home," called Dad.

Reid's bedroom door was closed, but I heard his excited murmuring as he investigated his space. Then I passed what had to be the master bedroom, where garish curtains of aqua and fuchsia bookended the picture windows—brazen colors Mom would never pick, not even for her container gardens.

Further down the hall, my bedroom was painted in the same shades as home: a deep plum on the far wall, soothing taupe on the remaining three. Even the windows were draped in the same linen curtains. Other than the air mattress topped with a rolled-up sleeping bag, there was nothing in the bedroom . . . except the brown box in the middle of the floor. I settled myself on the beige carpet and picked up the light box, cradling it on my lap as I read the printed label from a company I didn't recognize.

Inside, a delicate wrapping of tissue paper protected the small cardboard jewelry box. From that encasement, I pulled out a necklace with a square pendant. No note, just an etched inscription: LIVE EVERYTHING.

There was nothing else. But nothing more was needed. I knew who had sent this, but how had Jackson known that this precise message was what I needed right now? I slipped the long necklace over my head and pressed the pendant to my heart. The room, empty as it was, felt like mine.

"So what do you think?" Dad asked after I rejoined my parents in the living room a short while later and lowered myself to the marble floor beside him. My lips parted, ready to thank him for arranging my bedroom, when Reid hurtled down the stairs with a loud "Mom, you're awesome!"

Of course it was Mom's idea to re-create our bedrooms so we'd feel instantly at home. I flushed at my oversight, started to pull away from Dad, but his arm tightened around my shoulders to anchor me at his side.

"You like it?" Mom asked Reid.

"Love it!" he yelled, and held up a new set of *MythBusters* DVDs. "Thanks, Mom!"

"Did you find your moving-in gift, too?" Mom asked me.

I shook my head. "Just something from Jackson."

"Oh." Mom's forehead furrowed as she lifted herself off the cold stone floor. "Then it's probably in the closet. I'll find it."

As she did, Dad clapped Reid's shoulder with one hand. "You can thank Giselle, too. She orchestrated all this."

"Who's Giselle?" Reid asked, reading the back of the DVD case.

"One of the women at the moving company."

Mom halted at the stairs and turned around. Her eyes didn't waver from Dad. "We should get her a little something for all her help. Do you think she'd want a scarf? Or chocolate?"

I had a sudden image of Giselle—tall, fine-boned, long hair. No, she wouldn't be one to devour chocolate, to dare add a stray ounce on her body.

"Definitely not chocolate," I said.

Mom frowned as she leaned against the stair rail. "Why?"

Like an energetic puppy caged overlong, Dad sprang to his feet and trotted to the front door, saying, "I'm sorry about this, but I got to run to work. Emergency."

"But we just got here," I said, even as Mom took a step toward him with a "Today, Thom? Really?"

"I can't help it, but hey! I almost forgot." He crouched down to his briefcase resting against the far wall in the foyer, and withdrew two flat parcels. "Something to welcome you to Manhattan."

"That's so nice," Mom said, craning closer to watch Reid and me unwrap the presents: a membership to the Museum of Modern Art for me, and for Reid, a pass to the Museum of Natural History.

49

After breathing out a long "Wicked!" Reid demanded, "When can we go?"

"Maybe tomorrow. There's so much to see in Manhattan." Dad practically bounced on his toes. "You guys are going to love living at its back door! Just wait."

I caught Mom gazing wistfully at the thick concrete door as it shut behind Dad. Before she noticed me, she locked the door with a sigh.

"Oh, Reb, you did find your present," she said, smiling at the pendant I wore. "It looks great on you."

I cupped the pendant. "I thought this was from Jackson."

"No." Her lips pursed briefly, a faint line. Then, a scant moment later, my move-in gift forgotten, Mom ordered us, "Go unpack."

That evening Dad met us in the town square, where Mom, Reid, and I had been waiting for nearly two hours. All around us, happy, well-fed families were parked on their picnic blankets, content from their gourmet dinners. Reid had been getting progressively grumpier until Jackson reminded me by text of the emergency food Mom always carried. One of those just-in-case protein bars had saved Jackson on our Tuscany trip four months ago.

"Hey, there you are!" Dad said jovially, as if we were the ones holding him up.

He approached our fleece blanket that Mom had somehow

thought to stuff into her luggage. By then it was almost eight, and Dad had been gone for five hours. I didn't know why, but I watched him carefully when Mom asked him where he'd been and why he hadn't answered her phone calls. Dad simply shrugged and said, "The emergency at work was gnarlier than I thought."

I busied myself with making room for Dad on the blanket. Even then, I couldn't help wondering: If he had driven all the way into the city, why didn't we watch the fireworks and spend the night there, as Mom had suggested? As I had wanted?

"So, who's ready for dinner?" Dad asked, hefting two plastic bags that strained from the weight of our meal.

Reid asked ravenously, "What did you get?"

Dad settled himself next to Reid, sitting on the grass rather than on the blanket with the rest of us. "The works for Fourth of July."

No matter how much I tried to clamp down on the feeling that something was amiss, urgency needled me. For reasons I couldn't explain, I wanted to knock the ribs, the baked beans, the corn bread off my plate. And Mom's. This was the food of the fairies who tricked you into believing you were dining on chocolate, only to find yourself chewing a mouthful of dirt. There was no rational explanation for my panic, no logical reason for my complete loss of appetite. It was just there, as real as a frightened heartbeat.

Don't eat, don't eat, I wanted to warn Mom.

I needn't have worried. Under my watchful gaze, Mom pushed the gooey ribs around on her plate for a few minutes before she abandoned them, uneaten, too.

51

"Too hot to eat?" Dad asked me.

"Yeah," I said right as the first Roman candle burst in the sky, showering gold dust above us.

In the afterglow of a crimson starburst, I caught Dad shrugging as Mom waved off a piece of pie that he offered. He took a big bite, the juice from the apple pie dewing his chin. I couldn't bear to watch him eat so greedily while I was sick to my stomach with foreboding. So I lowered myself onto my back and stared up at the night sky splintering with fireworks.

Chapter Six

Breakfast the next morning was a grim affair of leftovers, since the refrigerator was the Sahara desert of food, desolate in its emptiness. Back on Lewis Island, Mom had vigilantly stocked our fridge with produce from local farms, and gallons of milk so fresh you could hear cows moo with every poured cup.

"But I want cereal," Reid said plaintively, his mouth curling in disgust at the cold rib glistening with coagulated fat on the paper towel that served as his plate.

With an elbow propped on the kitchen table, Mom leaned her head against her open palm, then methodically smoothed her hair off her forehead. Her eyes opened slowly and she said, "We'll have Dad drive us to the grocery store as soon as he's done with his shower."

"I'm going to learn how to drive a stick," Reid grumbled.

"Good idea," Mom said. "I told your dad it would have made more sense for him to buy an automatic in the first place."

By the time Dad appeared in the kitchen, hair damp, I had fashioned a spoon out of a binder clip for Reid. The rejiggered clip so appealed to Reid that he managed a few bites of the potato salad, enough to keep his low-blood-sugar grumpiness at bay. That won me such a heartfelt, relieved "Thanks, honey" from Mom, I felt exhausted but didn't know why exactly. Maybe it had something to do with the restless night I had had, too uneasy to sleep for fear of what I'd dream. I chalked that up to never spending any real time in a house this large.

"Hey, Thom, your mother left a message on my phone. She wants you to call this morning," Mom said as she set a paper towel in front of Dad.

With a sigh, Dad cast an exasperated scowl at the empty counter where our espresso machine should have resided. "God, I need coffee."

"Sorry, no coffee," said Mom, whipping around from the fridge with a flourish. "But . . . ta-da! Breakfast is served."

Dad's expression when Mom presented the ribs to him so mirrored Reid's revulsion that she and I laughed, and I made a mental note to text this to Jackson. Dad shrugged self-consciously without taking a bite of what he had so eagerly devoured the night before.

"I'll pick up some breakfast on the way to the airport," he said.

"You're leaving?" I asked. Dad's announcement surprised Reid so much that he stopped spooning potato salad into his mouth.

"But it's Sunday." Mom leaned back against the counter as if she had been punched.

Dad held up his phone, but whether it was the culprit or the alibi, I couldn't tell. "I told you about this last week."

"I don't think so," Mom said flatly. "Rebecca needs a way to get to her interview tomorrow, and I need to go grocery shopping. I thought we agreed you were going to drive us."

"God, Bits." Dad shook his head and stared out the kitchen window like he wanted to escape. "You can just rent a car."

The last time I had felt tension this sharp-edged, I had been a half-drowned girl in my hospital bed. Even though I couldn't understand what was so important that Dad had to leave us when we had just arrived, I assured him, "Dad, it's no biggie. We'll figure it out."

"That's my girl." Dad shot me an approving smile before trotting jauntily out the door to our one car that only he could drive. He sped away.

The idea of not making the most of a spare moment was about as appealing to Mom as stepping on a slime-yellow banana slug with her bare foot. Sometime between Dad's heading for the airport and her cleaning up after breakfast, Mom realized that she, Reid, and I could get acquainted with our neighborhood and go for a run at the same time.

"Why are we doing this, again?" Reid groused as he thrust his feet into his sneakers by the front door. I didn't have an answer to that question, or any of the other mysteries that were my mother's unfathomable decision-making.

"Speed Racer," I muttered after Mom's back as she ran well ahead of us. Wiping the sweat off my face, I wished I had swiped on another layer of deodorant.

Not a single other person was jogging in this sweltering humidity. A familiar rumble caught my attention. Jackson? I spun around, giddy even though I knew my guy was back at home. Instantly, I felt silly for grinning at a white-haired man in his air-conditioned Mustang, who cast me a look that was snagged between amused and bemused.

"Just look at that garden," Mom called out, slowing to scrutinize the raised vegetable beds in a neighbor's side yard. It didn't require too much imagination to picture her transforming our lush, green front lawn into a self-sustaining, organic farm . . . and dividing our bounty between ourselves, our neighbors, and the local food bank.

"I hope you like digging," I muttered to Reid.

My brother's visualization powers must have been fine-tuned during our vision quest of a run, too, because he groaned, "Oh no."

"Oh yes."

"Okay, let's head home!" Mom's cheer wasn't wind enough to blow Reid homeward. After one long block, he lagged so far behind us that I sighed like Mom, wishing again that Jackson were here in his Mustang to rescue us. But Mom had scanned the street, spotted a coffee shop at the corner, and asked, "Hey, kids, how about something cold to drink?"

We hadn't even begun to nod eagerly before Mom shepherded us inside to the welcome blast of air-conditioning. As I started feeling woozy from the aftereffects of the heat, we stepped behind a stylish woman with glossy black bobbed hair. Her son looked to be the same age as Reid. Mom asked me, "Green tea frappe?" while withdrawing a dollar and pushing the bill toward the cash register a scant second before the woman ahead of us discovered she was short some change for her iced coffee.

"Are you sure?" the woman asked. Her cherry-red shoes made her look like a modern-day Dorothy, and when Mom handed her the calling card that Shana's mother had designed as a bon voyage gift, I was positive the woman wished she could click her heels three times and be delivered far away from my mother.

"Just promise to call me," Mom continued breezily. "We're new in town. I need friends!"

Oh, geez, Mom wasn't bribing a stranger to be her friend, was she? Mortified, I turned away, distancing myself from my mother. Before I knew it, she'd finagled the woman's name—Angela—and arranged a playdate for Reid the next day, never mind that the boys didn't even register each other's presence. Never mind that Angela herself looked dazed, totally understandable since she had come for an iced beverage and left with an obligation.

Soon after we gulped down our drinks, Mom hustled us toward an ATM machine. Not one to let any teaching moment pass, Mom made Angela's empty wallet today's lesson. As she fed her bank card into the machine, Mom told us, "Never leave the house without your phone, key, and wallet. And always carry an emergency twenty dollars. Oh, and a tampon."

"Mom!" Reid groaned. "Gross."

"Well, of course, I didn't mean——" Mom started to say when the ATM rejected her request for a hundred dollars. The three of us read the bank message in disbelief; how could we have exceeded our maximum withdrawal limit for the day?

"Dad must have taken out cash this morning for his trip," I guessed as Mom tried—and failed—again.

"Hmmm." Mom pulled out her cell phone and called Dad, but he didn't answer. After she left him a hurried message, I expected her to transform seamlessly into our cruise director, herding us home to tackle five more things before the day was over. Instead, Mom stared distastefully at this crystal ball of an ATM machine that had spit out a prognostication about an unsavory future.

I couldn't squelch the slow bubbling of unease. "Come on, Mom," I said, and guided us home.

"Okay, can you say *embarrassing*?" Rather than dissect every last detail of the ATM Incident with Jackson, I focused on Mom's bribery for friendship, recasting that into an amusing anecdote. "Just you wait. I'm going to be able to write the best self-help book one day thanks to Mom, since everyone's mistakes are my lessons."

But Jackson didn't laugh the way I thought he would—not even a gratuitous chuckle. Instead, he asked, "Why would your dad need so much cash he'd max out the ATM?"

"I don't even know if it was Dad. Maybe the bank made a mistake. Who cares?"

Jackson was silent.

"Oh, please. It's not like he's buying drugs or anything."

"Hey, I didn't mean that." When I didn't say another word, Jackson continued, "What can I do? Wire you some money?"

"No," I said firmly, and winced. Even to myself, I sounded too emphatic. "Dad'll be home soon. And besides, we've got a credit card. It's no big deal."

"Well, if you need anything . . ." Jackson's voice trailed off, but he didn't need to finish his thought. Even if I was annoyed at him, I knew he'd help me in whatever way he could. But the one whose reassurance I wanted was off the grid, not answering any of our calls.

Chapter Seven

Mom's intentions were good—pushing what little cash she had left on me in the morning for a cab ride, despite my protests that I could take the bus and walk the three blocks to the architect's office. "You can't be flustered or sweaty for your interview," she had declared. All my appreciation disappeared when she added, "You have your questions to ask Sam written down, don't you? Like I told you to?" Of course, I hadn't. I knew I'd remember them, but Mom had frowned when I said so.

Like all good intentions, whether delivered via cab or not, I ended up flustered and sweaty in my form of hell anyway: waiting in a sleek lobby populated with beautiful people in tailored clothes, while I felt like a country bumpkin. Where my khaki pants, short-sleeved black T-shirt, and black flats would have been perfectly acceptable—and possibly even chic—in Peter's casual office in Seattle, here on the East Coast I might as well have been dressed for yard work.

The receptionist ignored me studiously, but twenty-five minutes after I was supposed to meet my potential boss, I approached her for the second time. She looked up at me from her awning of eyelashes, heavy with mascara—"Yes?"—as though I hadn't been sitting six feet from her.

"I'll try his admin again," she finally acquiesced, and didn't lower her voice when she actually got a real human on the line: "Mollie, Sam's interview is here. Yes, interview. Well, I don't know, but she says she has an appointment with him."

That did not bode well. Embarrassed and feeling unwanted, I flushed.

Another ten minutes, and at last I was escorted inside the architectural firm. Mollie, Sam's assistant, was a middle-aged woman with a mission-driven click to her step. Her heels might have been as sky-high as her boss's signature buildings, but she didn't so much as wobble as she led me down the long hall. The only sign of warmth in this building was Mollie's big smile, which she shared generously, as though she could feel my anxiety.

"Have a seat," Mollie said, gesturing me inside Sam's vast corner office. "A client meeting ran long, but Sam should be wrapping up soon."

I perched awkwardly on the edge of the black leather chair in front of the glass-topped desk and shivered, not because of the air-conditioning but because the office's aggressively modern lines made me feel insignificant and unwelcome. This was precisely how I had felt inside Synergy the one time Mom showed Reid and me where she used to work with the CEO. That corporate campus had been designed by Sam Stone, too. Strange thing was, if I told myself the truth, this remote distance was what I also felt inside our New Jersey house, built to be a statement, not an inner sanctum where you could safely retreat from the world.

A long twenty minutes later, Sam strode in, all efficient energy, barking a few instructions to his assistant. My stomach tensed. Finally, as Sam rounded his desk, he noticed me, and Mollie quickly introduced us: "Your interview candidate, Rebecca Muir."

"Interview? Since when did I have an interview?"

"For a summer internship . . ." Mollie said when I remained silent.

How could I answer? I blushed, wanting to escape Sam's intense, icicle-blue eyes that were sizing me up. His face was heavily wrinkled, though I doubted a single crease could be classified as a laugh line, since the corner of his mouth didn't so much as lift a millimeter. Rather, he demanded, "How did you end up in my office?"

All semblance of a response ran out of my brain.

"Here? At Stone Architects?" he repeated, as though I were a dunce who had mistakenly crashed his advanced seminar for geniuses. He leaned against the edge of his desk, one hand on his thigh. "Well?"

"Well, I'm going to Columbia this fall."

"Good, my alma mater. But who set up this interview for you?"

"Oh, my mom talked to my uncle, Adam Muir, and he—"

"Adam. That's right." At the mention of my real estate power-house uncle, Sam made his calculations and slotted me into his hierarchy. He held out his hand, but not to shake mine. "Let me see your sketchbook."

Every minute in this office had a lethal effect on my brain cells. All I could manage was to repeat one word: "Sketchbook?"

"Any good architect worth his salt carries around his sketch-book at all times," Sam said.

That, at least, was no different from what Peter had told me, even though he hadn't used the masculine pronoun, since I was clearly a *she*. On any other occasion, I might have been ashamed to show my doodles, but as I scrounged for my sketchbook in my messenger bag, I reminded myself that I had seen Peter's. His book, like mine, was a chaotic mess of tiny drawings and mus-ings, the creative process in action. What could Sam possibly have to denigrate about kernels of ideas and fledgling thoughts?

Apparently, a lot.

It took Sam all of five seconds to flip through my sketches of treehouses and research notes on sustainable materials. When he shut the book abruptly, it sounded—and felt—like a slap. I flinched.

He asked, "Why are you here?"

Sweat flooded my face. And under my arms. My gosh, I had no idea a body could leak so much fluid. I wiped my forehead nervously, wishing I had packed a bandanna the way Mom did—you never know when you're going to need to staunch a wound. "Excuse me?"

63

"You have decent ideas, but our aesthetics are diametrically opposed. You like small spaces." He flipped open the journal, noted a page. His tone was patronizing. "Fairy villages."

"I love corporate workspaces!" I protested even as my underarms dampened. Great, exactly what I needed: to liquefy from embarrassment. Self-preservation launched me into a robotic synopsis of my college application essays. For once, I was grateful that Mom had made me rewrite the essays so many times, I had memorized them. "I want to learn everything I can about large-scale applications of sustainable building."

How a single word could convey so much doubt, I had never known until Sam's dubious "Really." Then he asked, "Have you ever been on a job site?"

"Well, our architect back home—"

"Who?"

"Peter Nakamura."

"Does some nice urban fills."

Nice. The same damning word straight out of Mom's arsenal of PR vocabulary. *Nice* suggested forgettable and mediocre and, above all, derivative.

My voice might have been soft, but even I could hear its defensiveness: "Peter says it's important to expand your creative palette. So that's why I'm here."

"Do you always do what everyone tells you to do?" The slight shake of his head must have been a dismissal, because Sam parked himself behind his desk and punched a number on his phone. His assistant immediately rushed in to lead me to the lobby, far from Sam's epicenter of condescension.

"Someone will be in touch with you shortly." Mollie's look of compassion practically undid me. Before she sent me off to my regrets and second-guessing, she added, "His bark is a lot worse than his bite."

As I trudged to the bus stop, frustrated, I composed no fewer than five hundred different, scintillating answers to Sam's questions. Why had I sounded so stupid, so inept?

Later that night, I showered myself of sweat but couldn't rinse off my shame. I tore every one of the sketches of fairy houses from my journal and shredded them.

Not too surprisingly, the next morning Mollie called to tell me that Stone Architects was "unfortunately unable" to offer me an internship. So humiliated, I basically hung up on her. When I called Jackson right after that disastrous pseudo-conversation, he actually bristled: "As if you really wanted to work there, right?"

"Well, yeah, I sorta did. Sam's one of the best architects in the world. Plus, for the amount I sweated, I would have been model-thin in a week."

He didn't laugh, not even a snort. "Why? The guy sounds like my dad. Besides, you should see your face whenever you talk about treehouses."

How many times had I overheard this conversation before, except that it featured my grandpa George explaining to Mom why he was quitting yet another pursuit to start a new one—carpentry one year, glassblowing the next? At his every excuse, my mother's face would tighten with disapproval, while Dad reminded her later in private that they weren't Grandpa's retirement safety net.

This time it was me responding to Jackson's idealism with a pragmatic "Yeah, well, sometimes you have to pay your dues to pay your bills."

I knew I was parroting Dad and his career philosophy, but when had he ever been wrong? I was the one who failed, unable to reel in an internship that had been all but hand-delivered on a silver platter.

Three nights later, Dad came home from his business trip just in time for Reid's birthday cake. At the sound of his key in the door, Mom rushed to the kitchen to collect the chocolate cake we'd spent hours baking and frosting. Every last one of her attempts at conversation over dessert, though, sounded like interrogation: "Did you tell the board about your new marketing plan to target game developers?" I couldn't blame Dad for his flatline responses. After all, he was the sought-after executive; he knew what he was doing. The closest thing to a career Mom had this last decade was managing our lives. So now we sat at the dining room table, silent, as Mom nibbled her scant sliver of cake while the rest of us devoured large slices.

"Hey, little man, open your present," said Dad, handing Reid his gift, a large box artfully wrapped and tied with an impressive bow. Inside was an autographed football encased in a clear acrylic box. "Brett Favre signed it. See? You can display it on your bookshelf."

Reid nodded, uttered a perfunctory "cool," nothing compared with the awed "coooool" after he opened Mom's gift, a leather journal filled with hand-torn paper.

"To write your own fantasy novel," Mom explained. Incredibly, even though we hadn't coordinated, my gift to Reid was an old-fashioned fountain pen that matched the ancient-looking journal perfectly.

Leaving the signed football on the kitchen table, Reid rushed upstairs, cradling his new journal and pen. Hurt, Dad scraped the last cake crumbs from his plate, and I glared at Reid's receding back, wanting him to collect the football, fuss over the gift. Didn't he know how to keep the peace? Who cared if he hated the sport? All he had to do was pretend.

"Do you want another piece?" Mom asked Dad.

"Sure," Dad said as he retreated to the living room to work. After I served him his second helping, I escaped out the front door to text Jackson in the night air: *SOS.* He phoned me right away, as though he reciprocated my yearning.

"I miss you," I said.

"Me too . . ." Jackson paused, then asked, "What's wrong?"

"Nothing." I sat down on the front step and deliberately lightened my tone. "Tell me about today."

"So my dad sold the bird-watcher's sanctuary," he said.

In one magical morning, that property had become Our Spot, just as Tuscany was Our Beginning. "Ohhh . . ." I sighed.

"I know. But a really great couple bought it—the guy's a carpenter, and the woman writes children's books."

"That's perfect," I said, but what was even more perfect was how Jackson knew the type of people I'd approve to become caretakers of our property.

I clenched the phone in my hand, ached to tell Jackson that ever since our move, I was afraid to sleep, petrified to see what lay behind my eyelids. I toyed with sharing this unshakable sense of uneasiness about how Dad had been incommunicado on his long business trip.

But.

Even as Jackson and I traded stories now, I remembered the way Dad had smirked at Mom the few times she voiced her forebodings. Like the winter night when seventy-mile-an-hour gales shook our ancient cedar trees as if they were maracas, the boughs rattling crazily as they scraped my skylight. The winds shrieked so loudly that Mom ripped the comforters and pillows off our beds and made Reid and me sleep in the living room, even though Dad scoffed that she was making a big deal about nothing. But the next morning on our way to the ferry, we passed our next-door neighbor's house crushed beneath a thick Douglas fir. Mom didn't say anything, just stared at that severed tree trunk and the demolished roof before her gaze darted over to Dad. He kept his eyes squarely on the road ahead.

"I'm sorry, Rebel. I got to go," Jackson said suddenly.

"Oh, okay." Gone for less than a week and the bonds connecting us were already overstretching. I bit my lip, disappointed. At what point would those bonds break?

"I'll talk to you tomorrow, okay?"

"You bet," I said, even as a shiver made the phone tremble at my ear.

I knew that, yes, I would talk to him tomorrow. But no, I wouldn't reveal everything and risk Jackson thinking I was crazy. I hung up and stared at the dark cell phone screen that timed the minutes we had spent together. Together. So, like Mom, I kept my misgivings to myself. The price of admission was too high.

"Hey, kiddo," Dad said, peeking into my bedroom, where I lay on my stomach, journaling on the floor. He sounded more energetic and interested than he had during our entire dessert. "How's the internship going?"

"Oh," I said and sat up, ashamed. I hadn't even divulged the disaster that had unfolded in Sam's office to my mom, too ashamed to admit that I should have listened to her advice and been better prepared. "Sam hated my work. I didn't get the internship," I said, holding my sketchbook up as proof. My doodles of cottages and treehouses had given way to sketches of skyscrapers in Dubai. It was about time I embraced modern architecture.

"Well, here's a trick I've used. Just figure out what the hiring manager likes and regurgitate it," Dad said easily.

How many times had I heard my father declare that whenever he needed to rally his team: It's not about the gameplay; it's how we play the audience. I appreciated how Dad didn't dwell on my failure.

"Thanks, Dad," I said, sighing. "It was kind of a tough week."

The air-conditioning droned so loudly, there was no need to muffle his voice. Even so, Dad said in a conspiratorial tone, "As tough as the way Mom said it was?"

Glad Dad was home, glad to leave the uncomfortable memory of Stone Architects behind, I pictured the way Mom continually nagged at my father. Now that he was back, I realized how much I had missed him since his move from Seattle. I ignored the dull drumming of hurt I had felt all week from his neglect. Why hadn't he called? Or answered ours?

"Nah," I said, rolling my eyes. "We were fine."

"Hey, sorry I missed your interview," Dad said as he removed two hundred dollars from his wallet, handing me the bills. "Why don't you buy yourself a new outfit?"

"Are you kidding me?" I asked, grinning past the unsettling memory of Mom unable to access any cash while he was traveling. Whatever, he was home now, I thought to myself. Even if clothes were virtually the last thing I'd buy with this boon of cash, I was touched at his thought, and threw my arms around him. "You're the best!"

Exhausted for no good reason after Dad left my bedroom, I lay atop my sleeping bag. Then, restless, I flipped onto my side to pull a photograph of Jackson and me out of the back pocket of my sketchbook, the one he had taken with his arm outstretched before us. On our first-month anniversary, we had gone mountain biking on his favorite "beginner's" trail. I crashed, which freaked both of us out until I told him that I wanted to push on. For the picture, I had yanked my T-shirt down my shoulder to display the bruise collecting near my collarbone, an impressed expression on Jackson's face, a triumphant grin on mine. As much as I loved the quirk of his grin, the shape of his jaw, the picture was a cardboard-cutout substitute for the real guy.

The wind blew the sheep-wool clouds outside my window, the kind I used to dream about resting upon as a little girl. But now the only place where I wanted to rest was on Jackson's shoulder. I had already spoken with Jackson and hated the pathetic image of myself as the Needy Girlfriend who had to text him every five minutes.

A few hours later, I awoke to my stomach spewing fire and barely made it to the bathroom before I threw up into the toilet. Before I could raise my head to wipe my mouth, Mom was at my side. For once I was glad that her radar for our distress was on permanent high alert. After wiping my face with a cool, damp towel, Mom led me back to my sleeping bag.

The next morning, I was running a fever, and Dad had already run out the door.

Chapter Eight

No fair! Reb is totally faking it so she doesn't have to help us unpack," Reid grumbled as he propped the front door open for the movers with his foot while writing in his journal.

My head throbbed from all the commotion—the sound of heavy footsteps clomping on the marble floor and Reid grousing that it was a Sisyphean task to transfer our books from the boxes to the built-in bookshelves in the living room. Like a high-pitched violin above the cacophony, Mom voiced her wonder at the movers' personal stories along with her orders about where every box should go: "What brought your dad from Samoa, Antonio? Box one-two-one."

However much I wanted to nap, it was too mortifying to be tucked in my sleeping bag while the movers barged into my bedroom. So I nested in the living room, out of everyone's way, and shivered despite the comforter Mom had wrapped around my shoulders as if I were a little old lady.

The few times I ever got sick, I was powerless over my candy-colored visions of people I knew, moving in slow motion as they met their future. As soon as I was well, I would convince myself that I had only been dreaming the fever dream of the sick, that my memory of those dreams was faulty even if I worked to circumvent them. Like Shana in my dreams, slapped around by her college boyfriend when she was sixteen. Instead of telling her as much, I had casually suggested that the Bookster Babes do a community service project for abused women. Even though I didn't know whether the slap ever happened or not—Shana never said—I could console myself that she would be armed and ready if her boyfriend's hand contacted her cheek.

To take my mind off these uneasy inklings, I remodeled Mom's garish bathroom in my imagination, first stripping out the ornate brass fixtures and replacing them with a sleek faucet. That done, I installed a crystal chandelier with extravagant loops of glass that would catch the light and twinkle in a thousand rainbows. There had to be a good store for recycled building materials nearby, what with all these old mansions around us. . . .

My eyes drooped.

Old neighborhoods with brownstone buildings. Brownstone buildings in Manhattan, the kind Mom had hoped we would live in . . .

My dream drifted to Dad's voice: "Bits, we need to talk."

Mom's breath caught as worry sprouted like invasive

morning glory, entwining every nerve, every terrible possibility. She asked, "What's wrong? Is everything okay? Is it your
mom? Is she okay?"

"No, no, nothing like that. Can you meet me in an hour? At
the Starbucks near my office?"

"Is it your job?"

"No, we just need to talk. Can you come here?"

"Thom, I can't drop everything while the movers are here.
Reb's sick. And I've got to get Reid from his friend's. Remember,
only you have a car." There it was, her perennial accusation in full
bloom. Even sick, I could hear the constant chorus of her blame.

"Take the train. It goes direct from Newport."

"Just tell me what we need to talk about."

I wanted to wake up now. The sense of foreboding was so
overpowering, I had to claw my way out of this dream, this now.
I wanted to throw off my comforter, run to Mom's room, tear
the phone from her hands.

"Bits," Dad said as though he had practiced this a billion
times, "I've been seeing someone."

"Oh, Thom," Mom whispered, cell phone clutched to her
ear. "What have you done?"

"We need to talk."

"It's Giselle, isn't it?"

Pause. Then Dad, surprised: "Yes."

"How could you?" Mom asked, her voice fracturing.

Only then did I pry my eyes open. Only then did I realize
this was no fever dream but a vision I had seen and heard as if I
were in my mother's skin. A vision colliding with reality. A

vision unfolding into Now. Mom was racing up the stairs. Her face may have been hidden behind her hands, but nothing could stifle the raw and painful sobs that stole out of her.

"Mom . . ." I whispered.

Somehow I got to my feet, head whirling, the marble floor freezing my feet swaddled in thick socks. Somehow I stumbled to the stairs, unconquerable as slick, sheer rock face. There was no way I could climb to the second floor. One of the movers looked at me and said, "I think your mom needs you."

This perfect stranger held his arms out to me and waited in silent question.

I nodded.

He swung me into his arms and carried me upstairs to the dark-stained door, heavy and closed. Inside, I could hear the animal crying of a woman in pain.

"What should we do?" the man asked as he lowered me to my feet.

"I don't know," I said. I may have found my voice, but finding my balance was harder. I reached for the wall as my world tilted beneath me. "Maybe you should just go?"

Then I opened the door to find my mother collapsed on the floor. Instinct carried me to her, where I sank to my knees and cradled her in my arms, both of us surrounded by a wall of boxes filled with her hopes for our new life here.

Chapter Nine

This is what a girl does in crisis. When her world is shattering. When she is cut off from her friends back home because she doesn't have a landline phone or an Internet connection (her dad didn't think to add these functions before they moved). And the thick, stone walls block cell phone reception as effectively as they do her mother's sobs.

This is what a girl does.

She goes outside to call the Bookster moms and leaves messages with each one. And because she is afraid to leave her mother alone for too long, she texts her own friends. Then, her boyfriend.

She ignores the barricade of boxes in the living room that need to be put away.

She listens to the eerie silence after her mom stops crying. The silence is worse than the crying.

She falls apart on her own.

Half an hour later, her mom's friends haven't called back. Or her own.

So she calls her grandfather, the one her father has ironically called unreliable. She leaves a garbled message. The words are unclear, but the intent is not: *SOS. Your daughter needs you.*

Because he does not answer, she rings her grandmother, the one she hasn't seen in two years, maybe three. She doesn't leave a message, because what words can bridge the gap of silence between them?

And then, because she has no one else to call, she phones a neighbor.

A neighbor her mom bribed at Starbucks to be her friend. A neighbor she's met three times.

A neighbor whose last name she's forgotten or perhaps has yet to learn.

The neighbor flies into her house a mere five minutes later.

The neighbor takes one look at her and says, *Lie down, honey. I'll take care of this.*

The neighbor sprints upstairs to her mom's bedroom. And opens the door. And says, "Oh, Elizabeth."

Elizabeth? Since when had her mom started going by her full name?

The girl asks herself what else about her parents doesn't she know?

But then the neighbor tells her mom that Thom is a jerk. That all men lose their brains in their forties.

The neighbor says go meet him. Figure out what's really happening.

The neighbor picks the place to meet—a private bar in a hotel not far from here.

The neighbor says, *You won't know anyone there.*

The neighbor says, *I'll drive you and wait in the parking lot. However long it takes.*

The neighbor says, *Pull yourself together. You are strong. You must be strong for your kids.*

The neighbor leads her mom downstairs and puts her cell phone in her hand. The neighbor says, *Call him.* The neighbor opens the front door.

The neighbor says, *Fight.*

Chapter Ten

Around six, in lieu of dinner, Mom filled her white ceramic cup with water and placed it in the microwave. Watching the carousel spin, I had a sudden image of Reid, me, and Mom, our threesome whirling aimlessly while we waited for Dad to return home to us. I tiptoed to her, though I don't know why. She always knew when I was near.

"Mom, what did Dad say?" I asked gingerly.

"Do you want some tea?" she asked, as if we were in the middle of an entirely different, entirely meaningless conversation. I trembled despite wearing a thick fleece jacket. The problem was, I wasn't sure how much of my shivering was due to my being sick or my being in shock.

"Not really," I said.

"Okay, that's good, actually. I don't even know where Thom is."

"What?"

"Tea. I don't know where your favorite tea is."

We both heard the inadvertent slip of Mom's tongue. Worse, we both knew exactly where Dad was: precisely where he had been these last few months when he was living "on his own" in Manhattan. Disheartened, I sat down at the kitchen table, where I found Mom's ubiquitous list on her clipboard: *Call Schwab and Wells Fargo, contact divorce lawyer . . .*

Divorce lawyer?

My nausea now had nothing to do with the flu. Honestly, what kind of ice-pick woman discovers her husband has been cheating on her and a scant eight hours later devises a divorce plan? Disregarding my wish, Mom placed another mug of water into the microwave. Then she sliced an apple methodically, first in half, then in quarters. How could she be functioning normally when I felt so hollowed out?

"You should be in bed," Mom said after I sniffled, and set the plate of apple slices on the table. With a look of chagrin, she grabbed the clipboard and hastily set it facedown near her cutting board. Too late. I had already seen the damning contents.

I was about to demand an answer—*What the hell is this about a divorce lawyer?*—when, from the entry, Reid announced his arrival. "I'm home!"

"We're in here," Mom called back as she began cutting a block of cheddar cheese into bite-size cubes.

The hurricane of hunger that is my brother descended on the platter of snacks. Grabbing an apple slice with one hand, Reid shoved it into his mouth. "Mom, you forgot to core the apple!"

He spit out some seeds as he scooped up three pieces of cheese. Mouth full, he asked, "So, when's Dad coming home tonight?"

Mom froze, one hand midway to the cabinet, the plate she was about to fetch for Reid forgotten. Then, as if the floor had listed unexpectedly beneath her, Mom grasped the counter with both hands, steadying herself.

I glared at Reid.

"What?" he asked, cramming in another two cubes of cheese. "Dad's not on another business trip, is he?"

When Mom remained silent, I intended to answer, but how? What words do you use to tell your little brother that Dad has been cheating on Mom? On all of us? Whatever was said would end Reid's childhood. Mom dragged herself over to the table, aging three decades in that minute. Gently, she slid the barstool back as though a single sound would scare us away.

Steam warmed my cheeks when I lifted the mug to my lips, and I was grateful that I didn't have to break the news and break Reid's heart. Mom sat down heavily next to Reid, stared at her dry hands before she rallied like a general before a battle. She straightened and stated without preamble, "Your father's been dating another woman."

"But he's married." Reid frowned, refusing to look at either of us.

"Your dad is really confused right now. This has nothing to do with you. With either of you."

The room careened wildly as anger filled me. *Divorce lawyer!* "That's because this has everything to do with you. You've never once appreciated him."

Mom's eyes welled up like she had been twice betrayed—by husband and daughter, always the partners in crime. No way, had I really just said that to her? Had I? I felt like I was free-falling, limbs flailing. I don't know which of us shot out of our barstools first—Reid to punch me in the arm or me to flee the kitchen, Mom's hurt, Dad's lie, our messed-up lives, what I had said.

I bolted.

Jackson. I needed his voice. His belief that everything was going to be okay, that I was still a good person. That he loved me even when I hated myself.

Retreating to my balcony, I recounted everything that I could remember to Jackson. My mouth was dry and parched when I was done, but I still felt teary and welcomed the reviving power of Jackson's support: *Your mom's a great lady. Guys have been known to be inordinately stupid. Your dad will come back. My dad did after he had an affair. . . .*

"He did?" I asked, astonished. The breeze cooled my cheeks, which still felt flushed from bailing on Mom and Reid down-stairs. "When?"

"Five years ago."

"What happened?"

"He hooked up with my au pair." The sudden bark of Jackson's wry, embarrassed laugh hurt my ear. I moved the phone away from me a fraction of an inch. "What a cliché, huh?"

"How old was she?" I asked.

"Twenty-two."

I wasn't sure why I sought those tawdry details, as if someone else's worse transgressions could redeem my own father, but I did. "So," I continued, "what happened to her?"

"Her agency sent her back home to Brazil, I think. I've never seen her again."

There it was, a tendril of hope, so tender it could barely support the weight of my growing fantasy. Given another day or week, Dad would surely inventory all that he was sacrificing: our family, Reid, me. The balance sheet would tilt in our favor—how could it not?—and then Giselle would vanish from our lives, a shiny light that had temporarily blinded my father, blindsided the rest of us. So enamored with this homecoming vision, I was caught off-guard by what Jackson was now saying: "In a weird way, the affair was good for their relationship."

"Good?" I asked, honestly flummoxed. "How is that even possible?"

"I'm not saying it'll be good for your parents, but for mine, it was what they needed to appreciate each other."

The echo of my accusation at my mother—*you've never once appreciated him*—rumbled in my head. But I refused to follow Jackson's path of rationalization, not when I kept stumbling over the rocky shore of truth: How could "affair" be uttered in the same breath as "good"?

"Anyhow," Jackson trailblazed over my silence, "my parents went into pretty intensive counseling for a couple of years and threw me into therapy. My sister was already in college, so she escaped that torture. But you know, they worked through it. We all did."

"How can this be good?"

"It opened up their communication and made them deal with a bunch of issues they'd been brushing under the rug. Like money and Mom's shopping. And Dad's control-freak ways."

Suddenly, combustive anger flared through me. "So your father justified his affair because your mom liked to shop?"

"No . . ."

"And are you suggesting that sleeping with someone outside of your relationship is a good thing?"

"Rebel—"

I surged to my feet and gripped the metal railing. "Because if you are—"

"I'm not. Look, even though things worked out for the best for my parents, it doesn't mean it was easy."

"Why didn't you tell me this before?"

"Did you really want to know?"

Feeling more at odds with Jackson than ever before, I wrapped an arm around my middle. Shivering, I said, "You know what? I'm tired. I'll call you tomorrow, okay?"

Without waiting for Jackson's response, I hung up. Even though I set the cell phone far from me on the balcony floor, no amount of distance could fend off the foreboding that there was yet more hard news ahead. Jackson's secret was a boulder that had sheared without warning off a mountain cliff, marooning me on one side of a trail, him on the other.

Around midnight, I vacillated in that infuriating state of being exhausted but unable to sleep. Every time I thought I might drift off, my mind replayed the conversations from the day until they jumbled into one giant morass of Mom-Dad-Jackson confusion. The thought of organizing my space—despite my moving out in a few weeks—felt comforting. So I methodically opened the boxes stacked neatly against the back wall.

The first box contained everything I held most dear: the artifacts from my summer architectural program and the first present Jackson ever gave me. I set the smooth river rock down beside a framed photo of us, so easy with each other from the start that I had convinced myself we were fated to be together. But if I could be stunned by Dad and his ability to cheat and his capacity to lie, then how well did I truly know anyone?

What other secrets, unknown and untapped, resided within Jackson?

I dove back into the moving box and retrieved my clock, the one Grandpa had given me shortly after Grandma Stesha left. That clock had lulled me to sleep night after night, each tick a heartbeat of steadfast love. The journey across the country had broken its delicate inner workings. No matter what knobs I pushed or dials I twisted, the timepiece had stopped when none of us were looking, freezing us in the unchangeable past.

On my desk, my phone lit up with Jackson's text: *Rebel, call me.*

I yanked the comforter off my bed, draped it around my

shoulders, and escaped to the small balcony outside my bedroom. For the first time since we moved, I deliberately left my cell phone inside. The air had cooled off drastically from its earlier mugginess.

How was it possible that on this day when my family fell apart, the stars could twinkle so bright—especially the North Star, which Jackson, stargazer, had pointed out to me once. "Just look up in the sky and you'll find your way home, wherever you are." What we had lost in our home, I wasn't so sure we could ever find again. An invisible fault line had lurked beneath my family, and this move had triggered an unexpected seismic reaction.

A car came to a crunching halt in front of the house. In the dark, I could barely make out Dad's silhouette as he climbed out of his car and sauntered down the driveway, his arms swinging, absurdly carefree.

Dad had come home, just as I knew he would.

I sprinted through my bedroom to the hall. Mom must have been holding vigil for him, too, because she beat me to the stairs, racing down with hope-lightened footsteps.

"Thom?" she called softly, not wanting to wake Reid or me.

From upstairs, I leaned over the railing to find Dad in the living room. He looked neither somber nor brokenhearted. Not even guilty. With a start, I recognized the way his chin jutted out: defiance. That expression stopped me at the top of the stairs.

"You didn't know, did you?" Dad actually looked proud of

himself. Proud that he had conducted the affair so clandestinely that not even Mom's purported sixth sense could detect it.

"So when did it start?" Mom lowered herself onto the edge of the sofa. Her fingers were woven together like mine, gripped tight while I huddled in the shadows.

"You want to know how it started?" Dad smirked. I recoiled from this stranger masquerading as my father. This wasn't how I wanted to view him, even if, in a way, I could understand what Dad was doing. And why. Was it any different from how I wanted to skewer Mom with the truth, especially when she was caustic with impatience?

Dad remained silent for so long, arms crossed, that Mom had to ask: "How did it start, Thom?"

"It started in March. In Florida."

March . . .

I sucked in my breath. March was when we went to Tuscany. March was when we celebrated Dad's forty-fifth birthday and the launch of his new game. The back of my head rested against the cool metal slats, my mind stuck in March.

This last spring break, my family went on our first and only vacation where Mom was forced into the backseat, literally. Instead of Mom driving every decision down to the order of the sites we'd visit, a fancy tour company managed the details: the bikes waiting for us in Tuscany so we didn't need to ship our own. The air-conditioned van for riders who weren't fit enough to handle long, hot rides. The guides who pointed out all the interesting spots they'd scouted earlier so we could maximize our sightseeing.

I swear, the entire time leading up to the trip, Mom was fixated on the exorbitant cost because she could have done all the organizing herself. So when her "This is so expensive" monologue began yet again that first morning in Italy, I rolled my eyes. They landed on Jackson, who was standing across the posh hotel lobby. If I thought my first look at Jackson was thorough, that was nothing compared with his gaze: wholly male, wholly appreciative, and wholly disconcerting.

Maybe it was because Jackson flushed, embarrassed at being caught staring, but I found myself grinning at him reassuringly. That was invitation enough for my Jackson. Later, he'd tell me, "Oh, yeah. That was as come hither as a smile could get." In any case, he hithered around the couches in the lobby toward me.

Less than two minutes later, Mom ascertained from his parents that they had moved to Seattle at the beginning of the school year—"My husband went to Viewridge Prep, too!"— and that Jackson's dad, Stan, was a Navy officer turned real estate tycoon—"My husband's family is in real estate development, too. Muir and Sons."

"You're Adam Muir?" Stan said, looking at my dad, impressed.

"No, that's my brother." Dad shrugged without meeting Stan's eyes.

"What are the chances of this?" Mom marveled aloud, echoing my thoughts uncannily, as we followed the bouncy, cute tour guide outside. "Meeting you all the way here in Italy? Right, Thom?" Mom nudged Dad's arm. If she had elbowed me instead, my mouth might have opened. Words I didn't want to say aloud might have leaked out as I stared at Jackson and he stared back at me. Words like "Behold: proof of God."

"Before you know it," Dad said with a chuckle, "Bits will be telling you that this was"—his fingers waggled in the air—"fate."

"Why not fate?" Jackson asked so softly, I had to lean close to hear him.

"You actually believe in that?" I whispered as the soft breeze caressed my cheeks.

Jackson's grin was so roguish, I could feel my entire body flushing with sudden heat that had nothing to do with the temperature. With that, Fate herself might as well have caught me in one hand, Jackson in the other, and thrown us together with a stern command: "Connect."

Who was I to disobey?

How could Dad have started an affair in March when we had just had an enviable family vacation? When he and Mom announced our move to New York a few weeks afterward? How could Dad, my forever hero, the one I could count on to be the cool parent, do this to our family? And if he was going to leave us, why hadn't he told Mom back on Lewis Island? Why move her and Reid out in the first place . . . unless he loved us? Unless deep in his heart he wanted us to remain together?

I stood up now, heart and hope racing. There was a chance to keep our family together if Mom played this right. Profess her love, beg him to reconsider, apologize for being so critical. Instead, Mom asked as if she were checking off a list of prepared questions, "So, how much of our money have you spent on her?"

"Not our money," Dad corrected, and paused deliberately. "*My* money."

"Wow. Really. That's just . . . wow."

His shrug was nonchalant, as if they were talking about him buying whole milk instead of nonfat. "Look, I don't want to hurt you more. But Giselle. Well, she reminds me of you before we had kids."

The impact of his words—his damning words—slayed me. I knew I had been an unplanned pregnancy, a shocking rerouting of their lives: Dad forced to move back to Seattle from San Francisco, Mom eventually giving up her career. But didn't he want me at all? Or Reid, who was deliberately planned down to the hour when labor was induced? Didn't we, at least, make Dad feel loved?

As if Mom could feel my pain, as if his statement was a sin far worse than sleeping with another woman, she spoke loud and firm: "But we have kids, Thom."

Dad flinched, rearing back with an affronted expression, as though he were the victim. Even though Dad barreled toward the front door now, Mom didn't say anything, nothing at all.

That was it? That was all Mom was going to do to stop Dad from leaving us? Without thinking, I flew down the stairs. "Dad, wait!"

Too late. My father had already vanished outside.

"He left—and you didn't stop him!" I yelled at this frozen sphinx of a mother.

"There was nothing I could do," she said helplessly.

"You're giving up because of some stupid family curse that isn't even true!" I pushed past her, wrenched the door open, and yelled, "Dad! Dad! Wait!"

Immediately, Dad stopped at the car door and smiled sadly at me. "Hey, Rebecca."

"Dad, why are you doing this?" I trotted down the driveway to stand in front of him. No plan, just pure need. "Please, don't go."

"One day you'll understand. You can call me anytime you want, Rebecca. This has nothing to do with how much I love you and Reid. And always will. But I've been miserable."

I shook my head, uncertain how misery could justify Dad's actions. Even more unsure how I could commiserate with him about Mom and her dictator ways and still convince him to stay.

Then I recalled my conversation with Jackson. I said, "You could go into counseling with Mom."

"No," Dad recited patiently, as though he had rehearsed this speech—and I could guess who his adoring audience was. "I don't think people change. I just don't."

"So what are you saying?"

"I'm with someone who really cares about me." He jiggled his key chain as though he wanted to retreat to that someone now.

I wanted to tell Dad he was crazy. He had a family who adored him. Didn't Reid show it to him by playing football when he hated the sport? Didn't I? That question came so fast, so unbidden, I was shocked as the answering thought spooled from my heart to my head. And for the first time, I admitted the truth: I only wanted to create corporate buildings à la Sam Stone to please Dad. I felt empty now, deflated of both dreams and illusions. Still, I managed one last volley: "But, Dad, you're not just leaving Mom. You're leaving me and Reid, too."

"You'll be in college soon. On your own. It's just been so hard. All of it." Dad ticked off Mom's transgressions on his fingers and spoke as though she were standing in front of him, not me. "Your mom never supported me. She is always so task-oriented. And Giselle's so optimistic all the time, totally laid-back."

I stumbled back from Dad at this litany of wrongs. However much Mom annoyed me with her cross-referenced matrices and mission statements for our family, there was one thing I never questioned: Mom put us first. Besides, Dad was the one who had cheated. How could he blame Mom?

"Rebecca, I've been meaning to tell you something," Dad said conversationally, as if we hadn't been talking about his affair or Mom. He dropped into the driver's seat, inserted his key in the ignition, and paused.

My whole body tensed as I leaned toward Dad. "What?"

"You should go to UW. It's a great school, close to your friends, and you could intern with Peter. Plus, you'd be with Jackson."

"What?" I shook my head, utterly confused. Dad wanted me to go back home? "Why are you telling me this now, Dad?"

"I shouldn't have moved you guys out here. You'll be better off back at Seattle."

"But we want to be with you."

Dad didn't answer me. What he did answer was his phone. In the middle of ending his marriage with Mom and hacking apart our family and urging me to go back home, Dad actually took the call, placed a finger in his ear to block out the sound of my stunned silence. Who could have been so important? My mind raced to the only answer: Giselle.

Now, to my horror, I realized why he had sanctioned my long-distance relationship, assuring me that some were worth the effort. He wasn't justifying Jackson; he was justifying Giselle.

Dad mumbled a few indistinct words, hung up, and fired up his engine. "I have to go."

Chapter Eleven

et's say you've been unceremoniously dumped. Let's also say you're angry or distraught or confused. It is still a girl-truth universally acknowledged that for a week, a month, or—God help us—possibly a lifetime afterward, whenever your cell phone rings, your heart will lift, and you will think: Is it? Is it him?

So when the doorbell chimed the next morning, I trilled a long, high flute note of longing. *Is it him?*

We all must have believed at some level that Dad would return to us, because as one we wrenched from our breakfast to face the front door like antelope at the watering hole. Dad, it had to be him. Who else would visit on a Sunday morning at eight? He was going to explain the last couple of days away with a cavalier chuckle and an abundance of logical reasons: *Oh, it was nothing but your overactive imaginations, everyone! I would never leave you.*

Reid reached the door first, displaying never-before-witnessed track star speed. Plus, he body-blocked me with a fierce elbow-jabbing technique that would have shocked any number of his football, soccer, and baseball coaches. The pacifist on their teams actually showed some killer aggression?

"Hey!" I said, expecting Mom to run her normal interference, but she stayed behind, poised on the barstool like a hummingbird in torpor, alive yet dead to the world. As for me, I was prepared to launch myself into Dad's arms, forgive him everything.

Reid yanked the door open.

It wasn't Dad filling the doorframe, but our grandfather, a polar bear of a man whose profuse white hair sprang with riotous abandon from his head and eyebrows. In his wrinkled button-down shirt, Grandpa looked ill at ease, born instead to wear tattered flannel shirts and jeans faded light blue from honest, backbreaking labor.

With an arthritic slowness that concerned me, Mom rose to her feet and whispered, "Dad?"

Reid and I parted in the doorway, the guardians of a mother we never knew needed protecting. But once she reached the door, Mom hung back, shifting her weight from foot to foot like an uncertain girl, until my burly grandfather swept her into a tight embrace.

"You were right about Thom," she said softly against his shoulder.

"No, your mother was."

"He left me." Then she struggled out of his arms, transforming back to the tough woman who could author a divorce plan when other jilted women would be a puddle of heartbreak on the bathroom floor. "We're moving back to Lewis. And we've got a ton to do."

"What?" Reid asked.

Confused, I shook my head. "You and Reid are going back to Lewis?"

"You too. Until college starts," Mom said so sharply, I recoiled. Her tone spun me back to the hundreds of times I had felt that edge. That edge I never remembered as a little girl, never heard until after I almost drowned. Each word was hot oil. "We're leaving. The movers are coming back on Monday—"

"Wait, Mom, are you kidding?" I placed my hands on my hips. Was she for real? One measly day, and she was entrenched more firmly in drill-sergeant mode than I had ever seen. "Movers?"

"And I have meetings set up back home with an accountant."

"Betsy, stop," Grandpa said.

Mom continued, "And a counselor for you guys . . ."

"I can't believe you! You're not even giving Dad a chance. I mean, whatever happened to second chances? Whatever happened to learning from your own mistakes?" I said flatly, "I bet you have a meeting with a divorce lawyer, too? Don't you?"

Grandpa quelled me with a glare. "Stop. She's making a plan to protect *you*." Without another word, he placed his arms around Mom and tugged her close.

"Dad," she protested, trying to push herself free, "we're way behind. You have no idea how much I have to do."

"Shhhh." Grandpa rubbed her back like she was a child.

"Dad!"

"Shhhh."

Finally, Mom let out a sigh, her body shuddering, her face relaxing. I could feel her tension release. Her shoulders sagged as though she had laid down armor I'd never known she was wearing. I took the clipboard clenched in her hand like a shield. But who had she been protecting herself from?

My mind circled back to Dad smirking at her. Dad rolling his eyes at her . . . with me.

Grandpa continued in a voice gruff with emotion: "I've come to take you home, sweetheart."

Even I who dismissed Grandma Stesha's scrawled postcards about auras, I who laughed with Dad about how anyone could believe that colorful, angelic halos represented people's true spirits—even I could see the net of love my grandfather cast around my mother, as real as any used at sea.

Despite Mom's repeated hints and outright demands that Reid and I leave her to talk with Grandpa privately, we remained like stubborn ants unwilling to leave a newly discovered food source. Finally, Mom sighed and told Grandpa, "I don't want to discuss Thom now, okay?"

"You can't hide what's happening from them," Grandpa said, staring her down.

It was odd to see my mom being parented, after years of her managing Reid's football teams, my college admissions, and Dad's career. She drummed her fingers on the kitchen table, her short nails clicking the quick beat of her frustration. Finally, she sidled an uncertain look at first me, then Reid, before asking Grandpa, "So Mom told you to come? Just like that?"

"Well, Reb called me, too. And besides, since when has your mother ever been wrong?" Grandpa's bushy eyebrows lifted into twin arches of surprise, then furrowed in exasperation. "She always knows. You two, of all people, should know that."

"Come on, Dad." Mom shook her head.

"Why not? Investigators break cold cases with psychics. Artists, writers, researchers, and inventors are all guided by instinct. Thom might not buy it, but some of the best business leaders say they'd always trust their guts over analysis." Grandpa took Mom's hand in his, rubbing his thumb down her life line, as if the truth were written on her palm. "You know things no person can rightfully know. You have a special dialogue with God. I have no doubt of that." He stretched his hand out to cover Mom's, dwarfing hers. "She always said that there are no coincidences, only fate."

Now I remembered how Dad had smirked in that Tuscan lobby, dismissing Mom publicly. *Bits will be telling you that this was fate.* Now I remembered how Mom had blushed, ashamed. The same way blood rushed to her cheeks now, as though she remembered Dad's derision, too. She retracted her hand and scrutinized her fingernails. Their unpolished state had become critically important. Mom mumbled, "So why didn't she come herself?"

"She's in India."

"India?" I asked, and brought over the fourth cup of green tea I'd been using as my excuse to stay in the kitchen. I pulled up a barstool next to Grandpa George. "What's she doing there?"

"Leading another healing tour," he said, taking a sip of his tea. "Mystics this time. Anyway, there's been a strike at the airport. Not a single flight is leaving out of Delhi. Didn't you hear about it in the news?"

Both Mom and I shook our heads. Neither of us had been keeping up with the affairs of the world, outside of the one that had rocked our home.

As though the burden of her thoughts was weighing her down, Mom lowered her head and rubbed the back of her neck with both hands. I understood. My own mind spiraled to Dad, who had escaped to Manhattan...back to her...while we stayed in this cold igloo of a home. Suddenly I hated this house, selected by Dad, who never understood the magic of fairy houses, so I stopped building those fanciful structures. Dad, who told me that treehouses would be the first item cut from any

99

budget in a down economy, so I set aside my dream of creating treescapes. Dad, who told me that the big-league architecture programs only wanted people who were going to change the world, not a household, so I became the analytical Thom Girl he wanted.

I demanded to know what I already suspected deep, deep down: "But how did Grandma Stesha know what happened, when I didn't even leave her a message?"

"Didn't you know, too?" Grandpa asked me directly.

Guiltily, I averted my gaze and bit my lip even as my mind replayed all the times I'd heard the wailing. If I were honest with myself, I'd admit that I had known with certainty that something horrible would happen because of this move. But knowing was one thing; warning was an entirely different, entirely dangerous matter. I should have spoken up about the misgivings I had. I should have told Mom and prevented—

Interrupting my self-flagellation, Grandpa asked gently, "And what could she have done? Any of you? Even if you had said something?"

I clenched my mug so tightly, I was shocked it didn't crumble in my hands. True, while I might not have been able to stop Dad from cheating and leaving us, at the very least I could have prevented us from living in this isolation chamber of a house. I could have prepared us for the pain of Dad's betrayal.

Grandpa George placed a calming hand on Mom's arm. Whether to steady her or to prop her up for his next revelation,

I couldn't tell. He said, "Warn you? As I recall, your mother did that once, and look at what just happened."

Startled, Mom met my grandfather's gaze but remained silent.

"She predicted that Dad was going to leave us?" I asked, incredulous.

"She told all of us," Grandpa said flatly.

"Dad knew, too?"

"Your grandma accused him of it after your hospital stay."

No wonder Dad had wanted Grandma Stesha gone, banished from our lives. No wonder he dismissed her purported intuition so vehemently that his attitude verged on mockery. And no wonder Grandma Stesha had kept such vigilant tabs on him that he'd grouse to Mom: "She's always watching me. That evil-eye act is a little creepy." Then he had mimicked my grandmother, squinting his eyes so they looked beady, delighting me so that I laughed hard.

Grandpa asked quietly now, "So when she says you should come home with me—"

"Good," Mom interrupted. "Then she'll have nothing to complain about, since we're already planning to go home."

Grandpa George shifted in his chair and scratched the back of his neck. "Well, I didn't exactly mean Seattle."

"What do you mean?"

"I want to take you home to the Big Island."

"Hawaii?" I couldn't help interjecting then—not that Mom noticed, because her mouth had gaped open.

The power of speech revived in Mom with astonishing rapidity. She demanded, "When on earth did you get a place on the Big Island? How did you afford it?"

Reid chimed in. "Hawaii? I want to go."

"So how come you didn't tell me about the Big Island?" Mom asked.

"Spend a week there, then come back here if you want." Grandpa's broad gesture communicated what he didn't say in words: How could anyone want to be here? Here? That one gesture encapsulated everything about this house made of faux stone and fake plaster, starting with its lack of solidity, integrity, authenticity. *Just like Dad*, my inner voice whispered. I gulped down my hot tea, not caring that it scalded my tongue. Anything to stop that treacherous thought.

Mom confessed, "I don't know about the cost, Dad."

"Don't worry about that. Between your mom and me, we'll cover the trip."

There was a long pause before Mom asked, her voice soft, as though afraid to voice the question: "I didn't think you talked to each other?"

"Sweetheart," my grandfather answered tenderly, "I speak to her every single day. . . ." And then more faintly, as though echoing a confession he rarely admitted to himself, "Even if it's only in my head."

That sweet admission made me feel guilty because the flurry of Jackson's texts lighting up my phone had felt like harassing mosquitoes, annoying and unwanted: *Rebel, I'm here for you*. And *Rebel, call me whenever, wherever*.

I didn't want to talk to Jackson, not by text, not over the phone, not in my head. I didn't know what to say or what more I could possibly want to hear. Until our last conversation, I had been a thousand percent confident that Jackson wouldn't cheat on me. Now, after his blasé endorsement of his dad's affair, I could no longer be so sure.

Chapter Twelve

Perhaps Grandpa George's visit knocked me straight back to my childhood. Or perhaps I simply needed to escape the heaviness shrouding our home. Whatever the cause, I found myself in the backyard, foraging for materials to build my first fairy house in years. Kneeling on the grass edging the flower beds, I collected a few blue-gray pebbles and tiny fern fronds that would dry into a rich brown roof.

"Reb! Hey, Reb!" Reid stood at the edge of the deck, clutching his journal in one hand, my cell phone in the other. Even though Mom had instructed him to get ready for the day, Reid was still in his pajamas. No doubt he'd been lost in yet another one of his fantasy novels. "Your phone's driving me crazy."

Straightening, I approached Reid, knowing who had called yet again. I set my brown bag of building materials on the deck before taking the phone from Reid. Text message number three from Jackson was noticeably salty: *Silence is not golden.*

I sighed. Even though I knew it wasn't fair, I shut off my phone altogether.

"What're you doing?" Reid asked, disturbed as though his world had been rocked a second time by my setting my phone down instead of responding.

"I'm making a fairy house," I answered.

"Really? Like Tolkien's Lórien?"

"His what?"

If Reid raised his eyebrows any higher, his hair would be wearing a toupee. "The treehouses where elves lived . . ."

Startled, I realized that Reid had never seen me construct a fairy house. After all, I had stopped building them when he was four. So ignoring his pained disbelief that anyone could be so ignorant of *The Lord of the Rings*, I plucked a few rocks from my bag and placed them on his open palm.

"Here," I said, beckoning for his journal. "I'll design a hobbit house for you. Unless you want an elven treehouse."

I hadn't even finished my sentence before he entrusted me with his birthday gift.

"This is so cool," Reid breathed when we finished the sketch: tiny stones for walls and a thatched roof woven from strips of bark. For the first time, I experienced what it must be like to be an architect collaborating with a client, and I loved it. As Reid scrutinized our plan, completely absorbed, I felt at once how much I was going to miss my quirky brother when I was away at college . . . and worried that I was leaving him to navigate this torn home life by himself.

"Reb . . ." Reid began hesitantly.

I erased an errant line, blew away the rubber droppings. "Yeah?"

"Do you think we're going to be okay?"

I jolted, and the eraser skidded across the drawing but, luckily, didn't mar the sketch. I knew what Reid was requesting: ping the future, report back in the present. But that was an invitation to a secret society I wasn't sure I wanted to belong to, a faith in my visions I wasn't sure I deserved. Look at Mom, who was joining the women in our family as yet one more oracle cursed to stand alone in life without a partner, soul mate, helpmate.

"Do you?" Reid asked persistently.

"I don't know," I said.

"Don't know or don't want to know?"

I narrowed my eyes at Reid for having the audacity to ask me the question I was too afraid to ask of myself. It was one thing to have visions, but to court them deliberately? To look unflinchingly at all the other ugliness that might linger in the Pandora's box of our father's deception?

No, thanks. Maybe Ginny had it right all along. Maybe my wish was a curse, a self-fulfilling prophecy. With a start, I recalled my last wish on Lewis Island, that Mom's life would be as upended as mine. My God, what had I done? Had I changed her fate somehow, some way?

Reid stared intently at the drawing as though he wanted to vanish within the lines on that page. I would have gone willingly with him if I could. His question stretched invisibly between us, a taut tightrope. He deserved an answer, no matter how precarious it made me feel.

But what could I say that could possibly comfort him? A prophecy was no promise of solace. Just look at how mine about Ginny's dad had unraveled her. I grasped for anything and found inspiration in the unlucky source of our drawing, the treehouse from Tolkien's fantasy world. So I asked, "How would you get us out of this ick if we were a fantasy novel?"

"Us?"

"Mmm hmm. Us."

That one simple question filled Reid with ideas so rapidly, so abundantly, I could practically hear them collect like raindrops in a cistern during a storm. It was as though he had been waiting his entire eleven years of life to be a fantasy novelist. All he needed was the right trigger. Without another word, Reid leaned forward in his chair, plucked the pencil out of my hand, and began to write furiously. Whatever story he had begun to concoct in this wild, gasping rush of hope, I was confident he would write his way to safety. That was far better than I could manage. As much as I wanted to, I couldn't even string together a simple one-hundred-sixty-character response to Jackson's latest text: *Talk to me.*

"I'm not sure what you're doing," Grandpa George told Mom later that morning as he set a bag of Kona coffee beans and a box of chocolate-covered macadamia nuts on the counter, "but I'm hanging out with my grandkids."

"I thought you might like to go to the nature reserve. It's supposed to be just ten minutes away," Mom said, plucking a hot-pink binder from the bookshelf where the cookbooks were haphazardly stacked, some even upside down. "I've got the information right here."

"I've got this covered, Betsy. Relax today. Take a nap. Eat a chocolate." His brows drew together as he glanced down her scrawny frame. "Or the entire box. Do whatever you want."

Mom nodded quickly as her eyes filled with tears, and with chagrin, I realized how rarely I offered to help her.

"So, what sounds good to you?" Grandpa asked me.

"I'd love to check out Columbia," I said.

"Oh, honey, that's all the way in Manhattan," Mom started to protest.

"No problem," Grandpa said.

"You'd take her there? The city? You hate cities."

"Yeah, but I'd love to see where my granddaughter is going to learn to be an architect. And then she can show you around later."

Mom flipped to another section of the binder. "Oh, I have some info about Manhattan."

"Elizabeth, put that away," ordered Grandpa George.

Since Mom didn't look like she was going to obey anytime soon, I took the binder from her. Each section was neatly labeled with colorful tabs: gardens and nurseries, farmers' markets, architecture, antique dealers, bookstores and libraries, sports, and pubs. Every single one of these activities mapped to our interests, each meticulously researched from websites and blogs, articles neatly clipped from the *New York Times*, brochures Mom must have curated.

I flipped another page over and found listings for paint stores that Mom and I loved to troll for their colors. After that, a page with contact information for all the local treehouses featured in the three coffee-table books she had given me for Christmas.

"Mom, this is amazing!"

Pleased, Mom smiled, her first real smile in a day. "Really?"

"Yeah! When did you make this?" I asked.

"Before," she answered vaguely, as though she knew all her efforts to create a wholesome family had been futile.

Grandpa led the way out to his rental car. "Kids, what we need is a sense of adventure. And we've got plenty of that. Did your mom ever tell you about the time she thought she could fly?"

"What?" I asked.

"Oh, yeah. Your mom had just watched *E.T.* and got it in her head that if she hopped on her bike and launched off a big enough boulder, she could fly. She did . . . for half a second before she crashed and knocked out her front tooth."

I stared at my mother, who had followed us to the car, opening the passenger-side doors for us.

"Dad, sheesh!" she said with a smile, and only then did I

notice the slight discoloration in one of her front teeth. Despite her words, Mom flushed, a daughter beloved. "How did you remember that?"

Grandpa George added in a voice meant to carry to Mom before he shut his door, "My one and only job when your mother was growing up was to make sure she stayed alive. She's a daredevil but a terrible planner."

"Mom? She's the most detail-oriented person on earth," I said as I buckled myself into the passenger seat. "I mean, did you see that binder?"

"No, being organized is a foreign language she forces herself to speak to keep your lives in order. Your mom is a zero with details. So is your grandmother. Who do you think taught them to make daily to-do lists so they wouldn't forget anything?" He tapped his chest. "Did you know your mom broke her nose skateboarding down our steps?"

"Mom did?" Reid said. Both of us peered at her as Grandpa reversed out of the driveway. I didn't recognize the brazen girl Grandpa was telling us about any more than the broken woman behind us. *Carefree* and *adventurous*—those weren't the words I'd ever apply to my detail-obsessed, khaki-wearing mom. I rethought the binder: It wasn't to control how we spent our time but to direct it. She knew what we loved doing, which was why she knew to give Reid the journal to encourage him to write his own stories.

Mom followed us up to the edge of the driveway. There she stood, hugging the binder close to her, a shield that was supposed to protect our family in our cross-country move. I waved vigorously at Mom, and she grinned back at me, both of us touched by these simple gestures of affection.

Instead of eating in a restaurant, we brought our gyros, stuffed with cucumbers and dripping with garlicky tahini sauce, to the High Line, an urban oasis three stories above the city. Grandpa told us that this public park had been reclaimed from a defunct elevated railroad in the Meatpacking District originally built in the 1930s. Now birch trees and meadow grasses sprouted among the abandoned trestles. And we were stretched out, three peas in a pod of lounge chairs set on casters atop the rail lines.

One bite, and I was disturbingly full. Who knew that my heart and stomach had a symbiotic relationship: Both felt shrunken.

"Your mom would love this place," Grandpa said.

Humbled, I tilted my face to the sun. Even though Grandpa hadn't lived with Mom since she left for college, he knew the core of her: what she loved. What made her happy, filled her with joy. Years from now, would Dad know the same about me, considering he had dismissed my fairy houses, steered me to large-scale architecture, ignored my love for treehouses?

Grandpa crossed his arms behind his head while he stared up at the cloud-pocked sky. "You'll have to bring your mom here."

"But then she'd want to make a mini version of this back home," Reid said with his mouth full.

"Probably," Grandpa and I said at the same time.

We all laughed. I laughed again; I couldn't help myself. Nor could I explain my spontaneous burst of tears until Reid asked, "What?"

"Mom's home alone," I said, sniffling.

Grandpa reached over to rest his hand atop mine. "It's okay to feel happy even during this ordeal. In fact, you should grab as much happiness as you can, especially during this time. People are resilient. Your mom is. You are. You always have been."

We never talked about my near drowning off Grandpa's houseboat; none of us did. Grandpa tightened up whenever I mentioned missing his houseboat, sold shortly after the accident.

"Isn't it weird to think that you can find something this soulful . . . even here in a big city?" I asked as I watched a blonde girl with a birthmark like a cloudburst on her face sketch a robin bathing in a water fountain. The boy at her side wasn't studying the bird or her artwork or the GPS device he held, but her, as though she was the most beautiful being he'd ever seen.

Grandpa smiled, a Cheshire cat smug with a delicious secret. "When you come to the Big Island, you'll see. . . . There are sanctuaries everywhere."

I loved the idea of a sanctuary where people could find peace. That's what Mom had tried to create for us in the family binder she had assembled, a place for each of us to regroup in our new lives. This was no different from our personal spaces on Lewis Island, custom-designed without any of us appreciating her effort: my treehouse, Dad's man cave, Reid's library of a bedroom. When had Dad decided that he wanted to be a refugee in someone else's arms? I shut down the image of Dad with another woman. The thought, the idea, was way too disturbing. Way too revolting.

On the street below us, the rumble of traffic mingled with slammed brakes and yelling, so different from the lulling surf edging our island home. When had I decided that New York was my refuge? It was inconceivable that I would ever feel at home in nonstop traffic and thick congestion and crowds of strangers. Automatically, I pulled out my phone to text Jackson with that thought, only to notice he hadn't written to me. Trepidation shot through me, and I pushed my uneasiness down as I wedged my phone back into my messenger bag.

"Ready?" Grandpa asked, wadding up his soggy aluminum-foil wrapper. "We'll just hop on a subway, and you'll see how easy it'll be to get here. Plus, up closer to where you'll be at Columbia are the Cloisters. You'll love it there, too."

We retraced our way down the stairs and into the streets of this quaint neighborhood of boutiques and wine bars Mom had wanted to call her own.

Later, I would ask Dad and get a mumbled confirmation I didn't need. I knew as positively as I knew that Jackson would be mine, that my treehouse had been sited in the absolute right spot on our property, that I wanted to be an architect—I knew that this very street corner was where Dad lived with his mistress. An old brownstone home with a door freshly painted bright as a new beginning. An old brownstone home I had seen in a fever dream.

I could feel Dad and Giselle around me, laughing as they

strolled hand in hand along this charming street, not caring that we were home alone with our broken hearts. I could picture them, heads bowed together as they snuggled at one of the cozy outdoor cafés, their only concern their next trip together. All the while, Dad had been lying to us in his sporadic texts and infrequent phone calls about how his "business trip" was going.

People always say life is stranger than fiction. My personal experiences confirm that is true. What I tell you next is no lie, not even the slightest bit of exaggeration. Reid, Grandpa, and I were about to head to the subway when I spotted them far down the same street: Dad and Giselle.

You might say, *What are the chances of that?*

You might say, *Yeah, right.*

You might say, *Get your eyes checked.*

But I know what I saw.

It was as if my feeling Dad and Giselle had conjured them here near the High Line park.

What the hell was *she* doing here? I wanted to run to them and tear them apart; I wanted to run away. But then Dad threw his head back and chortled. It was the liquid laugh of a man without responsibilities. Suddenly, superimposed on the father I knew, I saw Dad at twenty-four, the hotshot MBA who had picked Mom out on the lawn in front of her freshman dorm. Dad before sacrifices in his career, in his travel plans, in his bachelor life had to be made because of unanticipated, unexpected me.

In that vision, I saw Dad as he wanted to be once again.

Reid's eyes grew fierce. He strode toward them.

"No, Reid," I said, holding him back even as I watched Dad pull Giselle into his embrace. She tucked her head on his shoulder so naturally, she must have done that a million times before. *That's my spot*, I wanted to yell at her, at him. My father's hands slipped down Giselle's tiny waist, then lower. I yanked Reid around, despite his protests.

"Let's go," I gritted out, tugging Reid along with me.

Even though it would cost us far more than taking a subway, Grandpa flagged down a cab. Gratefully, I slid onto the torn leather seat, ripped from overuse.

That unexpected encounter with Dad and Giselle left us too worn to visit Columbia. To lighten the shell-shocked atmosphere on the way home from the train station, I told Reid, "If Mom had been there, she would have marched right up to that woman and said, 'Move this.'" At that, Reid laughed. We all did as we imagined the mama-bear scene, but the Mom we found was slumped on the front steps, worrying her loose engagement ring around and around her finger as though our future was right there in her hands. But was our future here or back on Lewis Island? Give up or fight back? Broken family or simply bruised?

She raised her eyes, haunted, to meet mine in the car. She knew what we had seen. I had no doubt of that.

"Oh, Mom," I sighed.

No sooner had Reid and I left the car than Mom stood. She

was so achingly thin, her clothes billowed in the wind. She straightened, proud and rooted firmly in the ground as she waited for us. And what she told me with her hands heavy on my shoulders, as if she wanted me to feel the weight of her words, was this: "New York is just as much your place as it is theirs."

Chapter Thirteen

The first thing the next morning, I checked my cell phone. For once, there was no extra-late-night message from Jackson. No early-morning greeting. The reason was in his status update: *Heading to the boondocks with a good friend to watch the Pleiades meteor shower!*

A good friend? Sharp-edged unease prickled me. Since when did Jackson ever use the words *a good friend*? Buddy, yes. Friend, yes. But *good friend*, left unnamed? Never.

Unsettled, I sought girlfriend support, but knew better than to call Ginny at this early hour. She valued sleep as much as she did her flaming-orange KitchenAid mixer. So I phoned Shana, who was normally up and running by five to log her summer mileage.

"So . . . do you know who he went with?" I asked her as I laid out my harvest of found objects from the backyard: slender twigs and boat-shaped leaves, earth-toned pebbles and baby pinecones. This was my insurance policy. I needed to keep my hands busy to distract myself in case I heard something worrisome.

"No," Shana said without panting, since she was in such good shape, "but why don't you just ask him?"

Though I fell silent, the answer blared in my head: because I was afraid of what I'd find. Look at what full disclosure had done to my family. Nothing could soften the raw pain I felt after I spied Dad with his girlfriend in Manhattan. Nothing could muffle the sound of Mom's crying late at night when she thought everyone was safe asleep.

My voice rose a strained octave, then two, high-pitched with forced cheeriness. "Okay! I've got to go hang out with my grandfather."

When I hung up, I felt worse than before the call. I scooped all the materials for my fairy house into an untidy mound and went outside to scavenge more.

After helping Mom rent a car late that afternoon, Grandpa was reluctant to depart for the airport to fly back to the Big Island alone. With a dejected expression, he lobbed one last plea to Mom in the kitchen: "Sweetheart, if you change your mind, call me day or night. I'll get you the tickets."

Perhaps it was superstition, but suddenly I needed my broken clock—that timepiece of love—fixed. If there was one person who could repair anything, whether food processor or fairy house, it was Grandpa George.

"Wait a sec, okay?" I begged as he began to rise from his seat.

"Reb, he's going to be late," Mom admonished.

I sprinted upstairs to get the clock. Returning, I set the paralyzed timepiece before Grandpa on the kitchen table. Without saying a word, he cradled the device in his big hands, gentle as if it were a wing-injured bird. After inspecting the exterior, Grandpa slid on his bifocals to peer into the inner workings.

"I can fix it," he said, turning his steady gaze on me.

I nodded solemnly back at him as though this were a pact. If only a broken family could be so confidently repaired.

As soon as Grandpa drove away, my invalid clock carefully swaddled inside his carry-on bag, Mom grabbed the broom from the closet and announced it was time to tidy the house. That led Reid to retort hotly, "You're the only one who wants to stay here instead of go to Hawaii. So you clean the house yourself."

Mom's answer may have been just as pointed, but I heard the hurt coursing beneath her curtness as she swept the porch outside: "Stop being so disrespectful."

My breathing quickened during this spat, and I had to escape to the laundry room, not only because I had run out of underwear and Mom hadn't done the laundry in days, but because I finally knew why Reid's scowl looked so familiar. Dad had worn the same defiant expression when he told Mom about his affair.

After rewashing everyone's laundry, which had been left in untended piles for so long that all our clothes were wrinkled, I checked in on Mom in the kitchen. As soon as I neared, she mumbled furtively on the phone, hung up, and continued washing our breakfast dishes. Her hands trembled so much our dishes were in peril.

"What was that about?" I asked, worried.

"Oh, nothing." Mom nearly dropped a sudsy cup in the sink.

"Who was that?" I insisted. By the way Mom's lips tightened, I knew it had been my father. "What did Dad say?"

Mom countered, "What do you want for dinner?"

"I'm not hungry, thanks."

"You need to eat."

I studied my gaunt mom. "You do."

However much Mom protested, I was going to force-feed both of us a high-calorie snack at the very least. She had always maintained a strict five-day-a-week regimen of hot yoga and running, as well as her fresh-and-local dietary habits, but she was starvation-skinny now. Moments before I hustled downstairs this morning, I noticed that I, too, had become all jutting bones. Even my tightest pair of pants gaped at the waistband.

A smoothie, I thought.

Before I could open the refrigerator, Mom throttled full-force into our future as she picked up her clipboard from the counter, pen attached by a pink ribbon for last-minute list-making. "So, what should we do this week before we move?"

I forgot my smoothie-making intentions. "Wait. We're still moving?"

"Yes."

My vulture thoughts circled my parents' dying marriage.

Dictatorship was the first word that came to mind, *difficult* and *demanding* the fitting adjectives. Immediately, I felt guilty. My feelings teetered practically on the hour, every hour, first sympathizing with Dad, then siding with Mom. Angry at Dad, enraged at Mom. I felt like I was going crazy, mood-swinging dizzily between the opposite poles of my parents.

"You're just giving up because of some stupid legend in our family. The curse isn't real, Mom," I said as I wrenched the refrigerator door open. Cold air chilled my neck, my shoulders, my brain. Sighing loudly, I was about to slam the door shut when I beheld the nonfat milk instead of 2 percent. Over the last few months—surprise, surprise—Dad had become suddenly obsessed about getting in shape. There was the organic blueberry yogurt he loved for breakfast. On another shelf, I spied the six-pack of the dark ale Dad swigged during his nightly ESPN–and–e-mail marathons. Dad's favorite brand of Brie cheese, waiting for him like a faithful golden retriever.

Dad, Dad, Dad, Dad.

I sucked in my breath. This refrigerator was the still life of Mom's quiet and constant devotion to my father. For as long as I could remember, she had always kept these items stocked for him. In the refrigerator's chill, I could feel our family curse weave briskly around us.

At first I thought it was my scratchy sigh I heard, but I found Mom studying the refrigerator, too, her eyes filling with tears. Maybe neither of us could get our minds around the magnitude of Dad leaving us forever, what that meant for our family. But these little signs of lost love—an entire care package of a refrigerator—these we felt keenly. And maybe discrete, doable steps, like moving back home and arranging therapy, made pushing through this pain possible. And bearable.

So I took one doable step now. I grabbed the container of nonfat milk and poured its contents down the drain, every last drop.

Mom jerked when the plastic container thudded against the bottom of the trash can. I thought she'd rail about Dad and his "emergencies" at work. I thought she'd become one of those hell-hath-no-fury women who'd cut the crotches out of all his pants and sell his prized possessions for a penny.

Instead, Mom moved to the lonely outpost of the kitchen window and hugged her clipboard to her chest. Without turning to me, she urged gently, "Go check on Reid."

How little Dad—and I—knew my mother at all.

Late that night when my cell phone rang in my bedroom—not outside on the balcony, not in the one corner of our house with reliable cell phone coverage, but in my bedroom—I took that miracle as a sign.

Wouldn't you know it? The miracle was Jackson.

"Rebel," he said, "you're alive."

Not until I heard the familiar timbre of his voice did I realize how much I missed him. How much I ached to hear that "Rebel."

"Jackson." In truth, I sighed the two syllables of his name

with relief . . . and delight. I left my desk, where I'd been assembling Reid's hobbit house, and snuggled into my bed.

Instead of berating me for ignoring him, or explaining his own incommunicado absence, Jackson began with this: "So what's the latest?"

There are times when words tumble unexpectedly out of your mouth, expressing a wish you never knew you had until it was spoken aloud. This was one of those times. To my own surprise, I found myself revealing, "I don't know if I want to go to Columbia anymore."

"Why do you say that?"

"Well . . ." I studied the cracked skin on my heels. I swallowed, my throat parched as if these last days had sucked every last bit of me dry. "I'm not sure it's where I want to be. I mean, you should have heard Sam Stone! That's where he went to school. And besides, I don't even know if we can afford it."

My thoughts, I knew, were disorganized, a rambling path to an unknown destination. I turned around to fluff my pillow and felt irritated when Jackson asked what I knew was only a clarifying question: "So you're rethinking college because you think all the students are going to be Sam Stone clones or because of the cost?"

"I don't know. . . . All of the above, I guess."

"Well, this is a big decision. It could change your life."

To maneuver from a topic that made me feel stupid for not knowing what I meant, I deflected: "No, what's going to change my life is that Mom's not even fighting to keep Dad!" That deep-seated frustration pushed aside my overworked censor, the one that squashed every vision, the one that denied every premonition. I sat up in my bed. Now my confession flowed free. "She's giving up all because of my stupid family curse. All of the women on her side are single because every single man has left them."

"I thought your grandmother left your grandpa."

"She did. . . . When Mom started college."

"So that was some kind of preemptive strike? Kind of like you not talking to me?"

Darn it, I had forgotten how perceptive Jackson was. And how forthright. I said, "You're right. I'm sorry."

Now was a perfect time to ask him about his cryptic update post, about the "good friend" who had accompanied him to the boondocks. But I didn't want to know. So I changed the subject and told him that Grandpa wanted to take us to Hawaii.

Jackson said, "Escaping for a few days to regroup sounds like a good idea."

"I know, but Mom wants to move back to Lewis. I mean, she hasn't even tried to work it out with Dad." If it was hard enough for me to maintain a long-distance relationship with Jackson, how was Mom going to repair hers with Dad if both of them lived on opposite coasts?

"Does he want to work it out?" Jackson asked.

I sighed, flipped onto my side restlessly, and studied the hobbit house that I had left on my desk.

In Jackson's voice, I heard its echo, louder than the original question: *Do you?*

Louder yet was my answer: "I don't know."

Chapter Fourteen

When I got home from running to the post office to mail the bills for Mom, dinner for once wasn't on, and she was sleeping heavily. So pulling my best Mom, I called Ginny and asked her to step me through preparing a meal while catching up. Multitasking with the best of them.

"Where's all your food?" Ginny demanded after I had inventoried aloud the paltry ingredients in our pantry, refrigerator, and freezer.

"I guess none of us have gone grocery shopping," I admitted guiltily. Why hadn't I swung by the grocery store after the post office? I had assumed Mom would take care of us, the way she always had.

"I am so mad at your dad!"

"Geez, why are you so angry?" I peered into the pantry

again, as if a bounty of ingredients had magically materialized inside. "This is *my* father."

"That's just it. I mean, he's your *father*. Fathers are supposed to stick around. Fathers are supposed to put family first. Fathers don't just pick up and leave, not when they have a *choice*." That last word verged on a baleful wail, and I ached for Ginny at that unwitting admission. We may have both lost our dads, but mine was still alive.

"You're right," I said as I opened the refrigerator door. "So, we have some Brie cheese and pears. Beer and a couple slices of turkey."

"What are pears doing in your refrigerator? Never mind, take them out. Do you have bread? Please tell me you have bread. Or tortillas," Ginny asked in quick succession. "Tortillas will work."

"Bread!" I said, spotting the loaf with the relief of a ship-wrecked sailor at the sight of a rescue vessel.

Placated, Ginny carefully walked me through preparing melted Brie-and-turkey sandwiches punctuated with thin slices of pear. Pathetic as it was, I needed her detailed instructions because my kitchen skills were so abysmal.

"We should have read cookbooks for at least one Bed and Bookfest." Ginny sighed. After describing precisely how to cut the Brie cheese—leave the rind on—she added, "So I have to tell you something. Your dad's 'my money' comment has my mom worried. She thinks your dad might have been planning this for months."

I bit my lip and stopped slicing the bread for fear I might cut myself. The truth was, it worried me, too.

"We need a plan," Ginny said.

"Trust me, Mom's got that covered," I said, remembering her list: *divorce lawyer*! Nudging aside the bread, I made room for the pears on the cutting board.

"No, trust *me*. She doesn't. After Dad died, my mom got lost driving home from the grocery store. Did you wash the pears?"

Chagrined, I carried the pears to the sink and rinsed them off while telling Ginny, "Well, my mom was an accounting major. And if she wants to fast-track the divorce, she can be on top of the finances herself." My paring knife sank into the over-ripe pear with such ease, I wasn't prepared, and nearly sliced my finger. Hastily, I set the knife down.

"This is about you guys knowing what you have. None of us thought my dad would die when he was thirty-eight. Thirty-eight, Reb. My parents did zero financial planning. Zero." Ginny sighed, then added quietly, "Your mom helped me and my uncle sort through everything."

"She did?" I stared at the phone on the counter that I had just switched to speakerphone mode so that I could assemble the sandwiches with both hands.

"She did."

What else didn't I know about the people who were closest to me—Dad and Jackson's father with their affairs, Mom jump-starting Ginny's financial wizardry, Grandpa's Big Island property.

"Your mom's plan rescued us," Ginny said.

My mom's plan. That stopped me short from buttering the

thin slices of bread, and I remembered Grandpa's fierce defense of Mom: *She's making a plan to protect you*. Still, this paper trail I was supposed to construct, leading us sordid dollar by sordid dollar to all the details of Dad's deception? This was too much. I jerked away from the kitchen counter, strode to the oven, and turned it to BROIL.

Ginny added relentlessly, "I wish I could do this for you. Or my mom could. But your mom is so private. . . ."

Had I not known how dead-on accurate Ginny was about Mom and her intense need for privacy, I would have protested. But I knew Mom hated it when Grandma Stesha divined what she was thinking, what she was feeling. "It's like I have no safe spot from you," Mom had burst out once during a phone call with my grandmother before she realized that I was listening. On this point, I totally agreed with my mom. I hated the invasiveness of Mom's knowing what I was thinking even before I knew it myself.

"I have no idea how to do any of this." Panic made my voice squeak as I approached the phone again, wanting so much for Ginny to appear beside me. "I have no idea what our bank account numbers are or their balances."

"Um, hello, I remember your math score on the SAT. You're scary good with numbers."

I shrugged, but what Ginny had said was true. Numbers and formulas never intimidated me. It was another reason why architecture had seemed like such a natural fit.

"We'll help you," she said firmly. "This is no different from cooking: step-by-step."

"Really?" I layered the sandwiches with the wedges of Brie.

"Oh, remember to salt and pepper them before putting on the top piece of bread. Just one or two shakes should do."

I did as Ginny suggested. "I wish I could cook like you."

"You can. Remember? My only hope of eating well after Dad died was to cook. Otherwise, it would have been Top Ramen every meal, every day, since Mom had to work. But I'm lucky. That's how I found out that my Zen spot is the kitchen." Ginny's voice changed back to instructor mode as she reminded me, "So when you're about to serve the sandwiches, turn on the oven light and make sure the bread doesn't burn."

"Got it."

"Maybe you should make a test sandwich. Cut a sliver off one of them and stick it under the broiler while I'm on the phone."

As I did, I mulled over what Ginny had said. Petrified that I'd scorch the sandwich, I stationed myself in front of the oven. Finally, I admitted, "My Zen spot has always been my treehouse."

"I know."

From the moment Peter took me on a field trip to the recycled-materials store in Seattle's industrial neighborhood of warehouses and manufacturing plants, I knew I had come home. There, we had spent a blissful afternoon, choosing planks from a demolished barn to use as my flooring.

"Is it burning?" Ginny asked.

"Ack, I forgot to check," I said, chagrined, since I had been standing right in front of the oven. I grabbed two mitts and opened the oven. "It's black! I guess it's a good thing I did a test case."

"Yeah, and thank goodness you'll have dorm food."

"I'm not so sure about that," I said as I fanned the smoke.

"What do you mean?"

Hurriedly, I opened the windows and the back door, worried that the smoke alarm would blare at any second. "I'm not sure Columbia's the right place for me."

"You're not just saying that to spite your dad, are you? Because it's in New York, near . . . *them*?"

"Well, maybe it's got a little to do with him being there, but designing big, huge buildings? That was my dad's dream." What surprised me was my choice of words and the truth of them. I hadn't blamed Mom, but Dad. I took a deep breath of fresh air on the back porch. Then I swung the door back and forth, ventilating the kitchen.

When we were reviewing my college essay, Mom nitpicked the grammar, but Dad honed in on the topics. He never came right out and told me what to write, but his hints that "The admissions committee wants world-changers" and "Treehouses are a great hobby" and "Your heritage is in building some of the most important civic buildings in Seattle" had refocused not only my essay but my life itself.

"That, I can believe," Ginny said. Her voice changed back into teacher mode. "If you scrape off the black parts, you could still do a taste test."

Holding the hot sandwich carefully, I ran a knife quickly over the top piece of bread while Ginny asked, "So what are you going to do if you don't go to Columbia?"

"I don't know."

"You'll figure it out," she said, so confidently that I felt reassured. "How does it taste?"

Just as I had seen Ginny do a thousand times, I cocked my head appraisingly as I sampled a bite. "Hey, this is good . . . in a blackened Cajun sort of way."

Ginny laughed. "So we can thank your dad."

"Like, for what exactly?"

"Well, look at you. You're cooking!"

"More like creating carbon!"

We both chortled at that, laughing so freely we could have been at a Bed & Bookfest celebration. "Thank you!" I told Ginny as I placed all the sandwiches on the baking sheet.

"Well, now you know what to do. Just start over and make it even better for real," Ginny said before hanging up with an easy "Love you!"

Perhaps Grandpa George had it right when he told me to grab joy wherever I found it, especially in the midst of an ordeal. Perhaps it was time to reach out to Jackson. I glanced at the clock: six here, three o'clock Jackson time there. He'd still be at his dad's office. I brushed my hands off on my denim shorts, which probably would have made Ginny gag, and picked up my cell phone.

The moment Jackson answered, I could tell something was wrong. His voice was strained, reserved. I first thought he was going to announce it was over, that he was tired of the long distance, that more than the stars had exploded overnight when he was "watching" the meteor shower with his "good friend." I lowered myself to the top step and held the phone tight to my ear.

"I have to tell you something," he said, fueling every last dire scenario plaguing my imagination. Even as I tried to figure out a way to bypass this conversation that I so did not want to have, Jackson continued: "So last night, we were out for dinner, me and my parents, right?"

My grip loosened. "And?"

"And we saw your dad."

"Really? He's in Seattle? He didn't tell us that." But then again, why was I shocked, when my father had so masterfully camouflaged his affair from us?

"He was with his girlfriend."

I didn't think it was possible to feel the razor slice of betrayal any more keenly than I already had or witness any more clearly how Dad was forging ahead with his family-free Life 2.0. I was wrong. No longer could I deny that I had visions, so clear was the restaurant: Lola, the perfect place to bring his Lolita of a girlfriend, just ten years older than me. I'd been on Dad's side for years, us against Mom, us against her rules, us against her plans.

That image of Dad out in public—in our hometown—with Giselle short-circuited my brain. I could have been sitting in the restaurant with them, could overhear their conversation, could smell their richly sauced gnocchi. My stomach roiled from their poison meal. Who else had seen them? My school friends? My dad's family? And here I'd been Dad's biggest publicist, too, telling everyone how he loved us so much, he'd be coming back.

How could I have been so stupid?

"This is crappy," Jackson said.

"It is." My words were lethal bullets, as if he was my intended target, not Dad.

Despite my snippy tone, Jackson said, "I wish I were there with you now."

But he wasn't.

Ridiculous and unfair, I know, but I was suddenly, inexplicably furious with Jackson. The guy who had deemed his own dad's affair healthy—*healthy!* The guy who'd been out with his "good friend"!

I told Jackson abruptly, "I have to go," ending our conversation in a record ten minutes, our shortest phone call since we met. As much as I wanted to crawl into bed and yank the covers over my head, instead I sprinted down the street, dimly lit by intermittent streetlamps, only to trip on my flimsy flip-flops. My outstretched hands broke my fall. Sitting on the asphalt in the middle of the street, hands pressed on my stinging knee, I stared up at clouds masking the sky, so opaque it was hard to hope that the night might glow with starshine.

Slowly, I hobbled home, where Mom must have been waiting for me, because she opened the door before I rang the bell. She scanned my legs, which were scraped but not bleeding.

"Reb, what's wrong? Where did you go?" Mom asked, her eyes searching mine.

I didn't have the heart to tell her the truth about Dad's latest deception. Instead, I confessed my own omission of truth: "Mom, I didn't get the internship with Stone Architects."

"I know." Rather than berating me on the doorstep or even at all, Mom widened the door, letting me in.

"I didn't listen to your advice," I admitted, too embarrassed to look her in the eye, so I studied the marble floor that needed a good mopping. Without noticing, we all had tracked in unseen dirt.

"But now you know for the next time" was her frank reply as she led me to the dining room table, where Reid was seated, sure I would come home, the only question was when.

"Know what?" Reid asked. Hungrily, he eyed the platter of sandwiches that Mom must have broiled while I was gone, and removed just a few moments ago. The cheese was still melted.

"Know how important it is to prepare yourself." I sat heavily. "I should have written down all my interview questions! I should have practiced."

"Well, we can't go back in time, so it's no use beating yourself up now," Mom said, and served the sandwiches onto our plates. "This smells delicious."

And just like that, I was at the restaurant table in Seattle, watching my dad feed his girlfriend from his proffered fork. My throat burned with that betrayal. I swallowed. As if she knew what I had seen, Mom eyed me with concern.

"Eat," she urged. "You'll feel better."

I nibbled the sandwich, and Ginny could have been right here, nourishing me with a restorative meal made with love. When I told Dad about my lost internship, his advice was for me to regurgitate what the hiring manager wanted. Mom instead told me to rehearse so that I'd be prepared. Wasn't that what Ginny had meant, too, when she all but ordered me to broil a test sandwich so that the next batch would be perfect?

I recalled Ginny's admonishment, fresh in my head, that my mom needed my help. So I practiced. "Hey, Mom, can I borrow the car tomorrow? I'll go grocery shopping."

"Really?" Her face brightened but then turned into a frown. "I have to go to the doctor's tomorrow."

"I can drop you off, then hit the store and pick you up after. It's no problem." I was gifted with my mother's smile.

Chapter Fifteen

Exactly one day after my eighteenth birthday back in February, Mom chauffeured me to her ob-gyn in downtown Seattle in what I supposed was some happy-birthday/welcome-to-your-womanhood/coming-of-age ritual. Trust me: mortifying. First, their reminiscing about my birth was embarrassing enough—*Yeah, babies don't come much hairier than Reb!* And *She wasn't a baby; she was a Chia Pet!* But I have to believe that Mom's secret agenda was for my first gynecological exam to double as birth control. Can you say "cold metal calipers"?

So you can guess I wasn't entirely, shall we say, *comfortable* when I realized it wasn't just any doctor's appointment Mom had this morning, but one with a *gynecologist*. The parking lot was packed, so Mom pulled into the handicapped spot, where we could exchange seats and I could drive to the grocery store as planned. The only problem was that my mother didn't budge.

She just stared straight ahead, hands clenched around the steering wheel as if it were a life preserver.

"Mom?" I asked, worried. "You okay?"

"Yeah," she said, eyes misting. "It feels like yesterday when your dad and I were in the doctor's office, pregnant with you." Then with a firm, no-nonsense nod, she said, "Okay. I'll text you if the doctor's running late."

Worried, I started to ask Mom if she wanted me to go in with her when it occurred to me—duh!—why she was here. My face flooded with color. Of course, Mom had to make sure she hadn't contracted anything from Dad. The dirty aftermath of his affair hadn't sunk in, not really. Not until that moment. Because of Dad, Mom had basically kissed and touched and slept with every single person Giselle had. I bent over, sickened.

"I'll be fine," Mom assured me, her cheeks pink with shame as she hastily left the car.

No one—and I mean not even long-practicing gynecologists—should ever have to imagine their father and condoms, and their mother and STDs. Ever. Now I remembered how Mom would occasionally disappear with the phone, and wondered if those furtive exchanges were with Dad to discuss uncomfortable details like this.

I couldn't stand the sight of my mother vanishing alone through the office doors.

Don't do it; don't do it. But I found myself parking the car. I found myself crossing the interminable distance from parking lot to office door. Found myself hurrying down the antiseptic hall to slip through the office door, closing after Mom. Found myself in a waiting room full of visibly pregnant women and their even more visibly nervous partners. Found myself ignoring my mother's protests that I leave.

Instead, while Mom filled out a half dozen medical forms, I caught a puffy-fingered woman staring at my stomach, trying to gauge if I was the patient. Uncomfortable, I pounced on the magazines on the coffee table to hide my embarrassment. Underneath the crumpled copies of *Parenting* and *Car + Driver* magazines featuring radiant mothers and race cars, I unearthed a pristine issue of *Dwell*, my favorite home-design magazine. From the cover shot, I recognized the architect's distinctive style— organic and vital, brimming with creativity. Who else would construct a modern cabin out of rusty brown corrugated steel and rehabbed pulleys from abandoned shipyards? Excited, I flipped through the pages until I found the article. Just as I had thought: It was Peter's work, our architect. I lifted my gaze to tell Mom, but her face was averted toward the bland beige wall.

"You've got to look at this," I told Mom now, desperate to take her mind off the driftwood of her thoughts. I placed the magazine on her lap and tapped the article. "Look."

"Oh, Peter," Mom said. A wistful smile flitted across her face when she studied the small photo of our architect, geek-chic debonair in his trademark black jeans and black T-shirt.

The nurse barreled through the door, cast an efficient glance at her clipboard, and barked: "Elizabeth? Elizabeth?"

Mom's eyes watered as she glanced at me, face pale. "I'll see you in a little bit, okay, honey?"

Now, despite pressing her hand to her lips and clenching her jaw, her entire body shook from the violence of her fear, mine with anger at Dad.

"Mom, I'll be right here," I promised her with words that rightfully should have been my father's. Even if I wanted to flee this waiting room of curious stares, this STD-laced reality, I stayed.

Chapter Sixteen

What guarantee did I have that Jackson had been true to me these last few weeks? How could I trust that he'd be faithful these next couple of months? From the overgrown backyard where I had retreated after the doctor's office, I glanced up at the darkened windows in Mom's bedroom. No movement. I hoped Mom was resting, but I knew otherwise. I could still hear her soft sniffles on the long drive home, her restrained tears as she climbed the stairs, the unleashed sobs behind her closed door.

What assurance could I possibly have that a seventeen-year-old boy with raging hormones could be faithful when Dad couldn't remain true to his vows? To have and to hold—what was so hard about keeping that promise? In sickness and in health—how could Dad have been so reckless with Mom?

Since we moved in, the backyard had regressed from tidy

flower beds into a meadow of sprawling, puff-headed dandelions. I glared at the disarray of weeds, this enemy encroaching on my mother's usually well-tended territory. Rather than conscript Reid and me into her gardening crew, Mom had ignored the rioting yard as though she knew we were battling an even more insidious enemy. Now I knelt down to yank a dandelion from the mulchy ground, but its roots were so deeply buried, so stubbornly entrenched, that all I grabbed were flimsy green stems. Worse, my hasty wrenches had only blown dandelion seeds around the yard, where more weeds would take root.

How different was that from Jackson and his "my dad's affair saved my parents' marriage" philosophy? Didn't that kind of thinking sow more weeds in a relationship? What else could it justify? Maybe Shana had it right: It was better to be alone than with the wrong boy. Maybe the single status of all the women in my matriarchal line wasn't so much a curse as a blessing: Stave off heartache. Stave off betrayal. Stave off sexual diseases.

With cold recollection, I remembered what Jackson had told me when we first met: He believed in asking for forgiveness rather than permission. So what stopped him from cheating on me, then expecting my forgiveness?

The answer was as clear as if my sixth sense were a well-tuned, well-used instrument. The answer shivered its way down my spine, curved inward to my stomach, and nested in my heart.

What assurance did I have?

None at all.

It was weeding season.

Chapter Seventeen

You've been hard to get hold of," said Jackson, his voice serrated with irritation, as though he knew what I intended to do by conversation's end. The birds must have known, too. They stopped singing. The garden was graveyard-silent.

"I had to take my mom to the doctor's office. STD testing," I said bluntly, and moved to the shadows under the crab apple trees to escape the hot sun. Perhaps that was too much personal information to share, but was it, really? It was hard, painful truth no one should hide from, not when the risks were so real.

"How is she?" Even more gently, he asked, "And how are you?"

Strumming beneath Jackson's palpable frustration was a constant refrain of concern; it was in his every question, his every "Rebel." But that flash of intuition only threatened to change my mind, threatened to melt my resolve, threatened to reroute me from this path called self-preservation.

So I envisioned Mom on the examination table, her legs spread apart, her tears afterward.

And I remembered how easily that could have been me.

Before I could chicken out, I plunged in: "I don't think this is working."

"Excuse me?"

"This. Long distance. Us."

Silence answered me on the other end, stoic and chilly. Belatedly, I realized I should have broken up by text, the way Shana ended all her relationships—one hundred sixty efficient characters, clinical as Mom's examination room, cold as surgical instruments.

"I'm not your dad," Jackson said.

"I know that!"

"You're holding it against me that I told you that my dad's affair saved my parents' relationship."

"I'm not." Now I shivered in the shade, but I knew the sun was too hot. There was nowhere I could find a comfortable shelter. A neighborhood dog barked in agreement.

"You're scared that that's me," Jackson said, "and what I'd do to you."

"I'm not."

"Well, I'm not my dad. And I'm not your dad. If I wanted to date someone else, I would have ended this before you left."

"Good news: You can date other people now."

"Are you listening to me? I want to be with you. With you, Rebel."

Jackson's words felt too much like soothing aloe vera on

fresh sunburn, relieving the initial sting even before the damaged skin had a chance to heal. But I couldn't sink into his solace now, not when I could still feel Mom clenching my hand in the waiting room after her examination. She'd been so pale and shaken that the doctor herself had hastened after my mother to hug her in the lobby. When did that ever happen? I'll tell you when: when the gynecologist herself says, "You're better off without him. Trust me, I've been there."

"Look," I said, exactly as I had rehearsed in my head, "the fact is, it's hard to maintain a long-distance relationship. Everybody warned me about this, but I didn't realize how true it was until now."

One of the only advocates for staying with Jackson, despite our distance, was Dad. Of course he'd told me that some relationships were worth the effort, even if they didn't make sense. Dad had been gabbing about his girlfriend, justifying his actions. Words and promises, they meant nothing. Not even love itself. However much I loved Dad, that hadn't stopped him from leaving us.

"That could be because you haven't answered my calls today. Or my texts," said Jackson relentlessly. He paused, waiting for me to respond.

A part of me wanted so badly to give Jackson the answer he needed, to reverse my way out of this conversation, to assure him that a heart-damaged lapse of judgment had impaired my thinking. How easy would it have been to jump the divide between hope and fear, but the chasm . . . That chasm was littered with broken vows and lonely examination tables. I had almost drowned once because I had misjudged my ability to swim. I had learned my lesson. Stay safe. Step away. Don't jump in.

"Come on, Rebel. Don't run from me."

What neither of us realized was that I had a few days' head start on this breakup path, sprinting alone before I even knew I was fleeing. The truth was, a relationship—any relationship—was too risky. Shana had been right from the start: Heartbreak now was less painful than heartbreak later. As raw as I already felt, I chose now.

"Good-bye, Jackson," I said softly, and pressed the end-call button, a guillotine that cut myself off from Jackson and who we were together and what we could have been in the future.

Chapter Eighteen

Sobs shook me awake at four in the morning. My hand trembling, I flicked on my bedside lamp. A wave of fresh sorrow snagged my heart, a real weight pressing against my chest in both dream and reality. This ache went beyond missing Jackson; it was mourning stripped of blinders, a permanent lump in my throat.

Part of me wanted to run into Mom's bedroom now and ask her for reassurance. But she needed what little rest she could grab after yesterday's taxing visit to the doctor. Besides, all I truly wanted was Jackson's arms around me.

Too rattled to sleep and too scared about what I might dream next, I forced myself from my bed, shrugged out of my sweat-dampened T-shirt, and scrounged for a sweatshirt on my closet floor. I figured now was as good a time as any to tackle our finances.

Carefully, so I didn't rouse Mom on the off chance she was dozing, I tiptoed past her bedroom and downstairs to Dad's office. Despite the family photos on his imposing cherrywood desk and the wall of fame dedicated to his diplomas from college and business school, I didn't sense Dad in here. I sat at his desk, placed my hands flat on the smooth writing surface. No trace energy of him. He had been absent longer than we knew.

"What're you doing?" Reid asked from the shadowed corner. Partly startled and partly embarrassed, I yanked my hands off the desk.

"Reid! You scared me!" My voice was mother-sharp. I frowned at him and scooted back from the desk. "What are you doing up? It's late."

"Working." His challenging tone could have been me responding to Mom's terseness, Mom's questions. Now I wondered if I had misread her tone. When Mom demanded to know where I had been, what I had been doing, was it concern for me, rather than her need to control, that sharpened her voice?

More gently, I asked, "On your novel?"

Reid shrugged from the nest he had constructed in the corner out of a faux-fur brown blanket I recognized from Dad's man cave. My heart wrenched as I knelt in front of the protective wall of pillows surrounding him. It was as if Reid were wrapping himself in any proxy of Dad that he could. "How many nights have you been working in here?"

Again, Reid shrugged, keeping his eyes firmly on his leather journal.

If Mom were here, she'd nag him to go to bed, lecture about

147

how sleep triggered the growth hormone during this critical stage of his development. But I wasn't Reid's mother. So I switched to the safe topic of writing and said, "Tell me about your story."

"The oracle's chained up in the evil emperor's dungeon."

"Geez, Reid! Poor oracle."

"Oh, that's nothing compared with what's going to happen."

"Heartless." I squeezed his bare foot before covering it with the blanket.

"Yup." Reid turned a page.

Discomfited, I stood, then dragged myself back to the dungeon of Dad's desk. My first inclination was to keep my forensic accounting to myself, but Grandpa had a point: Reid and I were both old enough to hear the truth and old enough to help where we could. So I said, "I thought I'd figure out how much money we have."

"Did Dad use it all?" Over the last few days, Reid may have been acting all blasé, like he was cool, totally cool. But his wrinkled forehead belied how much he had been worrying inside.

It was tempting to pawn Reid off with feel-good platitudes, but real information and hard truth were the only way to allay our concerns now. Besides, I couldn't defend Dad anymore. The truth was this: Dad had left us before without ensuring that we had everything we needed. Had Mom been on the ground in New Jersey first, she would have made sure we had food, transportation, and emergency cash.

"That's what I'm going to find out," I told Reid. But as I rounded Dad's desk, I knew I could reassure Reid on two points with absolute certainty: "Even if Dad left, he loves us, so I doubt he'd leave us with nothing. Plus, Grandpa George and our friends will never let anything bad happen to us."

My words smoothed the concern from Reid's face. He flipped back a few pages in his journal and bent over his story again.

The most sophisticated my personal finances ever got was my savings account at Wells Fargo Bank, opened when I was five. A couple of allowance deposits here, a couple of withdrawals for gifts there did not a financial wizard make.

Accompanied by the comforting scratch of Reid's pen, I opened the first drawer and placed the main credit card file on the examination table that was Dad's desk. Taking a deep breath, I opened the file. Dad had said he'd been seeing Giselle for the last couple of months. So I started with March and found a four-night stay in Paris.

"No way," I breathed at the five-figure dollar amount. What was Dad thinking?

Quickly, I glanced at Reid, grateful he was immersed in his story. He hadn't heard me. And I needn't reveal anything yet.

On the statement from May, when Dad had moved by himself to New York, I found a long list of exorbitant dinners, not a single one less than a hundred dollars. Three hours later, I located my parents' investments. The sum total of next to nothing couldn't fund one retirement, let alone two. My first year at Columbia had been paid for, but what they saved couldn't fund all of our college tuition. Not for Reid. Not for me.

Where was all their money?

Two hours later, in the chill morning air on our front porch,

I called the university's financial aid office to arm myself with more facts. The woman there was polite enough about listening to my tale of woe, but her diagnosis was a rude awakening all the same: It didn't matter that our savings had dwindled alarmingly or that my parents might be divorcing or that Mom hadn't worked in eleven years. As long as Dad still made a heck of a lot of money, I wouldn't qualify for financial aid. And besides, we had a house that could be mortgaged.

I hung up with a heart drenched in worry. If I couldn't trust Dad to stay with us, if I couldn't trust Dad to safeguard our future, how could I trust him to pay for college? Maybe I should really and truly put off starting college this fall?

Enough, I thought, and pushed away from the front steps, intending to leave for a long walk to who knows, who cares where. I didn't have the strength to discover all the other betrayals that lurked within the recesses of Dad's office.

Even though it was early, I wanted to call Jackson.

Jackson would understand. Jackson would help me sort through all of this. Only then did I remember that I had ended our relationship. He was no longer mine to call.

Defeated, I began to lower myself onto the steps. As I did, I heard Grandma Stesha, her voice firm: *Isn't it better to know?*

In the still of the morning, my thoughts laced chaotically over and under each other like a crazy tapestry of memories, emotions, and realizations. I hauled myself inside to face the never-ending files. From the corner of Dad's office, I heard Reid rouse: "What? What did he do now?"

I wanted to say, *Nothing.*

I wanted to say, *Everything is going to be just fine.*

More than anything, I wanted to chastise Reid for assuming that Dad had harmed us yet again. But none of those could I say.

It was time to stop closing my eyes and face the dark truth confirmed in every file folder and by every document. Dad had concealed his affair from us with ease and deft skill. It was time for Mom to stop hiding from this reality, too. So I gathered the most damning evidence and set the papers on the kitchen table along with a note: *Mom, you need to see this.*

Chapter Nineteen

In my head, I still carry a snapshot of the kitchen table the morning Mom took over my reluctant role as the forensic accountant of Dad's double life: the tidy stacks of bank and credit card statements. A pink highlighter, uncapped, its tip drying out. A pad of paper covered with numbers, circled and underlined. And Mom's laptop opened to an Excel spreadsheet. Luckily, Mom wasn't in the kitchen—otherwise I'm not sure what I would have done if she heard the soft whimper-sigh that escaped me.

A small movement outside the window betrayed Mom's whereabouts on the back deck, arms gathered around herself while she stared, stared, stared up at the hazy gray sky. Way back two days ago, I was scared—and yes, wallowing in self-pity—when Ginny pushed me to help out. Way back then, I was furious that Mom wasn't being the adult. *You're the mother,*

I had wanted to scream at her. *You investigate. You decipher these bills and accounts.*

And way back twenty-four hours ago, I had heard my mother sobbing at the doctor's office, teetering on the thin ridgeline separating breaking down from broken.

Now I leaned against the barren windowsill. The last thing I wanted was for Mom herself to tackle the painstaking task of scraping the layers of intricate wallpaper covering her marriage and finding the insidious dry rot of betrayal.

Peter, our architect, had once explained at our job site the concept of sistering—how sometimes when wood was beginning to rot, you could add a new plank next to it. Side by side, the old plank could remain next to the new. Side by side, the two planks were stronger. Side by side, they could hold up a house. Side by side, they might hold up a heart. So I refilled the kettle and placed it on the back burner to start the water boiling while I walked out to the deck. There, I took hold of Mom's cold hand, and side by side, I led her back inside the warm kitchen.

As long as I can remember, Friday evening has been Muir Family Pizza and Movie Night. Tonight, when it was just the three of us on the sofa watching *MythBusters*, I literally couldn't remember the last time Dad had joined us, not even when he had lived with us on Lewis Island.

What I had been able to count on was Jackson hanging out at these end-of-week gatherings. Right on time, his text chimed on my cell phone as I went to open the door for the pizza delivery man: *Eat a slice for me, Rebel.*

It seemed so unnatural to ignore the text, which was what I was supposed to do, right? Delete the text because we had broken up? Instead, I found myself rereading those six words throughout the first half of the show, each one bombarding me with homesickness for my mountain biker.

Five slices of pizza later, Reid's distended stomach gurgled from his gorging, not that he noticed any personal discomfort. Too immersed in the MythBusters' quest to build a mammoth LEGO boulder, he didn't even notice the house alarm chiming as the front door opened. I flinched: *intruder.* Damn it, had I left the door unlocked? I jerked off the couch.

Not an intruder but Dad, who bounded into the entry, grinning at us like the father we knew and loved. I had missed that good-natured father so much, my throat clenched. The Thom Girl in me hastened toward Dad no differently than I had as a little girl of seven, eager to bask in his attention: *Yes, Dad, I can swim. . . .*

Reid bolted for Dad, too, throwing himself at our father first.

"Rebecca," Dad said, reaching one hand out to me as though nothing had happened.

I had almost drowned once stupidly trying to prove to Dad that I, unlike Mom, wasn't afraid of the water. As much as I wanted to burrow into his arms and smell his familiar Dad scent, I was drowning where I stood, no more able to breathe in this living room than I could underwater all those years ago.

This time, I didn't reach for Dad. He was no longer my solid and reliable hero.

I glanced back at Mom instead. But she, too, was immobilized, on the couch. By the time my gaze resettled on Dad, he had turned his back on us and was headed upstairs.

"See?" Reid said to Mom and me, glowing with triumph as Dad vanished into the master bedroom. "See, I told you he was coming back."

"Reid..." Mom cautioned softly. "I wouldn't get your hopes up."

"He's going to stay," Reid said, his jaw a stubborn line of boy bravado.

Despite her warnings, Mom rose and stared expectantly at the closed bedroom door, hoping in spite of what we all knew. It wasn't long before Dad trotted downstairs, carrying a small overnight bag.

"Wanna watch *MythBusters* with us?" asked Reid, rubbing the tip of his sneaker on the marble floor.

Dad dumped the overnight bag in the entry before tugging his cell phone from his jeans, his head bobbing—such a familiar gesture, my heart ached—while he calculated the time. I softened. How many times had he done that for me, opening his schedule when I needed a lift to the ferry? Or help on a problem set?

I didn't want to think beyond this minute, when we were still four, to the impending minutes that would whisk him to his weekend plans for two, whatever they were. Finally, Dad agreed, "For a little bit."

Without a word to Mom, he snagged her spot on the couch, with Reid leaning on one side of him. I sat on his other side but kept a gap between us where none had been before. That left no place for Mom, who stood near the entry, the odd woman out. Slowly, she walked over to us, perched on the arm beside Reid. From the window, I could see an old man strolling along the sidewalk, slowing down to peer in our windows to behold our cozy tableau: the enviably perfect all-American family. If he only knew.

One lone piece of pizza remained in the cardboard box. Cold as it was, Dad grabbed it before settling back, one foot propped on the coffee table. As I listened to him chew the pizza—our pizza—I suddenly grew angry. Now, heart, body, and soul overheated, I was sweating. I wanted to storm into the kitchen, snatch the spreadsheet Mom and I had created, shake all the zeros under his nose, and demand, *What the hell did you do?*

Mom may have been too proud to ask for help, but I had to. "Dad, our savings account is running low."

"I'll deposit half of my paycheck into it," he said easily.

"For how long . . . do you think?" Mom asked uncertainly, as though she didn't want to offend Dad and chance him retracting his offer.

Dad leaned back, arms behind his head, a man in command of the boardroom. "Into perpetuity, Bits."

I breathed out, relieved. This was the generous father I knew. The one who would take care of us forever, who would never claim it was "his" money. I grinned at him and snuggled into his side now. Right as the MythBusters debated the best way to transport their LEGO creation to the test site, Dad fidgeted. It wasn't long before he patted Reid on the knee and said, "Okay, got to go."

Reid demanded, "Why?"

"Where are you going, Thom?" Mom asked.

"Out," Dad said, belligerent as a boy defying his mother, disrespectful with curt, one-word answers. Shocked, I recalled hearing this very tone every time Dad spoke with his own mother . . . and mine.

"Well," Mom said now, standing slowly with her hands clenched so tight behind her back that her knuckles were white, "if there's an emergency, how are we going to reach you?"

"I've got my cell phone." Dad strode toward the front door.

How many times had I witnessed this conversation, too? Mom asking Dad for basic information, and Dad doling out responses in miserly monosyllables. Now I could appreciate Mom's position: How the heck could she have planned our week if she didn't know whether Dad could pick us up from the ferry station? Drive Reid to a football practice? With his scanty answer, I couldn't stay quiet, even if speaking meant incurring Dad's disapproval.

"Dad, you didn't answer our calls when we first moved here," I pointed out.

Just as I thought, he shot me a hurt look before grudgingly admitting, "We'll be at the Four Seasons. In Boston."

I couldn't help glancing at the empty pizza box that had felt like a reckless splurge of twenty bucks.

"That's where the party is," Dad said.

"Party?" I asked. Instinctively, I moved to stand at Mom's side.

"Giselle's parents are celebrating their thirtieth anniversary."

It wasn't me who spoke up against this new insensitivity. And it wasn't Mom who choked on Dad's tone-deaf intentions. But Reid. Reid who recoiled but refused to look away. Reid who maneuvered in front of me and Mom now, as though his one hundred ten pounds could protect us, and stated firmly, clearly, as if he were the man, not our father, "Dad, you're still married. Don't you think that's just . . . mean?"

Dad didn't respond but stared at his cell phone, wishing someone else would answer for him. There was no one else. The truth in Reid's assessment stretched taffy-thin before Dad answered in clipped words: "I didn't think about that."

Mom reared back as if struck in the face by the magnitude of Dad's disregard.

I can't take any more. I can't. Mom's voice was as clear in my head as if she had spoken, but she was silent, ashen-faced. Her bottom lip was caught painfully between her teeth. Fury gathered inside me as I studied this imposter of a father. Couldn't he hear himself?

I had ignored my inklings about this move. I had told myself that I was crazy when I predicted things. I had convinced myself that a sixth sense couldn't possibly exist. My scoffs echoed my dad's derision of everything and anything that couldn't be calculated and calibrated, explained and documented.

Whatever happened to us now—Mom, Reid, and me—was going to occur under my steadfast watch. Maybe it was time to admit to myself that I had visions.

Tired of nibbling after my father's trail of crumbs, stale and insubstantial, that led us in maddening circles, I asked myself: What should I do?

Then I listened.

There was no nausea, no listing ground, no pounding headache.

Get them to safety.

The voice was so adamant—my inner knowing unquestionably strong, a perfect-pitch ringing that ran from head to heart. I told him now, "Dad, you can keep doing whatever you want, but we're going to Hawaii."

Part Three

The mother art is architecture. Without
an architecture of our own we have no soul
of our own civilization.
—*Frank Lloyd Wright, architect*

Chapter Twenty

One call to Grandpa and we were bound for the Big Island two days later. I paused outside the open door of the airplane. There, I lifted my face toward the star-clad night sky, breathed in the balmy air of Hawaii, and felt, surprisingly, like I had arrived home. That unexpected sensation of homecoming only heightened at the sight of Grandpa George, in his vivid red aloha shirt, waiting for me and Reid and especially Mom.

As soon as Mom cleared security, Grandpa grabbed her heavy carry-on bag and threw his arms around her. A divot of concern creased his forehead, and he asked, "You hanging in there, darling? You look like you're going to faint."

"Doing fine, Dad."

He nodded. "We'll just get the truck, then, and head home."

"How far is it?" I asked.

"Two hours. You can sleep on the way to Volcano."

"Is that really what your town's called?" asked Reid.

"It really is," Grandpa said, mussing Reid's already bedraggled hair. As easygoing as my grandfather sounded, I caught his worried expression. Not that I blamed him. Three long flights had taken a toll on us: Reid smelled musty, I felt greasy, and Mom looked vampire-pale. She hadn't slept on any of the plane rides; I knew because every time I woke from my catnaps, Mom was either journaling or reading one of her books with dire titles like *He's History, You're Not: Surviving Divorce After 40* and *When Love Dies*. I never thought I'd miss her books on effective time management until now; this new batch of self-help was a heartbreak.

Six hours on the plane should have been plenty of time for me to compose a letter to Sam Stone, belatedly thanking him for meeting me . . . even if that meeting had been mortifying. Under any other circumstances, Mom would have been incensed that my handwritten thank-you note hadn't been signed, sealed, and delivered within twenty-four hours of my walking out of Sam's office. But my procrastination continued because I kept replaying our last good-bye with Dad and my final conversation with Jackson instead.

The twisting drive along the volcano's flank now stopped me from obsessing over what I should have said and berating myself for what I did say. One accidental jerk of the steering wheel would plow us through the sorry excuse of a guardrail, and we'd plummet into the ocean far below. While I was nervous, I trusted Grandpa to keep us safe. Mom must have, too, because she didn't nag him once to slow his mad-dash pace.

Reid had fallen asleep next to me, his head knocking against the window with every little bump. So I pulled him toward me, where he could rest on my shoulder. Who cared if he smelled like boy, sweaty and slightly sour? The comforting weight of his body slumped against mine made me feel less alone.

I wondered then about Jackson, wondered how he was doing, what he was doing. And who he was doing it with. As though my fretting had conjured Jackson, I received a text from him: *Heard from Ginny you went to Hawaii. Doing okay? Aloha.*

I found myself unconsciously holding my phone to my heart, as though I could feel the reliable clockwork ticking of his ongoing care. There were probably a thousand reasons why I shouldn't answer him—and Shana no doubt could list, footnote, and fact-check each one of them. Regardless, I was tempted to text Jackson back for the first time since we broke up: *Grandpa flew us to the Big Island. Aloha.* But we were never only friends. Instead, we had fallen immediately into a relationship. Flirting was our first language. I didn't know how to talk to Jackson without leading him on. Or worse, leading me down a yellow brick road that led to a fantasy called happily ever after. So I shut off my phone without responding and buried it deep, deep, deep within my messenger bag.

The sound of Grandpa's truck entering the gravel driveway woke me before his gruff "Welcome home." A pair of tiki torches glowed at the top of the driveway, highlighting the lush foliage edging the road. A wood sign nailed into a palm tree read OHIA.

"I'll show you to your rooms," Grandpa said as he parked the truck under a thatched garage, "and then I'll drop off your luggage."

Not even Mom protested with her usual polite "No, no, we can handle it"—we were all that tired. The narrow footpath from the garage forked off the driveway to a Japanese-style house but, surprisingly, Grandpa headed in the opposite direction. I could tell from the way Reid drew a deep, operatic breath that he was about to break into an aria of discontent, but the tiny building before us, not much bigger than my treehouse, silenced him. The hut exuded the same serenity that our architect had created for us back on Lewis Island. So organic, this hut could have sprung from the earth, but what were the chances that Peter had designed this property?

Two chairs flanked the front porch, a charming touch I wouldn't have expected from my gnarl-bearded grandfather. After Grandpa George opened the front door, labeled with a sign that read NOOKERY, he handed Mom the dragonfly key chain.

"Dad . . . what is this place?" Mom asked, peering inside curiously.

"Where you'll be staying."

At the far end of the room was a reading nook, deep enough to double as a twin bed. Fern-green curtains hung off to the side, ready to be drawn for privacy. Mom entered the space slowly, lingering at the built-in bookshelves on one of the walls. She ran her fingers along the spines of the faded old editions of classic children's books: *The Phantom Tollbooth*. *Half Magic*. *The Little Prince*. *The Witch of Blackbird Pond*. The Betsy-Tacy series. All the books I remembered Grandma Stesha reading aloud to me when she used to babysit on alternate days with Grandpa George while Mom was at work.

"Dad?" Mom asked haltingly. She pulled out *Betsy and Joe*, my favorite in the turn-of-the-century series, the one where Betsy falls in love with another writer, a boy who truly understands and appreciates her. "Are these my old books?"

Grandpa grinned at her uncertainly. "Do you like it?"

"Dad . . ."

"Just make yourself at home. I'll bring up your bag once I get the kids settled."

"Dad?"

But Grandpa had already backed out of the hut—Mom's Nookery. Who else could it have belonged to but Mom? If I were to design a room specifically for her, this was what it would look like: cozy and light-filled, stocked with books and the window seat she had always coveted. Only then did it occur to me that Mom had given me my treehouse sanctuary at our island home. A man cave where Dad could retreat and recharge. A bedroom that changed with Reid's ever-morphing interests: first a fire station complete with a replica of a 1934 fire truck as a bed, then a robotics laboratory. Even her gardens were intended for other people's pleasure: the healing garden for Ginny's dad, the vegetable patch for us. Other than her small container gardens, Mom never claimed a space of her own, never staked out a private spot to recharge, even after telling Dad how much she had always dreamed of a reading nook.

But Peter had heard her. I remembered their one argument during the remodel. Mom's reading nook was on the chopping block due to budget overruns, but Peter had insisted on retaining the window seat, overriding her protests. And he was the one who had the window seat upholstered in robin's-egg blue, Mom's favorite color, as a housewarming gift. I remembered her glow of pleasure when she first saw the seat, the way she had run to it and plopped herself down, precisely as she did now.

My last image of Mom before Reid and I followed Grandpa into the night was of her snuggling into her Nookery. Mom had arrived home, an entire ocean away. Despite my very best efforts otherwise, I wished I could snuggle into Jackson, but much more than an ocean separated us.

I fell asleep to the light drumbeat of rain on the upturned palm fronds outside the bunkhouse I shared with Reid. Hours later, I awoke to an exuberant birdsong that drowned out my latest nightmare of a vision: Dad slashing our spreadsheet with a red marker and smirking at Mom. *You may own the house, but the property is mine, not yours.*

So disturbing was the dream that I woke fully alert, without a trace of jet-lagged grogginess. What good was our cottage if Dad owned the land on Lewis Island? That was a question and this was a vision I refused to ignore. So I made a mental note to research property rights, then e-mail the Bookster moms afterward to double-check my understanding.

Across the room, Reid was sleeping so soundly, he didn't budge at the raucous gabbling of chickens in the garden, not even the loud cawing from beneath our window. Unable to rest a minute longer, I threw off the white quilt, appliquéd with fiery birds-of-paradise. The air was chilly, not the perennially hot, humid Maui I knew from my family's one previous trip to Hawaii. Though that vacation had been only a few spring breaks ago, it felt unfathomable that we were ever an intact family of four.

Shivering, I lifted my black sweatshirt from the foot of my bed, where I had cast it last night, and pulled my phone from my messenger bag. It was already ten, decadently late. Compulsive, I know, but I wanted to see if Jackson had texted. He had: *Surf up, Aloha Girl?*

Buoyed by his words in spite of myself, I practically bounced across the room to the front door. Closing the bunkhouse door gently behind me, I stepped into a jeweled paradise of variegated greens, bright against the clouds, and felt...happy. I remembered what Grandpa had advised in Manhattan: Seize joy. So now in the daylight, I reveled in this primordial jungle where wild spirals and alien antennae sprang rapturously from the mulchy ground.

Again, I was tempted to text Jackson back: *Volcanoes and jun-*

gles and sun, oh my! What harm would one little text be? But I knew. Any word from me would be an opening that I wasn't sure I wanted to create. Once again, I ignored the text, even if I could hear Jackson call me by my new moniker: *Aloha Girl.*

To reach the main house, I retraced our steps from last night, following the gentle bend of the trail. Like the Nookery and the bunkhouse, Grandpa's house was Japanese in style, Zen in spirit. If space itself could exude mystical healing energy, this one did. My muscles relaxed even before I reached the charming swing that dangled from a decommissioned crane next to the house. As enticing as that swing was, I followed the trail of river rocks winding a sinewy, black stream up the three steps to the front door. Two had words chiseled into them: *Live. Everything.* My eyes filled with tears at the familiarity of those words, etched on my pendant, unspoken in years. I could almost hear Grandma Stesha's butterscotch voice, sweet and husky, as she tucked me into bed: "The point is to live everything."

But it was Grandpa's voice that I heard this morning: "You're up." He had been sitting with such meditative stillness, I hadn't noticed him on the porch. The beginning of a smile softened his austere expression. "Sleep well?"

"Grandpa, this," I said, gesturing widely to encompass everything he had created, "is a masterpiece."

At that, he gifted me with his gathering smile, slow and wide and welcoming. "Would you like a tour?"

"What do you think?"

With an answering nod, Grandpa loped down the stairs,

gripping a metal water bottle, and jogged through the knee-tall grass behind the house. There, a muddy trail led into the forest, mired with thick roots and uneven with sharp rocks. I followed, laughing, as though we were playing chase the way we had whenever Grandpa babysat me.

The path opened to a vignette of art: a glass orb, vibrant cobalt blue. I thought back on the conversations I'd overheard between Mom and Dad, circling around how little ambition Grandpa had. Mom saying that was the reason why Grandma Stesha had given up on him, Dad saying my grandfather needed to grow up and get a real job. But if Grandpa had sacrificed the traipsing of his vagabond life for the trappings of a corporate one, would he have wrought this: beauty and sanctuary, security and love?

As I hustled to keep up with Grandpa, my gaze landed on a metal sculpture of an open hand, its palm a basin of water that cupped a pink water lily. Again, I thought of Jackson and how much he would love this place. I cleared my throat, trying to rid myself of my pining for a boy I could not allow myself to want. "Did you build your house yourself? Houses, I mean?"

"I had some help." He glanced back at me as if expecting me to grasp his meaning.

To our left, a hut with a whimsical roofline seemed vaguely familiar. But where had I seen it? Again, Grandpa's expectant look. I asked, "Are those solar panels?"

He frowned slightly, as though his star student had made a careless error. "Yeah, that's how I heat the water."

"And the cisterns?" Quickening my pace, I closed the gap between Grandpa and me so I didn't miss a single word. "Do you collect rainwater?"

"Most of us do up here."

"You're so . . . green. I had no idea."

Over his shoulder, Grandpa said, "I can show you the plans later."

"Cool!"

"But I'm just a builder." As proof, he held up his callused hands, scarred tools of his many trades. Then he looked at me proudly. "And you are going to be an architect."

"There's no 'just' to what you've created, Grandpa." Again, I was struck by his soulful vision for this property, the hours he'd spent crafting it. This work was no less important, no less impactful than Dad's in the office, shepherding a game to market. Who better than Grandpa to ask about my future now that I was questioning my college decision?

As Grandpa lifted another branch out of my way, I told him, "I'm not sure about going to Columbia."

"What do you mean?" He turned his attention fully upon me, letting the branch fall safely behind me.

"I'm thinking about taking a year off."

"Why?"

"Mom needs me. And I might have to pay for college myself. . . ."

Only then did Grandpa look concerned. His forehead furrowed. "Your parents have it covered . . . right?"

"The first year, but we don't have as much money as we thought. . . ."

Grandpa looked grim, his lips parting as though he wanted to probe further but thought better of it. He started down the path, this time slower. "How do you feel about a year off?"

"Confused!" A large rock nearly tripped me. "But in a weird way, I've been feeling like I've got to figure out whether I really want to go to Columbia. It's superexpensive." After I told him about my interview with Sam Stone, that mortification seared in my memory, I voiced my anxiety: "I'm not sure I'm meant to be an architect at all. You should have heard him talk about my 'little' ideas."

"Maybe you weren't meant to be his kind of architect. I wouldn't deviate from your dream just because of one naysayer. Life is littered with naysayers who are either insecure or pompous fools. In either case, it's best to ignore them." Grandpa's eyes bored into mine, and he asked, "Are you planning on going to college?"

"Yeah! Just not next year."

"Then it sounds like you could have an exciting year off."

I was so shocked that anyone—even Grandpa George— might support this radical idea, my voice boomed: "Really?"

Grandpa George was dead serious. "Really."

"What should I do next year, then?"

Grandpa stepped across a puddle. "There are hundreds of things you can do during your gap year."

"Gap year?"

"A year off for students. What you'll be doing." A pair of massive boulders anchored the pocket grotto of ferns ahead of us. Grandpa climbed atop one of the guardian stones, scaling it easily. Sitting astride the boulder, he gestured me to clamber onto its mate. "The tradition started way back in the sixties when kids began taking a year off to travel or volunteer. In any case, I'm all for it."

"A gap year," I repeated. It took me a bit longer than Grandpa to find my footing on the rock. Graceless as I was, I managed to haul myself up on my own. Traitorous mind, I could easily picture Jackson scampering up with a wicked smile. I refocused on Grandpa across from me.

"A year to explore. You never know what you'll discover about yourself or the world in a year." Grandpa tilted his head back as if he wanted to inhale the world itself. "You might decide you want to make furniture for a year. Or create paint colors. Or plant trees in a dying forest to learn about wood. No experience is wasted, Reb." He shrugged. "At least that's what I've found."

Another measure of burden released from me at Grandpa's permission to deviate from the path I'd been groomed to take. I slid off my boulder before Grandpa did, suddenly needing to be on the ground as a monumental thought occurred to me: I was secretly happy I didn't have to work with Sam Stone for the rest of the summer—not because I was scared of him but because I felt trapped every time I thought about designing his signature buildings: cold, gargantuan, imposing. That was his vision, not mine. The vision I'd prefer to follow and study was Peter's: small, soulful, sustainable.

"You know," I said thoughtfully, looking up at Grandpa perched on his boulder throne, "this place looks like what our architect, Peter—"

"Nakamura."

Grandpa unscrewed his water bottle and offered it to me, but I was so stunned that he knew Peter, I could only stare up at him. He laughed. I asked, "How do you know him?"

"He consulted on this project." Grandpa grinned at my surprise. He leaped down easily but winced, shaking out his legs. "Your grandmother always said there are no coincidences, that everything in life is connected. Stesha's the one who introduced him to your mom."

"She did? How does Grandma Stesha know him?"

As if that was a question for the oracles, Grandpa threw back his head and chortled. "How does Stesha know everyone? She collects friends the way other people collect salt and pepper shakers."

"That is so Mom, too!"

He recapped the water bottle and stretched from side to side before heading back on the trail. "Peter and his nephew went on one of your grandmother's tours."

I followed Grandpa closely. "He never said anything about this place."

"I asked him not to."

"Why?"

Grandpa shrugged. Another secret. The path led us to a large building made up of a single room, bare of everything except the bamboo floors. The far wall was painted a soothing orange.

"A yoga room?" I peered through one of the windows. "Do you practice yoga now?"

"More like for twenty years."

"I had no idea!" And there it was again, the troubling notion that I barely knew the people I loved. That I had so little insight into their lives beyond the intersection with mine.

"People are surprising," Grandpa said, leaning against the wall.

"Doesn't it scare you?" I asked. "Not knowing people the way you thought you did."

"As long as you know a person's heart, you know them. Everything else is exploration. And trust me, you want someone who'll take a lifetime to explore. Life is long, sweetheart. The last thing you want is to be bored." Grandpa walked us over to another garden alcove, trimmed with smooth stones. He motioned to the path ahead. "Why don't you take the lead?"

"I don't know the way," I told Grandpa, flustered.

"Just choose a direction." He shrugged as though he had all the time in the world for me to figure things out. "We're in no hurry."

So I stepped in front of Grandpa, and together we wandered home.

Chapter Twenty-One

As soon as we approached the main house, Grandpa oh-so-casually suggested that we take another circuit around the property so he could point out a few other sustainable features that might interest me. He didn't fool me. I knew he wanted to check in on Mom, no different from the way Jackson was checking in on me with his most recent text: *Call yourself a tea drinker all you want, but I know you're sneaking in a cup of Kona. . . .*

"Good news?" Grandpa said over his shoulder when he noticed that I had fallen behind.

I grinned. "Great news. How's your coffee?"

"Out of this world."

"Really?" In my head, I automatically composed a response to Jackson, even though I didn't send it: *Reliable source says Kona is awesome. Stay tuned.* Through the screen door, I spotted Mom tucked in the window seat with her computer. We hadn't made a sound, but Mom must have sensed our presence, because she looked up immediately and motioned us inside.

Grandpa pounced on the breakfast basket I hadn't seen at our feet, untouched on the welcome mat.

"You haven't eaten," he said, cradling the basket.

"I forgot," Mom admitted.

"Well, come on, then," he crowed almost gleefully. "I'll fix you something."

At that, instead of touring me around, he ushered us straight to his house, where he pulled an aromatic soup from the refrigerator.

"Dad, since when do you cook?" Mom asked when Grandpa waved us to the rattan stools at the kitchen island. After pouring the soup into a pot, he filled heavy glasses with iced tea. I could smell the sweet hibiscus as the tea splashed over ice.

"Don't believe the cynics who say people can't change," Grandpa said, and placed a tiny canister of raw cane sugar before us. He swiveled back to the cooktop to stir the soup. "And don't believe breakfast purists for a second. Soup is the perfect morning food, a little protein, not too heavy. I hope you girls are hungry."

"Better dig in, Mom, before Reid wakes up. You know he'll eat everything," I said.

Even more astonishing than Mom finishing the bowl of soup was her admission of truth: "Dad, Thom's wiped out our savings." A few weeks ago, that confession would have been a state secret if I were anywhere in earshot, but the boundaries of our

178

relationship had blurred, no different from the weeks before graduation when teachers started talking to us as college students. Mom might not see me as an equal, an adult, exactly, but I was no longer a child who needed to be sheltered, either. I liked that.

Grandpa stopped chopping a spiny pineapple to give Mom his full attention. "What about your Synergy stock options?"

"We sold the last of them for the remodel, and the earlier options to diversify our portfolio. It takes a couple of bad investments before everything's gone."

"Bastard."

"Dad!"

Grandpa set the knife on the bamboo cutting board and propped his hands on the counter. "How much do you need?"

"Dad, I don't want your money." Mom's words were so emphatic, her rejection so visceral, I could feel Grandpa's hurt.

"All I'm saying is I'm here to back you up. You don't have to worry, sweetheart." His gaze stayed on her, his blue eyes unwavering. "You're not alone. You never have been."

The conviction behind those words was so definitive, so healing, tears welled up in my eyes. Mom's, too. She sniffled and pressed a napkin to the corner of her eye. "Dad, he's going to her parents' anniversary party. While we're still married. I don't think he's coming back."

I lifted my hand toward Mom's arm to comfort her, but she shook her head slightly, an almost imperceptible movement. I had become so used to observing her closely these last couple of days—overseeing the few bites she managed, watching her reaction whenever Dad called—I caught her unconscious signal. So as Grandpa scooped fresh fruit on top of yogurt, I walked around the kitchen island to give Mom a modicum of privacy.

"This one's for your mother," Grandpa told me, adding an extra dollop of Greek yogurt to her bowl.

"Thanks, Dad," she said, "but you can't support me for the rest of my life."

"I'm just your bridge."

"I know." Mom smiled ruefully. "You always have been." Then, as if she felt the full weight of what she had acknowledged so easily, her eyes widened. "Dad, you've always been there. You."

Mom rarely spoke about her past. The most I ever heard were veiled allusions to the privations of living with a tarot-reader-turned-teacher of a mother and a pursuit-of-the-moment father. In fact, once at book club, Ginny's mom had pointed out, "Betsy, you never talk about growing up."

Mom demurred: "Trust me, nothing much happened. We didn't have the money."

"But what was your dad like? Is he anything like Thom?"

"Like Thom? No." Her laugh was uncharacteristically harsh, accompanied by a swift shake of her head. Not a hair moved, trapped stiff with hair spray. "Thom's rock solid, Mr. Dependable. It's why I married him."

Now, at Mom's visible appreciation, Grandpa's cheeks flushed. Self-consciously, he turned to check the soup, but not before I caught his touched expression.

"What's scaring me is that I'm forty, and I have to start all over," Mom said, spearing a wedge of pineapple with her fork. "I seriously thought I had hit the lucky jackpot with Synergy, made my killing, and was done working. I know. Spoiled. How many people win the lottery like this? But . . . it's all gone."

"That asshole."

"Dad, that's not productive."

Grandpa grunted.

I skewered a chunk of mango from the cutting board and waggled it in the air with my fork as I said, "But it feels good to say it."

We all laughed because it was true. My thoughts echoed Grandpa's: Dad really was acting like a jerk. Grandpa finished heaping the remaining bowls with the fresh pineapple and mangoes, and I placed one next to Mom for Reid, ready for whenever he woke from his Rip Van Winkle sleep.

"I need a job, and I haven't worked in eleven years. Eleven," Mom said, picking up and then setting down her spoon without tasting a drop of the yogurt. "Remember, I left my job when Reb was seven. Thom stayed at work, I stayed at home. That was our deal. Now he's a titan, and I'm a relic."

"You've got plenty of options," Grandpa said, and he winked at me.

"Options? I'm a stay-at-home mom. I'm good at chaperoning dances and driving carpool." She laughed wryly at this paltry inventory of skills.

"Come on, Mom, just think about it this way: You're taking a gap year with me," I said, and pulled out the stool beside hers. "You get to figure out what life after being a stay-at-home mom looks like."

Strategic mistake. Mom frowned ominously. "Gap year? What are you talking about?"

"We don't have money for college."

"Your freshman year is paid for."

"But what about the next three?"

"Your dad will cover it."

I hadn't intended to share my plans for the upcoming year in quite this way. My eyes dropped to the mango, now drooping precariously from my fork. "Mom, I'm not even sure Columbia is where I want to go. And the last thing I want to do is go there for a year, then transfer somewhere else, where I'd have to start all over." I looked Mom square in the eye. "I called Financial Aid, and they said divorced or not, savings or not, Dad makes too much money for me to qualify for a penny."

"I'm telling you," Mom said sternly, "you're not postponing college. Period."

Grandpa intervened before our argument could escalate. "Let's first figure out the money situation. Then we can tackle college."

"Fine, like there's anything I can do." Mom threw her hands in the air, frustrated. "I don't think anyone's recruiting for housewives. The last time I worked, cell phones were bigger than bricks!"

Grandpa wiped a few droplets of soup from the counter with a dishrag before answering. "Well, take a look at me. I didn't settle on a career. Now I'm about to run this inn, and I realized that this is what I'm meant to do—and everything I've ever done has led to this. Who would have pictured me doing this? Not me. So, sweetheart, reinventing yourself is actually a rush."

"Inn?" Mom and I asked at the same time. I continued, "What do you mean?"

Shyly, Grandpa nodded. "Ohia is opening in a few weeks. You're my first official guests. I can house six total. What do you think?"

"This is awesome!" I said, glancing at Mom, since she was silent. Eyes dark with despair, she pushed away from the kitchen island. "Mom, what's wrong?"

"Dad, this is great, really great," she said, scooting off her stool unsteadily. "You may be fine reinventing yourself every two years, but all I want is my old job back. I want to be a wife and a mother."

"You're still a mother," he pointed out.

"I need to lie down."

I tried to hold her back. "Mom——"

"We can talk later," she said softly as she hurried to the door.

I was about to follow, but Grandpa laid his hand gently on my arm. Mom receded down the path, a lonely figure, before disappearing into the thicket of rain forest.

"She needs to process. This is a shock; it's all a shock. I pushed her too hard." He cupped Mom's empty bowl between his palms as though it were a child's rounded cheeks, but I wasn't sure whose concern he was allaying—his, mine, or Mom's. "But don't worry. We'll figure this out."

By then I had lost my appetite, too, and stirred my soup idly.

"Dad told her he was giving her half of what he made into perpetuity. That's what he promised. So why is she so worried?"

Grandpa didn't answer. Instead, he busied himself with refrigerating Mom's unfinished fruit bowl.

To fill that damning silence, I said loudly, "Dad wouldn't leave us without anything. Not us. You heard Mom. He'll pay for my college." Despite my insistence, despite my own doubts otherwise that had spurred me to call Financial Aid, I begged for him to agree: "Right?"

But Grandpa was a man who did not apologize for his life choices—not to Dad, who questioned his long list of short-lived jobs; not to Mom, who worried about his retirement. Above all, Grandpa was a man who did not lie, opting to say nothing rather than say something he did not believe. And he was pointedly silent while my phone rang. It was Dad. Now was my chance to talk to Dad, ask him point-blank, prove Grandpa wrong.

And yet . . . I couldn't. I didn't want to hear Dad's voice or his all-veneer-no-substance promises.

I turned off my phone and felt Grandpa observing me closely.

On the verge of bawling, I didn't want Grandpa to witness my meltdown. So I escaped outside, sprinted toward the driveway with my arms hugged tight around myself, as if that would keep my jagged heart together. Without warning, a peahen darted from the thick foliage. I yelped.

Trying to calm down, I breathed big gulps of dew-infused air. How were we going to make money in case Dad didn't come through with his promise to share half his income—or any at all? Whatever skills Mom had were lost a few generations of technology ago. Besides, I had serious doubts that she'd be able to take orders from anyone. Reid, what could an eleven-year-old boy do other than get a paper route? That left me.

Me, the girl who couldn't even lock in an internship that had been practically handed to her.

What the hell could I do?

Three matching mountain bikes, all shiny silver, leaned against the garage; not one looked used. Biking hard and fast away from my worries, away from Dad's lies, away from Grandpa's damning silence, had its appeal.

But the bikes weren't mine.

But Mom might need me.

But I didn't know my way around.

My mind raced to Jackson, who would have grabbed one and gone, no plan, no destination. It's better to ask for forgiveness than permission, he'd have chortled with a rebellious grin. What was I waiting for? Another long list of *but, but, but* excuses to stop me from what I yearned to do?

I snatched one of the bikes, snapped on a helmet, and pedaled hard down the driveway. With a sharp bank to the right, I aimed for a path called exploration that I'd never charted solo before.

I don't remember much about the beginning of my bike ride except that I prayed in earnest for the first time in a long time. Dad wasn't a churchgoing man but an atheist who categorized religion in the same cracked bucket as sixth sense, soothsayers, and pretty much all of Mom and her drowned-witch family lore. And Mom was the fair-weather kind of churchgoer, attending only on Easter Sunday and Christmas Eve.

En route to the volcano, my prayers flooded from me with a fervent power that might have scared the most devout: *Please, God, take care of us. Please, God, keep us safe.* I pedaled even faster, crouching low over the handlebars.

The one thing I did not pray for was my father's return.

I steered hard to my right, so fast I could have taken flight. Unholy anger propelled me into the mist shrouding the two-lane road in the Hawaii Volcanoes National Park. If Dad were here, I would run him down. How dare he sound all self-righteous when he spoke to Mom—"I never felt loved by you"— which, when you came down to it, was a backhanded way of blaming her for his affair.

Coasting on a hill, I flew into the headwind of truth. Dad prided himself on sticking to the letter of the law, when all along he had been fraying its edges. His lies made me sick; his smirk, even sicker. At that moment, I hated him and never wanted to see his face or hear so much as a word—not one "sorry," not one "love"—come from his lying mouth again.

Down the park's main arterial road, I sailed by the scoured landscape—here the 1917 lava flow, there the one from 2003. Not that it mattered exactly when the lava had flowed; the effect was the same: utter obliteration of everything in its path. No different from Dad.

So involved in my private diatribe, I didn't see the jagged

lava rock on the road. My tire careened off it. I skidded. The bike toppled. I fell. It was a miracle that only my knee was scraped. A trickle of blood slid down my calf. My breathing was hard and labored, more from being scared than from being winded or hurt. Oddly, the shock of the fall combined with the intensity of my uncensored anger at Dad actually calmed me.

To my right, a roadside sign warned about the volcano's toxic fumes, hazardous to your health. I gasped for air, almost laughing. Grandpa was right: Life itself was a risk. Here I was, atop a volcano, inhaling poison and potentially damaging internal organs. But what was I going to do? Stop breathing? Stop living? Stop loving . . . ?

Go home. Now.

Without any hesitation, I heeded that voice and climbed back onto the bike for the long, uphill ride to Grandpa's inn and home. The road curved around a large heart-shaped chunk of lava. Instead of appreciating the shape, I only wondered guiltily whether I was any different from Dad, in the abrupt way I had ended my relationship with Jackson. Ended it without giving him a chance.

Even as I made my resolutions to stop dwelling on the past, and the wheels on the bike made their revolutions propelling me forward, my mind circled back to Jackson.

Jackson, whose texts had greeted me this morning and wished me sweet dreams last night. If I were being honest with myself, I missed his voice. I missed being in his arms.

And as vulnerable as it made me feel and as weak as it sounded, I had to face the truth.

I loved him.

Even so, love was no guarantee that any relationship was worth the risk. Countless books, movies, songs were about broken-down love. Eighteen, and I already counted myself too much of an expert on betrayal. At last, sweaty and exhausted, I veered off the main highway and into Grandpa's jungle of a neighborhood. Everywhere I looked, verdant green bloomed in lavish defiance of the very real, very persistent volcanic threat underneath us.

Skidding to a stop on the graveled driveway, I saw a tiny woman standing alone before Grandpa's porch. Her voice was as insistent as any rooster crowing in the morning, and so, so beloved to me: "George! You get your butt out here right now. You kidnapped my daughter. And I want to know where the hell she is."

For the first time in these tundra weeks, I felt a spurt of joy: buoyant, unbidden, true.

Grandma Stesha had returned.

Chapter Twenty-Two

From behind, Grandma Stesha looked no different from the last time I had seen her: still skinny, still bedecked in jewel tones. Her hair was short and salty white. Hands on her hips, feet spread apart, Grandma was an Amazon from the land of Lilliputians, dressed for battle in a purple tunic, black leggings, and her trademark motorcycle boots.

For such a small woman, her bellow was elephantine. "George? *George!*"

How long had it been since I last saw my grandmother? Right before she embarked on her tour of Scotland, scouting out fairy glens and stone circles two years ago? Three? My heart lurched toward Grandma Stesha, but something stopped me from flinging myself at her. A hand could have reached out to hold my arm: *Wait.* A voice might have whispered, *Hold on.* Whatever it was, I listened and didn't move.

Perhaps it was the same hand that kept Grandma Stesha grounded on the pathway instead of mounting those three steps to pound on my grandfather's front door. Perhaps it was the same whisper that cautioned her from storming through the door that Grandpa never locked, day or night. She waited.

And then, there was Grandpa, first silhouetted behind the screen door, then standing on the porch. If I thought he had emitted protective vibes when he came for us in New Jersey, that strength was anorexic compared with what I felt today. Gone were all my doubts that people can exude an aura, because Grandpa's energy swirled from the porch, cascaded down the steps, and roared throughout the sanctuary.

"Don't you stand up there lording over me, George Price," Grandma Stesha snapped.

"Then you better come on up here."

The fight left Grandma's body at this unexpected challenge. Her hands fell from her hips as if she was so stunned, she had lost traction in the world she had known and defined.

"Fine," she said, regaining some rigidity in her posture.

The women in my family, as I've said, are not known for great height, but neither are we women easily daunted. At least, not according to family history, which I now remembered like a tired echo that had finally reached me after a long, detoured journey. Now I could hear Grandma Stesha shut *The Witch of Blackbird Pond* with finality, and now I could remember her declaring, *Reb, stand tall like Kit, even when everyone else doubts you.* Now Grandma Stesha strode up the stairs to face my grandfather. Now she stood before him as if she belonged here in the sanctuary.

"I asked you to bring her home, George," she said.

"I did. This was supposed to be our home, remember?"

"I meant home to me. In Santa Fe. Not here." Only then did Grandma Stesha take her eyes off Grandpa and gesture at the buildings that he had built with his own hands. The paths that he had carved around native plants, connecting one building to another, connecting her to me.

Perhaps it was that thought that called Grandma Stesha to me. Whatever it was—psychic knowing or energy reading—she spun around, her eyes locking on me. For the first time in years, I saw my grandma's face. Worry lines creased her forehead, and deep laugh lines bracketed still-lush lips.

She flew down the steps, pulled me into her arms, and held me so tight, the sweet scent of her gardenia perfume churned together dream and memory and reality. Grandma Stesha pressed kisses on my cheeks like I was a little girl recently fished from a lake. And then she kissed the backs of my hands, first the left, then the right, as though blessing the girl I had become. With one last squeeze of both hands, she drew back to study me. This was no cursory glance but a head-to-heart inspection.

Surprisingly, I was Grandma Stesha's exact height. In my memories, she towered over me, a force of nature whose clear-eyed stare could snap burly paramedics into action.

Satisfied, Grandma Stesha said, "Reb, I thought that was you."

Dad would have scoffed at those words. Not so long ago, I

would have scoffed right alongside him, renouncing Grandma—
and my own sixth sense—simply to win his approval.

But Dad wasn't here. And I no longer needed to deny that at
some deep and immutable level, I had known that Grandma
Stesha would come back, here, now, today. That I had felt her
barreling down the road toward us even as I biked from the
volcano.

Time may have passed, and the world may have separated
us, taking Grandma Stesha from Peru to Turkey, India to Bhutan. But she still knew me, always loved me. I had no doubt of
that. And I? I knew and loved her, too.

Even before Grandma's smile of homecoming widened, I
knew she sensed Mom. In that moment of recognition, Grandma
Stesha transformed back into the grandmother I last saw: powerful and protective. My mother emerged from the forest like
some mystical creature who had come when she was called. She
clenched her arms around herself.

From the shadows, Mom said, "You were right about Thom."

"I'm so sorry I was. You don't know how sorry I am."

At that, Mom's face softened, and she stepped from the forest's shadow, closer to us, though a heart's beat away. In the dap-
pled light, she admitted, "He hurt me, Mom."

"I know, Babycakes. I know. . . ."

"I should have listened to you."

"You were trying to save your marriage," soothed Grandma
Stesha, padding slowly to Mom, a tiny bird, too broken to fly.
"You had the kids to worry about. I wasn't helping. I shouldn't
have said anything, not to you and not to him."

Perhaps Grandma's tour business wasn't so much to pursue her life's dream as it was to escape the premonitions she had about Mom. A breeze blew the hair from my eyes. I almost lost Ginny's friendship once with my prediction that her father was going to die. So how much harder would it be for a mother to know about her own daughter's breaking point and be powerless to stop it?

"Why didn't I listen to you?" Mom asked now.

Grandma Stesha merely opened her arms wider in answer, creating a space that only a beloved child could fill. "Babycakes, come here."

At the moment my prodigal grandmother encircled my mother in her embrace, their foreheads touching, all the years separating them vanished, along with every misunderstanding and every ignored premonition. Homecoming—I saw it clearly and felt it myself when Grandpa wrapped his arm around my shoulder and nestled me close to his chest. I felt it again at noon when Reid finally bolted into the main house, so ravenous he was practically frothing, but he launched himself at Grandma Stesha, crying, "Grandma! You're home!"

Homecoming—I wanted it badly with Jackson. I felt a sharp pang, an actual physical hurt, from yearning for him. But I wasn't ready to risk myself, not when I caught the look of longing on Grandpa George's face in his swift, surreptitious glance at Grandma Stesha before he switched his attention to the cooktop. That palpable heartache so perfectly mirrored mine.

Chapter Twenty-Three

While I could ignore Dad's voice mails and texts as much as I wanted, Mom had other ideas. She answered his call on the first ring, then handed her phone to me with a dejected expression: "Your dad wants to talk to you." I shook my head, backing away from the phone, but Mom glowered at me and whispered, "He's still your father."

It was all I could do to respond to Dad's chipper "Having a good time?" as though we were vacationing while he was stuck at work. But I was done with his innocence-clad denials, his words that were lies in sheep's clothing. My distant and disinterested "Um . . . yeah, I guess so" reaction was nothing compared with Reid's.

"Are you still seeing her?" he asked Dad point-blank.

Dad squirmed from the truth: "Of course, we have some paperwork from the move to finish up."

Reid simply grunted and handed the phone to Mom, who looked at the device as if she had never seen one before.

After that call, Grandpa declared that a visit to the volcano would do us all some good, which rejuvenated Reid, making him whoop. That's how, for the second time in the day, I found myself at the Volcanoes National Park, a place I had already grown to consider my personal backyard playground. Ten minutes down the main road, the Chain of Craters, Grandpa blew past the disconcerting warning sign that had stopped me in my path earlier.

"Um, Grandpa, should we be worried?" I asked as I checked every window to make sure they were rolled all the way up, sealing us inside safe, recirculated air. Around us, plumes of steam escaped the black rock, and I could imagine poison fumes pooling in our lungs.

"Nah," said Grandpa, all blasé unconcern about the possibility of losing a few critical organs. "If the air was really bad, I wouldn't have brought us here."

Even though no one said another word—maybe because none of us other than Grandpa wanted to chance inhaling more toxic air than necessary—I caught the look of surprise that Grandma Stesha shot my grandfather, as if she had never witnessed this responsibility, this protectiveness. The road twisted past a forest of mushroom-shaped trees embalmed in lava and ended in thick, pitch-black lava that had coursed across the street before spilling into the ocean.

"It's so strange," Mom mused as Grandpa edged toward the side of the road. "Miles of moonscape, and then paradise down here. Who would have known?"

"That's why we fell in love with the Big Island on our first visit," said Grandma Stesha, turning around in the passenger seat to smile at the three of us in the backseat. "There's a primal wildness in this land that we both fell in love with. Remember, George?"

"How could I forget?" he answered, gazing steadily at her.

Grandma Stesha's face colored slightly. Maybe she, too, heard her easy reference to "we," so easy you could forget that they had been divorced for more than two decades. Adroitly, she changed the subject. "Every place can be an adventure. Even your own backyard."

Grandma launched into a story about a woman from Taos whose abusive husband died of a sudden heart attack in his home office fifteen years ago, and since then everyone, including her cat, refused to enter the space. The man from North Dakota who swore his farmhouse was haunted by his wife, because every morning, he'd find his bedroom door cracked open . . . even when he double-checked to make sure it was locked when he went to bed. The old lady in New Jersey—not far from our house . . . yikes!—who heard jazz from her locked attic late one night, only to find her son's long-lost sheet music when she investigated the next morning.

"Why don't they just move if they think their houses are haunted?" Reid asked, so frustrated that he flung his head onto his headrest. "I mean, wouldn't you just move?"

"Inertia. Sometimes moving is the hardest thing to do," Mom said softly.

"Not inertia. Incubation," Grandma Stesha corrected her.

"Sometimes staying in one place is the healthiest thing to do while you regroup. And then, watch out. There's a whole lot of pent-up forward momentum to make some changes. That's why people want to go on my tours. They want resolution from the past so they can live in the present and plan for the future."

The tours Grandma led weren't about gallivanting around the world, having a grand old time, leaving us behind. They were about healing people of pain. How far would I have to travel to stop longing for Jackson?

A car sped up behind our truck, trying to overtake us as though we were racing. Rather than speeding, Grandpa edged to the side of the road to give the other car maximum passing room.

"Everyone, breathe in," Grandpa said.

Instead, I breathed out and squeezed my mother's hand.

Our surroundings could have been a movie set for an apocalyptic movie, human civilization on the brink of destruction after a devastating volcano. But shimmering like a promise before me was the powerful, undulating ocean. Leaning over the stone wall, I snapped a picture of the waves crashing against the cliffs of lava, knowing how much Jackson would love this, when he texted me: *Found paradise yet?*

The synchronicity of the moment, the two of us dwelling on each other at the exact same second, warmed me. That had to be a sign of something. . . . Whatever it was, I could no longer resist the siren call of texting Jackson back.

I promised myself, just one text a day.

I promised myself, no signing off with an XOX.

I promised myself, keep it friendly, not flirty.

So after agonizing about the right words while the seagulls cried and the waves pounded, I broke my long days of silence and sent him the photo with the message: *Paradise found. Aloha.*

But as soon as I hit Send, a million questions fired in my head: How would he interpret my texting him? Did I strike the right tone—friendly-warm, not girlfriend-flirty? Were my words so cryptic and innocuous that he wouldn't understand that I meant we were doing well? Interrupting my second-guessing, I received his answering text with a photo of his work desk piled with official-looking real estate forms: *Purgatory found. Hello.*

I laughed and, without thinking, shot off an answering text: *Who knew paradise serves Kona coffee?* Right as Jackson responded— *Now, that just hurts*—Reid jogged over to me, tugging Grandpa along. No doubt this was my brother's thirtieth question in five minutes: "Is the volcano still erupting?"

"More like leaking." Though Grandpa answered Reid's question, his eyes were trained on Grandma, ever the tour guide, who was educating herself by reading the sign explaining the science behind the lava flow. "Maybe tomorrow night we can drive to where the lava's still flowing. You've never seen anything like molten lava at night."

Mom marched ahead, bearing down on the hardened shelf of lava that overhung the sea. I understood: I yearned for the wide expanse of horizon, too. At my side, Grandpa continued to watch Grandma. It was easy to envision her leading groups to sacred spaces, pointing out details that tourists would have missed without her sharp eyes. But those sharp eyes completely missed the tender way Grandpa was looking at her like a long-lost treasure he had misplaced. A long-lost treasure he had spent a lifetime regretting.

What had I done? I looked with horror at my phone, this mobile Cupid I thought I had exiled.

Five minutes. I hadn't even respected my own set of rules for engagement with Jackson for five minutes before I broke two of them: flirting over multiple texts. His newest message—*Wish I were there with you*—only reinforced how easy it was for each of us to draw the other back in. I didn't want to be Grandpa, still pining for a woman rooted deep in his past. I didn't want to be in Mom's shoes, aching when Jackson moved on to someone else.

"Isn't living here like playing chicken with Mother Nature?" Reid asked Grandpa.

I almost choked. What was I doing but playing chicken with Love?

To keep myself from any further temptation, I powered off my phone. Attempting to take my mind off yet one more mistake I'd made, I gestured at the acres of death-black lava sprawled before us. "Isn't this one of the most dangerous spots on earth?"

Grandpa thought for a moment as he nudged an errant lava chunk away to clear my path. "Actually, you could argue this is the safest place on earth."

"How can you say that?" I demanded.

"Well, Seattle is basically right smack on top of a fault line. They've been predicting the Big One to hit in the next hundred years, right?"

Both Reid and I nodded.

"There are no early warning signs for an earthquake, unless you count watching animals."

That was something Grandma Stesha would have said. As if we had called her, Grandma glanced in our direction. I waved at her to join us as I asked Grandpa: "Do you really believe that?"

"Sure. There've been reports that cows get antsy before an earthquake. And snakes get more active, slithering all over the place."

I knelt, picked up the lava rock he had brushed out of my way, porous and pitch-black and surprisingly light. In my head, I could hear Dad mocking Grandpa, snickering about animal sense, which he believed no more than he did women's intuition.

"So living on a volcano, is that any more dangerous than any other place on earth?" Grandpa asked as he placed his hands on an enormous boulder. Reid and I copied him, the hardened lava rough against our palms. "At least here, the volcano is literally letting off steam. And you get enough warning to evacuate."

"But aren't you worried that the lava is going to wipe out your home? All your hard work?" I asked.

"It's a risk, but historically, the lava flows down the other side. When you think about it, life is a risk. Every day is a risk." His eyes may have been on me, but I knew he was totally aware of Grandma standing behind him. He continued. "Getting in a car is a risk. Loving is a risk. But, darling, losing it all means that you have a chance to rebuild, better than before."

Wanting to give my grandparents some much-needed alone time, I knocked my shoulder against Reid's. "Hey, let's go find Mom." When we reached her where she was staring out at the sea, she said, "Well, kids, I always said I would go to the ends of the earth for you. And here we are."

Together, we stood on the black shell of destruction, where the flow had indiscriminately scorched and suffocated everything in its path—road, trees, shrubs, sand. Enormous, rippled piles of lava resembling fossilized elephant dung (Reid's observation) converged with table-flat chunks of lava that could have been upended by some burrowing monster (Mom's). There was no trail across the lava floor, only trail markers made of stacked totem poles of rock.

"Let's go up there," I said to Reid, pointing at a hill of lava.

We darted from trail marker to trail marker, and at the third, I recalled rock piles like these on postcards Grandma Stesha had sent us, first from Scotland, then from Tibet: cairns that marked memorials. It was mystifying that certain rituals and beliefs could cut across countries and transcend cultures. This universal emblem of death didn't sit well with me, and I glanced uneasily at the steam wavering at my feet. Perhaps my imagination was overactive, but I swear, the rubber treads of my sneakers were melting, sticking to stone.

I had expected Reid to follow me to the lava mound, but not Mom. Yet there she was, scrambling hands and feet up the hill with us. A veil of mist engulfed the three of us, not thick enough to cloud our vision but enough to be living proof that the earth was breathing.

So warm, I unzipped the sweatshirt that Dad had bought for me to celebrate my acceptance to Columbia. As I peeled it off, a sleeve snagged on the uneven lava. I tugged, but Mom freed me before it ripped.

Had Dad vented—literally vented, instead of stuffing his misery deep, deep inside himself—would things have been different? If he had spoken the way Reid had earlier, firmly and decisively, would his needs have been met? Instead, Dad erupted, not in words but in actions. Actions no less violent than this volcanic eruption.

I shut my eyes on this destruction and concentrated on the power of the earth beneath my sneakers. No matter how impractical and financially unstable designing small spaces was as a profession, I loved tiny places that enlarged a person, no different from this minor hill within an acreage of lava. I loved spaces that lifted people's spirits and allowed them to recuperate after a miserable day.

Yes, I heard the ringing of rightness. *Yes.*

When I opened my eyes, Mom was holding out a single flower to me.

"Where did you get this?" I asked.

She gestured to the ground below, where a pink-tinged shrub had sprung improbably from black death. Across from the low bush was a spindly tree, taller than me. I spun around, no longer noticing the consuming force of the volcanic eruption but instead seeing the hardscrabble life that had eked its way back. This was no different from the High Line park in Manhattan, which could only have been rebirthed into an urban oasis because the railway had first been abandoned. No different from Mom, whose face was angled toward the sunlight, her natural curls bouncing freely around her shoulders. No different from me, freeing myself from a mantle of expectations I no longer wanted to wear.

All around me, the burned floor was sprinkled here and there with a flowering of glorious red.

Chapter Twenty-Four

Immediately after dinner, Mom apologized that even though it was only seven, she needed to sleep, blaming her exhaustion on jet lag. Her excuse was only partially right. It wasn't just our bodies that were jet-lagged. So were our emotions. Coming to terms with Dad's betrayal and all the aftershocks of new hurts and the reappraised past had sapped me more than I cared to admit. What toll did that take on my mother? I accompanied Mom to the Nookery, our pace slow in the dimming light.

"Dad totally screwed up, Mom. You deserve better than this," I said softly. Instead of feeling like a traitor for admitting out loud that Dad had messed up and let our entire family down, I felt . . . unburdened. And relieved.

Unexpectedly, Mom began to cry as if her illusions were shattering all over again, shoulders heaving with sobs I hadn't heard since her appointment with the gynecologist.

"Mom, Mom!" Panicking, I fluttered around her, not knowing what to say to assuage her sorrow. "I'm sorry! I shouldn't have said anything."

Even in her distraught state, Mom must have sensed that she was frightening me, because she shook her head. "No," she said, drawing in a shaky breath, "I'm okay. Better than okay, Babycakes."

That nickname—the one I heard Grandma use with her, the one I had snapped at Mom never to call me ever again in front of my friends when I was in sixth grade—was healing balm.

As though she had foreseen this moment, Grandma caught up to us, toting a basket loaded with a flask of Kahlúa, a Thermos of coffee, and three tiny cups. She told me, "It's time for a girl talk."

Designed for one, the Nookery was snug for two and crowded for three. Even so, we squeezed inside, all three of us on the window seat.

"Girls," Grandma said without any preamble, "I've been wanting to tell you something for a long time. You both have spent practically half your lives—yes, you have—denying your intuition. Let me tell you something. Your sixth sense is a God-given gift." She held up her hand to stave off Mom's protest. "Let me finish. It is no different from your gift in creating gardens." Then she turned to me. "Or yours to design buildings." Straightening her back and placing her hands on our knees, Grandma said, "Denying your intuition is no different from squandering those gifts. So when people talk about callings, you should know that you've been twice blessed. It will be a shame, a darn shame, not just for you but for everybody around you, if you don't use your gifts, all of your gifts, to their full potential."

"Thom said—" Mom began.

"I can guess what Thom said!" Grandma smoothed back her hair to calm herself. Her eyes were button-hard as she considered us. "There are plenty of CEOs who talk about trusting their guts. What's that if not sixth sense? In any case, what matters most is you being authentically yourself. And if you cut a part of yourself off—especially to please someone else—do you think that you're really being celebrated for who you are? Do you really think you're being truly and completely loved?"

My mind wandered to Jackson as I pondered what Grandma was telling us. I had never trusted him to accept all the parts of me when I saw firsthand how Dad mocked Mom's inklings and scorned her forebodings. Had I been wrong about Jackson? After all, not once had he ever asked me to be less than I was. But then I thought of Ginny. Her reaction to my premonition about her dad's death had all but censored my visions.

"How do you know that our visions aren't . . . I don't know, wrong?" I asked quietly.

"Because we help people," Grandma answered simply. "How could that impulse come from anything but goodness?"

I thought of Mom and her healing garden for Ginny's dad and the salad bowl container gardens that she gave as gifts. And I thought of my few visions, even the prophetic one about Ginny's dad. After my revelation, she had flounced to her mom in hysterics, demanding to leave. Didn't that give her time with her father that would have been otherwise spent on Lewis, away from him before his unexpected death a few days later? For the first time, I found peace over that event.

"I'll put it in another way," Grandma said, as she took my hand and my mother's and squeezed gently. "When you're in tune with your inner voice, do you feel completely aligned: head, heart, and soul?"

I nodded. It was true. When I denied my visions, that's when I felt nauseous. Mom murmured, "Yes."

"The women in our family have always been helpers. I don't mean that you have to save the world. But you do have to listen to your intuition. That is our true calling. I believe it," said Grandma, quiet in her conviction. Silent now, she poured the Kahlúa and coffee in cups for herself and Mom, just coffee in mine. Lifting hers, she said, "*Salud.*"

Through unspoken understanding, Grandma and I left Mom to rest after we finished those drinks. We found ourselves drawn back to Grandpa's home, his front door propped open with a coconut. Through the screen door, I saw him puttering in the kitchen, filling the next morning's breakfast baskets on the countertop. I counted one for each of us.

"Do you think everybody will want macadamia-and-banana pancakes tomorrow morning?" he asked uncertainly when we ventured into his kitchen.

"Who wouldn't?" I answered.

Before I could offer to help, Grandma did so, grabbing the Ziploc bag crammed with fat macadamia nuts from the refrigerator. Without a word, in perfect synchronicity, they assembled the other ingredients. Feeling left out, I knew I should leave them alone. But where should I go? Even though there was light left in the waning day, I didn't want to bike any more than I wanted to drive down to admire the lava glow in the dark.

Grandpa blurted, "You know, there's a treehouse here. . . ."

"A treehouse? Really?" I asked, startled. "That wasn't part of our tour."

Grandpa shrugged. "I wanted you to find it on your own. . . ."

"But don't you need help?"

"No," said Grandma quickly, too quickly.

When she wasn't looking, I winked at Grandpa. With a grin, he handed me a flashlight.

"Where is it?" I asked. But then I shook my head because I knew where Peter had sited the treehouse, where I would have hidden a secret sanctuary on these lush grounds. Even without any guidance or direction, my gut knew the way.

There were no twinkle lights, no tiki torches, no wooden signs to announce the existence of the nondescript path beyond the yoga hut, just a discreet archway of boughs. I ducked, even though I didn't need to. The arch was the perfect portal for someone my size.

After winding around primordial ferns, the path curled to a stout tree before connecting to a spiral staircase made of wood. Those stairs opened to a treehouse, ten feet off the ground, high enough to gain perspective on my life.

On the bookshelf, tea lights were piled inside a palm-size

bird's nest. Three thick glass votives, each the color of sea grass, anchored a column of hand-stitched journals that were crafted from rough banana paper. A bouquet of multicolored pens filled a tiny canister painted with a path that led not to a watery rainbow or a buried treasure but to a heart wide open. Above that heart, one word: *Follow*.

And there, lining the window ledges, were the tiny fairy houses I had crafted with Grandpa when I was a little girl. Offerings I had placed around his houseboat because I truly believed that the fairies themselves would call back Grandma Stesha, tell her we missed her. He had kept them all. I had never known.

The treehouse rocked gently in the wind, soothing as a cradle. Now I cupped my favorite fairy house delicately in my hand, studying its steeply pitched roofline punctuated with a hawk's tail feather that I had found floating past Grandpa's houseboat.

I followed my instinct now and lit three candles, marking this as sacred time with myself. What better way to begin than with a fresh journal? I selected a green one. Then I settled on an orange floor pillow, the fairy house before me.

It had been so long since I had consulted my heart about anything, relying as I did on my head. I was at a crossroads with college and Jackson, and it was time to make some decisions that felt right both in my mind and in my soul. Until I figured out what it was that I truly wanted, I didn't want to talk to Jackson. He deserved better than me jerking him around with texts that suggested I was getting back together with him. He deserved a girl who knew with a thousand percent certainty that she wanted to be with him, only him. I wasn't there yet.

By the time the sky had dimmed to indigo, my sketches and flowcharts and ruminations filled fifteen pages, and I had run out of answers to the tough questions I had posed to myself. One thing I knew for certain: I didn't want to go back to Seattle and apply to UW for next fall solely because a boy was there. That decision—that life change—had to make sense for me, too.

So I composed a final text to Jackson for the time being: *I can't do this right now. Life is too chaotic. I'll be in touch when I'm ready and sure of myself again. . . . Please understand.* Before I lost my resolve, before I could edit and rewrite the message a hundred times, I hit Send.

Later, much later, when the tea lights had burned out and I rested my fairy house back on the bookshelf, I heard Grandma Stesha's incredulous voice: "You built this all on your own?"

Leaning out the window, I could see the merged shadows of my grandparents before they stepped into view.

"Well," said Grandpa as he leaned against a tree trunk, "with a lot of help."

"But you created a place for writers and artists. You dismissed that idea when I told you what I wanted to do with this land. You *hate* what I do."

"Stesha, I was a kid. I was threatened by all the people who swarmed around you, wanting something from you."

"Solace about their future." My grandmother's arms were

crossed in front of herself protectively, defensively. "What was so wrong about giving them that?"

"I was afraid that I would lose you."

"We lost each other."

"Angelheart, you didn't think I cared, but I was listening. I always listened to you. I wasn't man enough for you back when we were kids."

Rain clouds must have clustered while I was journaling, because they released a soft mist. Grandma's face angled skyward, as though she were washing away the cobwebbed remains of their troubled past. Birdsong erupted at that moment, much louder than the raucous score this morning.

This wasn't a regular plot of land Grandpa George had developed to be his second home. And it was a heck of a lot more than an inn whose bookings would fill his retirement coffers, more than a retreat for writers and artists, more than a sanctuary for a wounded family.

Arms hugged around myself, I looked upon the beautiful, improbable truth, lifting my eyes from the rooflines of the fairy houses to the matching roofline of Grandpa's creation. No wonder Ohia had felt so familiar. Its inspiration came from our original fairy village. But this was conceived and designed and built with love—only love—for one woman: Grandma Stesha. I wanted to hold her hands in mine. I wanted to stare into her beautiful violet eyes that had looked upon parts of the world that few ever saw, those eyes that penetrated people's souls where few ever ventured. Most of all, I wanted to tell her, *For a woman who can see far into the future, you can be awfully shortsighted about people. Just look around you, Grandma. Really look.*

The moon rose, illuminating the new night, but it was still dark enough to conceal large roots on a path that might trip up an older woman. As if my grandmother had heard my thoughts, she linked her hand safely through my grandfather's rock-solid and dependable arm as they made their way back home.

After my solo bike ride early the next morning, my heart nearly broke when I found no response to my text to Jackson. Just the silence I had asked for. What did I expect? Still, the space I had requested was harder to handle than I'd imagined it would be. What was Jackson doing? Thinking? Feeling? For the first time since March, I had no idea.

Inside Grandpa's kitchen, I found Reid already seated, heeding the siren call of those macadamia-banana pancakes. His was the desperate hunger of the shipwrecked and starving. Five short minutes of watching Reid's plate-to-mouth shoveling would have beat any weight-loss program for effectiveness. Trust me. I wanted to snap a quick close-up picture to document this wholesale piggery for Jackson. But I recalled my resolution to remain incommunicado until I knew for sure what I wanted.

So it was a testament to Grandpa's amazing culinary skills that not only did Reid completely forgo writing his novel to focus on gorging, but I held up two fingers when Grandpa asked me, "One or two?"

Grandpa attended to the cooktop, crowding the griddle with large pancakes, far more than one famished, growing boy could eat. Far more than I could finish on my own. As though he had expected them, Grandma Stesha and Mom now walked through the front door, laughing at some shared joke, with my grandmother's gaze lingering on Grandpa George. More than that tender look, I loved the relaxed ease of Mom's expression, as though Hawaii—or perhaps this sanctuary itself—was healing her. In a gesture I had last seen in my childhood, Mom placed both hands on my shoulders and kissed me on the top of my head. Where before I might have been irritated at being treated like a little kid, now that simple affection filled me.

Without a word, Grandpa George plated their breakfasts, fanning caramelized bananas across their pancakes. The table was already outfitted with warmed syrup and a platter of fresh-cut papaya and pineapple. And there, beside a place setting that must have been Mom's, was a mug of her favorite green tea, steaming hot.

"You cook?" asked Grandma Stesha, looking at Grandpa with astonishment, as though she had never seen him so clearly before. Maybe she hadn't.

Grandpa merely shrugged before wiping his hands on the dishcloth. He glanced over at Reid's plate, with its rapidly disappearing pancakes, and immediately poured more batter onto the hot griddle.

"Yeah, I do," he said finally, serving himself last, sliding two misshapen pancakes onto his chipped plate.

What I remembered with chagrin was this: how I had gotten

up from countless breakfasts, abandoning Mom to clean up after a meal she never ate herself. How I dumped my dirty clothes atop the clean, neatly folded ones in my laundry bin and thought Mom was being shrilly irrational about my not putting away my clothes.

I hadn't even finished my pancake when Grandpa approached me with another, so large it draped over the ends of the spatula. There we were, reaching across the table to help ourselves to the warm syrup, drinking our mugs of freshly ground Kona coffee and hot tea. All of those fixed for our pleasure, placed for our convenience.

"Here," I said, beckoning Grandpa close. "Sit down and eat with us."

Without a word, Mom dragged over a barstool, not caring that it was too high for the table. Just as she was about to take the odd seat for herself, I wriggled onto it, brushing off her protests. Grandma Stesha in the meantime had rearranged the table settings and was now opening the space next to herself. I noticed that. Meanwhile, Reid was fetching Grandpa George a clean fork. In our own ways, none of us saying more than a word or two, we all made room for one another at the table.

Chapter Twenty-Five

L ate that night, Grandpa and I fell into what had become our routine of assembling breakfast baskets and delivering them before everybody roused the next morning. On tomorrow's menu: chocolate–macadamia–graham cracker muffins, apple compote, and homemade granola. We didn't talk. It was enough to stand beside each other, Grandpa fixing me what had become my favorite beverage—freshly ground, rich Kona coffee with a splash of whole milk and coconut syrup—while I spooned thick batter into muffin pans.

Looking more energetic than she had in two weeks, Mom breezed into Grandpa's home, holding not her usual clipboard but a new hot-pink journal, embroidered with a vivacious spray of sunrise-orange orchids.

"It's over," Mom announced as she set the journal on the

counter with a satisfying sound like a single drumbeat that signaled the end of one stanza, the start of another.

I admit: Part of me had been holding out for a miracle, that my parents would get back together. But I didn't contradict Mom, not when I noticed that she had removed both her wedding and engagement rings, and certainly not when she finally looked at peace.

As I was about to fetch the green tea for her, Mom interrupted me: "You know, I think I'll try some decaf coffee myself tonight." So instead I handed her a tiny jug of milk.

"I'm going to find a job," Mom announced purposefully, and opened her journal, the first page labeled in all caps: IDEAS. I had wondered what she'd been up to for the bulk of the day, and now I knew. She was gathering herself together in her Nookery, concocting her famous to-do list, which I never would have guessed could actually make me smile. But I was beaming now. Mom continued, "A fabulous job. I've got a few ideas."

Grandpa nodded proudly at her before he pulled a bag of decaf coffee beans from the refrigerator. "Of course you do. What're you thinking?"

"I could go back to PR," Mom said, and uncapped her pen. "Maybe work at a PR agency, or one of the nonprofits where I've been volunteering for the last couple of years."

Even a tone-deaf person could hear how lackluster Mom sounded as she reviewed the other top contenders for her re-entry into the workforce: marketing at Synergy, project manager at a tech company, account manager at an ad agency. It reminded me of how Jackson had challenged me when I bemoaned the internship at Stone Architects—*Why would you want to work there?* Now I understood. Listening to Mom recite her reasons for why each job made sense, all drily practical without even a suggestion of passion, made me picture a hummingbird caught and caged.

After a moment, Grandpa leaned against the kitchen island and said, "Maybe instead of thinking about what you've done and can do, you should begin with what you love to do. And you've always loved gardening. Creating planters, outdoor spaces, herb gardens. You've done that since you were a little girl."

"Yeah, Mom, you were offered a segment on TV for your container gardening," I said as I opened the oven door and slid the muffin tin inside. "Why don't you create your salad bowls as a business?"

"I can't make a living by potting plants," Mom objected. She flipped to a page scribbled with figures. "The numbers don't work out."

"So design gardens," Grandpa said.

"Then I'd have to get a degree in landscape architecture," Mom said, even as she circled one of the bullets in her journal. "There's so much I don't know. And it's entirely possible that I'll need to get a job before I can go back to school."

"You could work and go to school at the same time," said Grandpa. "People do that all the time. And I could help you."

"How? You've got this inn to run, and the cost of a master's degree . . ." Mom sighed, and her gaze unconsciously slid over to me. I could read the worry in her expression, the trade-off calculations in her mind. How could she pay for her education when we might not be able to afford mine? Mom was going to insist in a thousand different ways that I attend college this fall, employing every bit of persuasion in her arsenal and hocking every one of her possessions to make it happen. But I wasn't willing to add to Mom's burden.

"No censoring, Betsy," said Grandma as she strolled into the house, sweaty in her yoga outfit. For a woman of seventy, my grandmother had an enviable body. She smiled at Grandpa, who grinned back before he filled a glass of ice water for her. "We're just ideating right now."

Between Mom's list of career ideas and her equally long and well-prepared objections, I knew she had brainstormed becoming a landscape architect on her own earlier and rejected it soundly. But why? How many times had I found Mom bent over her horticulture books? How many hours had she spent researching plants for Ginny's dad and his healing garden? And what about all her doodles of gardens I'd find around the house, wallpapering the kitchen bulletin board and bookmarking her cookbooks?

"I have to do something soon." Mom's hands rubbed against her denim skirt.

Perhaps Mom's infamous lists weren't created because she was compulsive. Nor were they only methods to cope with disorganization, as Grandpa told me once. But could they be emergency plans to change a vision of the future Mom had foreseen and didn't like? Perhaps her knee-jerk rejection had nothing to do with the impracticalities of applying to graduate school and everything to do with being fiscally practical to protect us from an impoverished future she saw and didn't want for us.

"Frank Lloyd Wright never got his architecture degree," pointed out Grandpa.

Grandma Stesha wiped the sweat off her forehead and chimed in, "And Bill Gates never got his college degree. Didn't stop them."

Like the other half of a practiced tag team, Grandpa finished, "They both did what they loved, even if people thought they were crazy. And look at them."

Instead of considering other successful people with nontraditional beginnings who had pursued their passions, I studied the ones flanking us: first my grandfather, then my grandmother.

"That's what you both did, isn't it?" I said now. "I mean, look at this place, Grandpa. This is what you've loved doing. Creating places. And taking care of people."

"Oh, this is nothing. Let's keep brainstorming," Grandpa said quietly, but he stirred the still-hot granola on the cookie sheet so vigorously that chubby clusters of oatmeal, honey, and macadamia spilled over the edge.

My eyes widened because for the first time, I saw the likeness between my freewheeling grandfather and my task-oriented mother. "Mom, this is just like you . . . and your healing garden!"

To my ears, Grandma Stesha's sudden intake of breath was as loud as a shouted cry: *Eureka!* But what she murmured softly was this: "Exactly." Her eyes gleamed as she nodded in encouragement at Mom, then beamed at Grandpa with such warmth, Cupid would have blushed, which is precisely what my grandfather did.

"And, Grandma, you love to take care of people, too," I said now, wondering how I had missed that critical heartbeat in her work.

Grandma shrugged, then added humbly, "And travel. I love to travel. That's why my tours are the perfect job for me. You know, when I first started, I thought I'd have enough clients for a trip or two to some Native American medicine men. I never thought that almost twenty-five years later, I'd still be at it and traveling around the world."

Mom picked up a fallen chunk of granola from the counter, popped it into her mouth, and chewed thoughtfully. While she may not have said anything, I could hear her mulling over what we were suggesting: Live your dream.

Could I dare the same?

"You know," Grandma said, nudging Grandpa in the shoulder, "I think we need to take a road trip and show them our favorite place on the island. Tomorrow."

"Where?" I asked.

"It's a surprise," said my grandparents in perfect unison, as though no time or history had separated them at all.

Chapter Twenty-Six

The truck bounced uncomfortably along the bumpy one-lane road that wound past endless fields of—what else?—black lava. Unbothered, as though we were driving on smooth tarmac, Grandpa kept explaining the strict laws that had regulated ancient Hawaii. Taboos had dictated every part of life, from eating to worshipping, marriage to childbirth.

"Break one," Grandpa said, "and the penalty was death."

"Harsh," said Reid. I could tell from the glint in his eye that this tidbit had spurred new thinking for his book.

"You'd have to paddle madly to a Place of Refuge, eluding every single pursuer. That's where we're going this morning, a Place of Refuge," Grandpa said, grinning in the rearview mirror.

"So you could be a coward who flees in the middle of the bloodiest battle in history?" asked Reid.

"Forgiven."

"And all your soldiers are killed because of you?"

"Forgiven." According to our grandfather, Pu'uhonua o Honaunau, now a national park, had been a Place of Refuge where defeated warriors or hardened thieves could undergo a purification ceremony to absolve them of all their wrongdoings if they paddled safely to its shores.

"Whoa," said Reid as he slumped against the car door and began writing madly in his leather journal. His fingers were gripped around his pen so tightly, they looked frostbitten white. I leaned over to peek at what he was writing, but he angled the book so I couldn't read a single word. "Geez, Reid, what's happening to your poor oracle now?"

His response was a wicked cackle. Not comforting.

Before long we reached the sanctuary's parking lot. As we strolled toward the visitor center, Grandma caught my hand just as she stumbled on the uneven asphalt. I grabbed her around the waist to stop her fall.

"Grandma, you okay?" I asked anxiously as Grandpa ran to her side, concerned. No wonder Grandpa was anxious. Regardless of how limber Grandma Stesha was for a woman her age, she really was getting older, and she really was slowing down. How was she going to manage her overseas tours two years from now? Five?

At the stone altar laden with fragrant plumeria and smooth stones, Mom and Reid decided to stay with Grandma when she declared, "I'm sitting down here." Grandpa nodded approvingly.

So it was just my grandfather and I who trekked across the lava rock toward the ocean, as if we were both on a mission for forgiveness.

"Are you sure we're allowed to do this?" I asked, looking around nervously, since I could almost imagine security guards and ghosts of Hawaiians past hauling us to our immediate death. "I feel like we're breaking a hundred taboos."

"Respect this place. That's the only rule that counts," Grandpa answered over his shoulder. "So this particular refuge happened to be reachable only by swimming." He pointed at the bay. "That used to be called the sharks' den."

I shivered, imagining these dark waters infested with all kinds of lurking dangers: man-eating sharks, tentacled jellies, and who knew what other beasties that could bite, attack, and drown a girl. Making my way to the water's edge required my full attention, the black rock was that uneven. I didn't want another lava scrape as a souvenir of my time here.

Up ahead at the point, whitecapped waves crashed over rocks. The water swirled violently below us, and I grabbed Grandpa's hand. He was our family's guardian, who'd brave even the most threatening tsunami waves for any of us. What would compel me to paddle through waves, risk being capsized, flirt a second time with death by drowning?

I knew who I'd risk my life for: my family. My friends. My Jackson.

Boyfriend or friend, I knew I would be Jackson's personal Place of Refuge whenever he needed. There was comfort in owning that. And even more comfort in acknowledging that Jackson would be the same for me. No matter what happened, he would be at my side, supporting me, even at three in the morning. With a hundred percent certainty, I was confident of that.

223

If only I could say the same about my father, but my emotions swirling around him were chaotic, a deadly whirlpool.

"I don't know if I'll ever be able to forgive Dad," I said, feeling guilty and disappointed in myself at the same time.

"Forgiveness is a process, and sometimes it's an entire life's work. What we can aim for is understanding and peace," Grandpa said, gazing over my shoulder. I knew who he was studying: Grandma Stesha.

"How can you even get to peace?" I asked. The surf crashed hard, spraying me with droplets of salt water. I wouldn't have been surprised if the waves had gouged a chunk out of the rock. "Half of the time I'm so mad at Dad for leaving us . . . and right after moving us, too! And what about college? What about Mom and Reid now? And then, other times, I miss him so much."

"We'll figure the college part out, darling. And don't you worry about your mom and Reid. What's more important is that you don't let what your father did eat you forever. I've seen what happens when people let themselves marinate in bitterness."

True, I didn't want to drown in my anger at Dad any more than I wanted my joy to wither because I was so mired in the past: past hurts, past roadblocks, past betrayals. The wind picked up. I shivered but shook my head when Grandpa asked if I wanted to leave. Not yet. I had more questions.

"But what are the steps? How do you get to forgiveness?" I asked, knowing that I sounded like Mom, charting our cross-country move down to the last detail. Look how well those plans had turned out; life and Dad had thwarted her.

Grandpa spread his arms out. "You're already here."

224

"Here?"

He grinned as though he had eavesdropped on my doubt and skepticism.

"Here, as in this place is the destination?" I asked, crossing my arms over my chest. But then I remembered Jackson and his self-assuredness in bucking his family tradition of attending the Naval Academy, defying his father even if he didn't have a step-by-step plan, only a destination point: the life he wanted. Maybe forgiveness was another destination point, and getting there a journey each of us had to take—each a different adventure, each coming with its own threat of shark-infested waters. Each requiring hard paddling through setbacks. And each gifting moments of unexpected beauty.

Perched at the ocean's edge, I breathed in the sea. Here we were, on the Big Island, famous for its mystical healing, standing on top of devastation in a place called forgiveness. It was only because of the volcano's very destructiveness that this otherworldly beauty could exist. I gulped and looked—really looked—at this austere moonscape within a tropical paradise.

Only because Dad had an affair were we here, enjoying Grandpa George's inn.

Dad's affair brought Grandma Stesha back to us.

And healed my relationship with Mom.

And opened the possibility of finding my true passion in life, not the one that had been prepared and handed to me on a silver platter stamped MUIR & SONS.

Grandpa tugged me close. "Forgiving others is easier when I remember that I'm human and stupid, too. I haven't treated the ones I love well all the time. I mean, look at how my revolving door of jobs has impacted your mom and your grandmother. Your mom's so anxious about financial security because I didn't provide that for her."

Now I wrapped my arm around Grandpa's waist and absolved him: "But you provided so much else. You were always there. You still are. And that counts." Smiling up at my grandfather, I announced, as though I were an oracle, "Life is very strange."

"Very."

With my gaze refocused on the frothing ocean, I realized to my complete surprise that I was content. I relished watching love fill every crevice that had separated Grandma from Grandpa, Mom from her mother, and me from mine.

A sense of peace filled me as a burden I hadn't even known I was lugging around released in an enormous wave of relief. Did it matter what had compelled Dad to do what he did? Would I ever know the truth?

Adulterer, liar, cheat.

All those labels could be applied to my father. That was true.

But he was also the father who taught me how to ride a bike after I'd fallen for the thousandth time and was scared to climb back on. Who helped me with my physics homework when no one else could explain optics and Schrödinger's cat in a way I could understand. He threw himself into the lake without hesitation to rescue me when I was drowning, and he camped out in my treehouse every summer, my spider slayer who would sneak up the forbidden food of marshmallows and sugary cereals.

No matter what Dad had done, no matter the choices he had

226

made, I still loved him. He was my father, and that was a destination point I could cling to tightly.

The sun dipped behind a cloud, and the crispness in the air could no longer be called refreshing. I clasped my freezing hands together. Without my needing to ask, Grandpa George slipped his steady hand over mine. As he did, I noticed that the scrapes from my solo bike ride on the volcano were already scabbing over. Without even being aware of it, I had been healing.

Chapter Twenty-Seven

All of us snickered at the name of the inn where we would be staying that night: Napoopoo Plantation. Even Mom chuckled when Reid intoned the name in three different voices, none of which, I'm sure, used the correct Hawaiian pronunciation. I rolled down my window in hopes that I'd catch a whiff of coffee—after all, we were high up in Kona coffee country—but the air that blew back my hair held only a sweet floral scent.

The truck chugged up the steep, plumeria-lined driveway to the five-room inn overlooking the coastline. In advance of opening his bed-and-breakfast, Grandpa had teamed up with a few other inns, so we were able to snag the two vacant rooms at a special price.

The wraparound lanai was painted a sky blue so glossy, I was thankful I wasn't wearing a skirt as I took the stairs. Flip-flops, water shoes, and sandy sneakers lined the steps. A walkie-talkie was propped inside a rattan basket on the small table near the front door. A hand-printed sign leaned against the basket: IF YOU NEED HELP, TUNE TO 2 AND SAY, "ALOHA, DAVE OR WILL."

"Who knew the world could have so many sanctuaries?" I asked Grandpa, already in love with this inn.

Grandma nodded. "And there are so many more to find."

Perhaps it was the day spent at the Place of Refuge or the early evening down at the beach, where we watched a cloud of gemstone fish flicker in the sea. Perhaps it was being full from the fresh ono we bought at the local market and Grandpa grilled for our dinner. Or perhaps it was simply relaxing in the hot tub, watching the sky blaze with stars.

Whatever it was—the sea, the food, the stars—the rest must have freed my mind to brainstorm that night in Kona. Ideas knocked around inside my head. Why not work on the Big Island during my gap year and learn about innkeeping? While these properties were much larger than a treehouse, their charm lay in the specially crafted private and public spaces for the guests: Grandpa's small huts and yoga room, for instance. The tiny sitting area outside the room I shared with Mom and Reid in this inn, fitted with a petite lime-green armchair and a basket of sea glass–colored yarn. There was a ton to learn here about creating a feeling of aloha welcome. So why not ask Grandpa to hire me as one of his helpers? I could prepare and deliver the breakfast baskets for guests and clean their rooms. And then maybe on my days off, I could embark on my own tour of sacred spaces on the island, visiting inns and private residences, waterfalls and refuges.

The last thing I remembered wondering before I drifted off to sleep back in my bed was how I could possibly capture this soul-restorative experience within the four walls of a treehouse.

Before six the next morning, Mom roused us to drive fifteen minutes to a horseshoe bay at the bottom of the hill. There, in their historic refuge from predators, a pod of thirty-some dolphins rested and calved their babies. Across the bay, a stark white monument memorialized the spot where Captain Cook had been murdered. Even paradise and refuges had their shadows, their murky pasts, their sorrows.

Locals, dressed in ratty flip-flops and stained T-shirts, lined the edge of the tiny parking lot and nursed their coffees.

"Have you seen anything?" Mom asked, sidling up to the group as though she were part of their community. These last few weeks hadn't stripped Mom of her ability to make friends with just about anyone. I admired that.

"They've been here for the past couple of days," answered a handsome, white-haired man whose opened aloha shirt showed off some serious chest muscles. His tanned face was the perfect canvas for navy-blue eyes that crinkled appealingly. I could hear Shana as she twirled her hair around her finger while studying this man appraisingly: *You know, for an old guy, Mr. Aloha is pretty hot.*

"Do you see them regularly?" Mom asked, brushing her hair off her face.

Mr. Aloha turned toward her, smiling. "I come here every day when I'm in town to check. You visiting?"

Weird doesn't even describe how strange it was to watch a man flirt with my mother. My grandmother, I noted, didn't find anything uncomfortable in this. She practically shoved Mom into this stranger's muscular arms.

I thought about how unfair I'd been to Mom, accusing her of using the family curse as a lame excuse to let Dad go without a fight. Accusing her of going straight into taskmaster mode, plotting the divorce before Dad had made up his mind. But maybe he had. And maybe Mom was simply stepping aside rather than languishing in unrequited love. Now she was free to find the soul mate who would accept and celebrate her: sixth sense and detailed lists, throw pillows and manic weeding weekends, wild curls, hot temper, and all.

An hour slipped by without any sign of dolphins; it was just a peaceful morning, aside from Reid's dramatic impatient sighs and Mr. Aloha's lengthy conversation with Mom—he was from New York, recently retired from a thirty-year career in banking (*bor-ing!*), and was searching for his next big adventure. Most of the other locals had drifted away, some venturing to a beach farther south, where the dolphins had also been spotted in the past week.

Suddenly, Mr. Aloha leaned a mite closer than necessary to my mother to point out a dolphin surging from the water. "There!"

"What's it doing?" Mom whispered as the dolphin spun in the air before dropping back into the sea.

Mr. Aloha grinned down at her. "Playing."

"Playing," she repeated slowly, as though having a good time was a long-forgotten concept. Even so, her face glowed with the rapture I felt when another dolphin took to the sky, and she missed the appraising *aloooooha!* look the man gave her. I had to glance away quickly; that look reminded me all too painfully of the caressing way Jackson studied me whenever he thought I wasn't paying attention.

Mr. Aloha nodded over to the rocky cove. "Going in?"

"Ohhhh . . ." Mom shook her head, suddenly self-conscious. She waved to the dolphins. "They're so far out. I'm not that good of a swimmer."

"You're not supposed to swim to the dolphins anyway," said Reid as he gestured to a sign requesting that people maintain a fifteen-foot distance from the spinner dolphins.

Mr. Aloha shrugged and explained, "They usually come to us. It's like they want to interact. And if they're asleep, we stay away." Instead of cajoling us to join him, Mr. Aloha crouched to grab his banged-up flippers. "You girls can be like fisher wives and wait for your men to sail back."

That comment rankled almost as much as the truth of his observation: Mom, Grandma, and I were watching from the safety of the shore while Mr. Aloha, Grandpa, and Reid prepared to swim in the cove. Dad would have been the first to frolic with the dolphins had he been here, pressuring Reid and me to join him, rolling his eyes if we didn't.

While Dad didn't believe that people could change, Grandpa did. And I chose to side with my grandfather's philosophy. Ever since my near drowning off Grandpa's houseboat, I've been leery of any body of water—oceans, rivers, ponds, pools. My friends lost count of the number of times I "felt sick" or "had my period" at pool parties and lakeside picnics. The one and only stroke I had mastered was a modified breaststroke where I could keep my face above water.

Reid's and Grandpa's laughter washed over the waves. My lucky brother: He floated free of our history of water-phobia. A dolphin dove near Reid, but my brother didn't shy away, nor did he swim to the safety of the shore. He didn't just stay; he played. In the echo of his laughter, I could almost hear Jackson now— not pushy but confident, the way he had been about my non-existent mountain-biking skills the first time we went: *You can at least try.* Even if Mom, Grandma, and I were scared of the water, we could at least stand at the shoreline and feel the waves on our toes.

"Come on," I said as I headed down the treacherous black rocks for the shore. When Grandma Stesha balked, I said, "Grandma, just because one of our ancestors may or may not have been dunked in water—"

"She was drowned, not dunked. She may or may not have been a witch. That's the only *may or may not*," Grandma Stesha replied, arms crossed. But I noticed that she followed carefully.

"Fine," I said, slowing so Grandma wouldn't rush on the uneven lava. "But that doesn't mean that we're going to drown if we get too near to water."

"You almost did."

I continued to make my deliberate way down, not too proud

to crouch and use my hands for balance. Never again did I want to be a helpless girl who needed to be scooped out of the murky lake because I was too afraid to dunk my head underwater, too afraid to see all the scaries that lurked below the surface, too afraid to learn to swim. I swiveled around to my mother and grandmother, who were following me at a distance, and told them hotly, "History doesn't have to repeat itself."

Support came from an unlikely ally: Mom. She agreed so adamantly—"Reb is right"—that I knew she was talking not only about swimming but our family curse, too. There was a long line of women with sixth senses in our family, and an equally long line of men who had left them. Men who couldn't handle our divining the future and reading their moods and knowing their thoughts. The dissolution of relationships wasn't entirely our fault, nor the men's. Could it be a confluence of everyone's fear of being completely vulnerable and easily hurt?

Mom stood on a bulbous rock with her hand shading her eyes from the sun. She finally said, "We need to know how to swim." Had I been mistaken about Mom yet again—that she was our crossing guard, safety patrol, fun police, not because she was cautious by nature but because protector had become her role in our family?

"Girls, remember who we are!" Grandma Stesha planted her hands on her hips, each foot on a different lava rock.

That was just it. I did remember who I was, finally, after all my denials. I studied my hands, pebbled with volcanic grit, square hands that came from Mom and Grandma. I may have been a Thom Girl, but I was also my mother's daughter. I knew my limits, and I knew when to test them.

I bent down to the cool seawater to wash my hands of rock dust. Without warning, I spun around and flicked first my mother with water, then my grandmother. I grinned as they both squealed. "When we get back home, Mom, we're signing up for swim lessons. That's the first thing I'm going to do in my gap year."

"I'm still not so sure about that," Mom said.

"But I am. I know this is what I'm supposed to do: take a year off, figure out my next step." I straightened, wiped my hands dry on my T-shirt. With Mom's hand clasped in mine, we watched dolphin fins flash above the surf, then vanish, the ocean's answer to a shooting star. "We can take lessons together. It'll be fun."

"You know," Mom said as her eyes sparkled in the healing sun, "your gap year just might be growing on me."

Chapter Twenty-Eight

Telling me that we were leaving for home in two days was easy compared with telling Reid, whose eyes reddened, a hidden volcano of anger. He kicked one of his sneakers so hard, it bounced off the door of our room at the inn, where Mom had taken us for a private talk after dinner.

"I don't want to go to Seattle," Reid said, slumped on his twin bed. His lower lip jutted out like a petulant toddler's.

"I know you don't," Mom soothed. She reached out to stroke Reid's arm, but he flinched away. "But Lewis is our home."

"Dad's in New York," Reid argued.

"But we'd be in New Jersey, not New York."

I didn't want to move back to Seattle any more than Reid did. With my head lowered onto my hands, I slumped on the queen bed I shared with Mom. If anything, heading home felt like a concession of defeat, as though somehow we couldn't hack it in our new lives. Plus, with all my classmates off to college, I was going to feel like a loser, left behind. And worst of all, we would be the gossip du jour among our neighbors and everyone at school, our lives flayed open for dissection. It made me so sick, I crossed my arms over my stomach, thinking about people feasting on every last salacious detail of Dad's affair.

"You move, then!" Reid's eyes flashed hot and he flung his pillow away.

Those could have been my eyes, my frustration, my anger, but after our nights at the kitchen table and our trek through the volcano, I knew how to translate Mom's soft sigh. It was a sigh not of exasperation but of resignation. I could practically hear Mom doing the accounting: her need for home versus our need for Dad. If she thought it'd be best for us, she'd move back to New Jersey, to a house she despised, to a city where she had few friends, to Dad's affair that would be rubbed in her face. That wasn't a sacrifice I wanted Mom to make, nor was it one that Reid should request.

"Reid," I said firmly, crossed the space separating our beds, and placed my foot atop the other sneaker he was preparing to kick. "We're moving back to Seattle because it makes more sense." He started quibbling, but I held his hand. "Mom needs a job, and all her connections are there. And I'll be going home with you."

"You're only saying that because Jackson's in Seattle," Reid said, scowling at me.

"Maybe a little bit," I admitted, "but our home is in Seattle." Only then did I lift my foot off the missile of his sneaker.

Mom chimed in, "It'll all work out." Her laser-beam eyes that never missed anything settled on me. It was disconcerting. No wonder she had needed distance from Grandma Stesha if her every thought could be plumbed so easily. "Even going to the college you really want. If it's Columbia where you want to go, you'll go there. I promise you."

"How can you say that? That it's all going to work out? Huh?" Reid demanded.

"Because it always works out" was my answer, spoken with finality because I knew at a soul-deep level that we had survived the worst ripping apart of our family. Our lives were knitting back together into a different but stunning design of our choosing.

Before Mom or Reid awoke the next morning, I grabbed my journal and ambled outside the inn to the row of whitewashed Adirondack chairs. Under the protective shade of the mango tree, Grandma Stesha was cycling through her morning yoga routine. A strand of gray hair curled in the shape of a heart on her sweaty cheek. I poured two glasses of cucumber-infused water from the pitcher on the table and doodled while Grandma finished. She brought her hands together in a prayer position and lowered them to her heart. Only then did she open her eyes, step off the thick yoga mat, and greet me.

I held out the glass of ice water to her. "Mom said we're going back to Grandpa's today, then back to Seattle the day after."

"It's hard to leave," Grandma said, taking a grateful sip. "But we can always come back."

"You're right," I said, nodding. "We can always come back."

Just as I wanted to get to know my grandfather beyond a make-breakfast-together way, I wanted my understanding of Grandma to be more than a label: tour guide to the weird and the woo-woo. So, like my mother, I asked a question that would invite a deep conversation rather than an exchange of surface niceties: "Grandma, why do you do your tours?"

Without any hesitation, Grandma Stesha plunked herself down in the adjacent chair and replied, "It's my calling. Traveling to some of the most special places in the world while giving people closure on old hurts? Or helping them find meaning in their terrible, horrible lives? Or when terrible things happen to them—tragedies—showing them that there is hope on the other side? This is what I'm meant to do." Grandma Stesha finished her water in three gulps. "Do you know how many people I meet who just float through their days without any real passion? Who are stuck in jobs they hate? I'm lucky to do what I love."

A light breeze blew my hair into my eyes. I brushed the strands back impatiently so I wouldn't miss a single expression on her face. "But how do you know it's your calling?"

"You know. In here." Grandma tapped her heart and then pointed at mine, as though she knew I was asking about myself. "Trust your instinct, Reb. No amount of planning is going to confirm what your gut can, especially when life changes our best, most detailed plans. When your passion and your power collide, that's when you know you're on the right path."

"Passion and power?" I asked, not understanding.

"When what you love intersects with what you're good at. And when that happens, you have to lean into your calling, even if people think you're absolutely crazy."

Matchbox cars raced on the road that ran alongside the meandering coastline. From yesterday's dolphin-watching expedition, I knew the beach was closer than it appeared, a scant ten minutes' drive. Maybe in the same way, what I wanted wasn't impossibly far out of my reach. My passion kept circling me back to my treehouse and the sense of magic and peace I found high in the boughs. If Grandma's calling was to heal people through travel, then I wanted to do the same, but with their homes. I sat up, bolt straight. My calling wasn't to build treehouses but to create special spaces for people to experience the same joy and healing I found in my sacred spot.

Grandma Stesha remained silent even as I felt her watching me carefully, lovingly. She waited, giving me time to find my own way, allowing me to stumble from insight to idea.

"And people find closure on your tours? The meaning of their lives?" I asked, my hands clutching my knees as though my epiphany had knocked me off balance. "Just by traveling?"

"Just by confronting the truth, no matter how hard or uncomfortable it is . . . whether it's hurting someone you love or accepting that a relationship is over or coming to terms with a terrible childhood."

Or having a sixth sense that could predict one version of the future.

I lowered my gaze to my bare feet. Ever since Dad walked

out of my hospital room after my near drowning, I had tried to deny my sixth sense just as much as I had denied that I loved designing intimate treehouses—because I was afraid he would turn from me the way I had seen him dismiss employees, Grandma Stesha, and my own mother. A wind blew a ripe mango off the tree, landing hard at my feet. Startled, I cringed, then bent to pick up the sun-warmed fruit, cupping the egg shape in my hands.

The truth had to be faced: Call it sixth sense, gut instinct, visions, or intuition. Since I started heeding my inner voice, look at all the riches I'd been given. A recuperation on the Big Island with the healing presence of my reunited grandparents. And time to explore a future I wanted to call my own.

"I think you're right," I said as I set the mango on the table between the two of us. My mind swept to Ginny, who hated learning about her future. "But, Grandma, what's the purpose of our intuition? I mean, are we supposed to change fate?"

"I'm not sure about that. What I do know is that we're supposed to listen hard. Be alert when our inner voice tells us we're off course. Our job is to be deliberate about how we live our lives and what we invite into them—the people we choose to spend our time with, the opportunities we choose to take and the ones we choose to let go. For me, I think of intuitions as early warning signals when we need to correct our course."

I took a sip of my water as I thought about Grandma's words. "But what about our visions of other people?"

"We can choose to tell people what our intuition says about them, but ultimately it's their choice about how they want to live." Grandma leaned back and closed her eyes. "We can't take responsibility for what other people decide to do."

I thought about Dad and his choices, made to optimize his happiness alone. The last words I remembered Grandma Stesha saying before she left us—*But, Betsy, isn't it better to know?*—pealed in my memory.

"It really is better to know." So now I asked the question I'd wondered but had been too afraid to ask: "Grandma . . . was it hard to leave us on your trips? We haven't seen you in years!"

Slowly, Grandma Stesha held out her upturned hand, as if she wanted to both receive and support me. I placed my hand atop hers. Our palms touching, she answered: "Leaving you and Reid and your mom, knowing what your father was going to do, was the hardest thing I have ever had to do. But it would have been worse if I had stayed, despising your dad for something he hadn't even done and coming between him and your mother."

I leaned back to study the overhanging branches, dangerously laden with fruit. There was comfort in the image of Dad struggling with his decision and grappling with the unfairness of his actions—no different from the way I was waffling about Jackson. Perhaps deciding to leave us had been the hardest decision Dad had made, too. Perhaps staying would have been worse for reasons I didn't understand now—and might never understand.

Grandma Stesha squeezed my hand tight in both of hers. "I missed you all so much. But I knew I'd come back for good when the time was right."

It helped knowing why Grandma had made her decision to leave us, even if I might have made a different choice. The wind blew, and a handful of mangoes on a branch swayed. Since I wasn't a little girl who was a victim of my circumstances, I stood up, uneasy about remaining underneath this mango bomb of a tree. Grandma mistook that for me leaving: "Reb, I hope you'll forgive me someday."

"Grandma, I'm just moving us to where it's safe," I said, smiling as I held my hand out to help her to her feet. As soon as I saw the tears of relief brightening Grandma's eyes, words flew out of me in an eager, heartfelt rush: "I'd love to go on one of your tours. With you."

With you.

Those were the same warming words Jackson had given me in the bird-watcher's sanctuary: a promise, a plan. Words that made me feel united with him, as if we were stronger together. Words that made me yearn to reach out to him now.

"We'll have to plan that soon, then." Grandma spread her age-spotted hands out in front of herself. "It's getting harder to get around airports. All those lines! And hauling luggage and dealing with clients. My gosh, my clients and their special dietary needs . . ." Mildly exasperated, she shook her head and rolled her eyes.

I could easily envision traveling with Grandma Stesha— sampling spices and produce I'd never encountered before, befriending strangers, all the while weathering stomach woes, high-maintenance tour guests, and lost luggage. Every bit of those experiences, the fateful coincidences and the accidental setbacks, would become our history together.

"I've been thinking it's time to start arranging tours in the

U.S.," said Grandma Stesha as I pulled her chair, then mine, into the sun.

"Like Sedona?" Another wind rattled the branches. I was glad we'd moved, particularly when a green mango fell right where Grandma Stesha had been sitting.

"You listened to yourself," she said, smiling before continuing. "And Santa Fe. Maybe even Seattle."

"Seattle?" I stared at Grandma, shocked, as she refreshed my glass of water. "What's in Seattle?"

"Not what but who. There's a Native American ghost whisperer who a lot of real estate agents hire to clear old houses of spirits."

"For real?"

"For real. And a woman, Belly-button Grandmother. She divines your future through—"

"Your belly button? Really?"

"Really."

A plan began to coalesce as Grandma smiled to herself, reminiscing privately about tours past. Or perhaps she was divining my private brainstorm, this bounty of ideas ripening in my mind. What if I spent my gap year traveling with Grandma, working as her go-to girl? I could deal with people's luggage and complicated dietary requirements. Or I could do reconnaissance work for her stateside tours, researching amazing places to visit in Sedona and Seattle, the way Mom had done for us with her binder of activities. What better way to learn about sacred spaces than to study and see them for myself?

Grandma Stesha leaned closer to me, as if she wanted to

share a secret: "I would love to take you with me to Taktsang Monastery in Bhutan, and Machu Picchu in Peru."

My grandmother's words must have unlocked a secret yearning I hadn't even realized I possessed. "I'd love to see the world with you!"

"Me too." Her face softened with fond memories. "I absolutely adore traveling."

"Why?" I asked.

"Traveling gives me such startling clarity that I can see the life I have . . . versus the life I can choose to create." Grandma Stesha stared out into the vast horizon as if she were brailling all the possibilities as boundless as the sky. She gazed at me fondly. "There are places in this world that are so imbued with spirit, you become rearranged just by breathing the air."

"Rearranged." I breathed in that idea and grinned back at Grandma Stesha, feeling as if I had completed the first expedition of my gap year. "I love that." And because it was a benediction worth repeating, a barometer worth using to measure life, I whispered as I wrote the word in my journal: "Rearranged."

Chapter Twenty-Nine

S tay right there." Mom sprinted toward Grandma and me, sitting in our matching Adirondack chairs. She held a camera in one hand and her hot-pink journal in the other. Then she added in a firmer voice when Grandma started fussing about how she hated having her photo taken, "I hardly have any pictures of you two together."

That was true, but we could change that fact.

"Come on, Grandma, humor us," I said.

The breeze sent Grandma Stesha's long earrings bobbing and blew back her short hair so I could see the fine lines on her beautiful face. A pang clenched my heart; my grandmother really was getting older, and our moments really were finite. Like Mom, I wanted to document this.

"Smile," I ordered as I pressed my cheek against hers and grinned for the camera.

Standing in front of us, Mom looked more carefree than I had ever seen her, dressed in what I recognized as my grandmother's flirty little skirt and vintage Hello Kitty T-shirt.

"Mom, what are you doing in Grandma's clothes?" I asked after what felt like a thousand shots.

"I forgot a change of clothes."

"These are actually your clothes from college," Grandma said, her eyes twinkling. "Don't you remember? I've been borrowing them."

"Those were yours?" I asked in disbelief, unable to recall Mom wearing anything but her boring uniform of boyish khaki pants, a pressed skort or two, and practical flats.

Mom laughed again before she sank onto the grass, legs out and leaning back on her hands. "Your grandmother was always raiding my closet."

"You used to dress so . . . funky," said Grandma, frowning momentarily, as if she, like me, wanted to bomb Mom's conservative wardrobe and start all over. "So think about it this way: They're going back to their rightful owner."

"You know something? I feel like me again." Mom tossed her hair that had air-dried into a mess of curls. Each strand sprang with life, as if glad to be free from the flattening constraints of corporate life. Stay or go? Married or divorced? Maybe those had never been the questions Mom had been asking herself, but this one: Was she Bits or Betsy? Or was she someone else altogether: Elizabeth?

In a funny way, as I touched the sun-warmed pendant from Mom that I had never removed since I found it in New Jersey, I felt like I had reclaimed a part of myself, too. The dreamer who constructed whimsical fairy houses and the bold creator who declared, "I want to build a treehouse." And just possibly the one who said "Why not fate?" when it made no sense to start a relationship at the tail end of my senior year in high school.

I closed my eyes and imagined my life on the trajectory it had been on before everything happened. There it was, the deadening dread of sitting in a birdcage of a cubicle, trapped and unable to fly. No wonder both Grandpa and Grandma had shunned the corporate world, trading steady income for a life of their own authoring. I took a deep breath and let myself speak freely even as I watched for Mom's reaction: "Mom, I don't want to build big, huge corporate buildings."

"Are you sure it's not because you don't like Sam?" she asked, probing.

"It's not that I don't like him; I'm afraid of him!" I said.

Even Mom laughed at that before saying, "I can understand that, but we don't run from anything just because we're scared. We'll talk about different strategies for you to work with people like him, okay?"

"This doesn't have anything to do with me being scared. It's everything to do with me creating what I love." I squeezed Mom on the arm.

Before, she might have argued with me, citing ten different reasons why my decision wasn't prudent. Today, she nodded, respecting my opinion, and opened her journal, which was half full of her thoughts. "You weren't the only one doing some more thinking this morning," she said as she flipped through pages of numbers and sketches, others covered with writing in bold capitals, and still more dotted with long lists of bullets, some circled and crossed off. "I feel like I'm at a standstill."

"Maybe it would help if we made a list of people you could talk to?" Grandma suggested. "How about listing all your mentors? All the people who love you. Like Ethan Cheng, from your first job."

"Oooh," I said, leaning down from my chair to tap Mom's journal. "And his daughter, Syrah. Didn't she want to hire you to make all the centerpieces for some fund-raising event for bone marrow transplants?"

Mom's list grew rapidly, with people added every time we jogged her memory—"Remember your volunteer work with the pediatric camp?" and "How about your college friends?"

"I keep coming back to gardening, decorating, and PR," Mom sighed. "None of them feels exactly right, though."

"Maybe there's something you could do that combines all of them," suggested Grandma, looking at me thoughtfully, expectantly.

I remembered what Grandma had advised me. "Mom, maybe you should think about your passion and power. What you love doing and what you're best at . . ."

Those words—spoken first by Grandma, shared by me with my mother—created an earthquake effect, shaking loose a deep wish I never knew I had. Now I felt compelled to open my own journal. I listened to that urgency.

My gaze fell on sketches of my treehouse and the urban refuge that was the High Line park in Manhattan. Without any plan, without knowing what I'd find, I turned a few pages to the ob-gyn's office, cold and sterile compared with the healing Place of Refuge and the dolphin cove and my grandfather's soulful inn. Past the frayed remains of the pages I had ripped out after my disastrous meeting with Sam Stone, ashamed of my whimsical fairy houses. I flipped back to a study of our backyard: the pergola draped with purple-blossomed wisteria, the sleek fire pit, the stone-paved path. And finally the healing garden.

As these images dangled like loose threads in my mind, the back of my neck prickled, no longer a warning sign of an impending premonition but a welcome inkling of a future I sought.

"Maybe there's something that combines what we all love doing. . . ." Electrified, I had to stand. With my hands on my hips and the breeze playing with my hair, I felt like a sea captain overlooking a coastline that was taking shape, clearer and clearer as I drew close. And there, there it was. Land ahoy. The vision that had been waiting for me all this time. I welcomed it.

"What if one day we created a treehouse sanctuary?" I asked aloud. "Where people could come heal . . . like us? Or people who are recovering from cancer. We could design a place where they'd be nurtured with awesome food. And gardens they could roam and experts to guide their journey? We would pamper them."

It wasn't my globe-trotting grandmother who encouraged me to explore further, but my mom, whom I once believed to be deathly dull. She built on my idea: "We'd want people who couldn't afford fancy spas like Canyon Ranch or Miraval. They'd flock to us to rejuvenate."

Grandma chimed in, "And we'd have a mud bath. Oh! And a labyrinth. Must have a labyrinth."

So in the welcoming space that we created, for a long hour we sketched with our words, painted with our dreams, drew from our experiences. How Mom could design the landscapes, including her fully realized healing garden, and Grandma could supply the wisdom and gurus. Grandpa could oversee the construction. And one day—one day when I had thrown myself into seeing the world and finished my schooling—I could be the architect. Or work alongside an established one, like Peter, as an intern to bring our vision to life sooner.

At last we fell silent, not because we had run out of ideas but because each of us was envisioning this sanctuary that would demand every bit of our talents. For so many years, I had squelched my premonitions, clenching my body against the first sign of them until I ached. Never before had I experienced this flood of belief that I could create my dream, or this surge of passion that made me ache to start building it this moment. Never before had I imagined the pure joy of embracing a future where my skills were aligned with my calling.

"It'd probably cost a ton of money to start this," I said, then pointed out the obvious. "And we don't exactly have the money."

"Yet," said Mom.

Grandma Stesha said, "Plus, we're envisioning. So let's stay in the yes."

Stay in the yes, I thought. Why not? Why not dream boldly because I was so enthralled with this idea? When had I seen

Mom this excited in a long time, too? I said, "It's as if everything has led us to this."

"Maybe it has," Mom said, scribbling in her journal. I peeked. She was brainstorming names for our sanctuary.

"What's going on here?" asked Grandpa, strolling to us with Reid next to him. "Because whatever it is, it looks like some serious subterfuge."

"We're envisioning," I said, repeating my grandmother's word. Then I added the concept my grandfather had introduced to me, "our own Place of Refuge." Gazing at my family now— every last one a dreamer who turned romantic windmill-tilting into a life's work—I knew what to do. I flipped to a fresh page in my journal, smoothed it with the back of my hand, and invoked my mother's favorite magical words: "Let's make a plan."

Chapter Thirty

On the day of our departure, I finally made time to enjoy the swing beside Grandpa's house. I left Mom and Reid on the porch, where they were reviewing the novel growing in the leaves of his leather journal. The seat was so high, I had to hoist myself up with the ropes stringing it to the construction crane. I swayed gently to the chorus of birds and thought about how much I wished Jackson were right here with me. He would have loved how this crane had been repurposed into playground equipment.

I sailed forward as though he had pushed me hard enough that I could fly into the limitless sky. Mom's phone rang. I recognized the high-tech ringtone: Dad.

My heels dug into the macadamia shells beneath the swing, halting my flight. I hadn't spoken to my father or answered any of his texts since we arrived on the Big Island. It wasn't like I was going to ignore Dad forever, I knew that. But as Grandma said, I was incubating my feelings, allowing myself to get stronger before I spoke to him. Reid, on the other hand, must have prepared for this call, because he went straight for Dad's jugular: "I'm not playing football this fall."

Stunned, I swiveled toward the porch to find Reid standing, facing the volcano. When had my little brother gotten so tall? Gone was the little-boy petulance. Now he sounded as sure as a man, looking straight ahead to his future instead of backward at Mom and me for approval.

"No," Reid said firmly, shaking his head as though Dad could see him. "I'm not doing this to get back at you. It's just that football is your sport, not mine."

Whatever Dad said, Reid simply grunted, leaped off the deck, and thrust the phone at me. He muttered, "He wants to talk to you."

Reluctantly, I took the phone, eyeing it as if it was a snake invading Eden. I knew I couldn't put off talking to Dad any longer. But as soon as I heard his boisterous "Rebecca!" as though he believed everything was perfectly wonderful, I wished I hadn't answered.

"So your mom e-mailed that you guys are going to Seattle today," Dad said now. "When are you coming home?"

Home?

That word disrupted the peaceful nirvana I thought I'd attained at the Place of Refuge and triggered all my feelings of revulsion and resentment in one wild rush that left me shaking. Afraid that I was going to fall from the swing, I scooted off and rested against the metal backbone of the heavy crane. What would Dad define as home, now that he had uprooted us? Suddenly, I wanted to punish Dad by telling him that life didn't just go on without him, but life was pretty damn good, thank you. Without him we'd watched dolphins, hiked the volcano, stood on the edge of earth, hung out with my grandparents—

My grandparents.

Our guardians, they strode onto the deck now, hand in hand, a united front of hard-fought love and hard-earned wisdom. I breathed in deeply, remembering what Grandpa had taught me: The path to forgiveness was fraught with hidden crevasses. I remembered what Grandma had shown me: Count all the blessings that have showered upon us because of Dad's affair.

My future was unfettered by anyone's expectations but mine.

Blunt as the truth was, I spoke it the way my brother had: "Lewis is our home, Dad."

"Lewis?"

"Dad, do you really think we're going back to New Jersey?"

"Well, doesn't Columbia start soon?"

I hesitated. Standing up for myself was harder than I had imagined it would be. I wiped one of my sweaty palms on my shorts. Even now I found myself circumnavigating the one subject I needed to discuss forthrightly with him: my gap year.

Dad's vehemence about college was only one reason why I hadn't told him about my plans. More than that, I worried that he'd discard me just as he had discarded Grandma Stesha because she knew his character, and Mom for reasons only he knew. Love me all he wanted, but the truth was, Dad had left us to create the life he desired. It was my turn to architect my own.

I cleared my throat and remembered Jackson's motto: Ask for forgiveness, not permission. At one time, I thought that was the mantra of cheaters to excuse their actions, but now I wondered if it was the rallying cry of explorers who defied conventional lives. So I told my father clearly: "I'm not going to Columbia this year, Dad."

"Oh, you got in touch with UW. Great!"

"No, Dad. I'm taking a gap year."

"Gap year. In my day, that would be called dropping out."

"I'm not dropping out," I said, digging a hole with my foot in the bedding of macadamia shells. "I'm going to be working in my gap year."

Dad's disapproval was distilled down to a single question: "Why would you do this?"

I couldn't believe Dad had the gall to ask me why when he was so obviously the reason. "We don't have the money—"

"I've already paid for your freshman year."

"What about the other three?"

"No problem," he said dismissively, as if what we were discussing was as easily solved as a run to the ATM. At stake today was a quarter million dollars of college tuition, room and board, and books. "We'll figure it out."

We.

But I now knew what "we" meant in my dad's lexicon. "We" meant Mom and me contorting ourselves to do his bidding. But "we" hadn't just done the research. "We" had created a plan.

"I've talked to Financial Aid," I told him. "You make too

much money for me to qualify for aid, even if you and Mom are divorced." There, for the first time, I voiced the very real possibility of a divorce. Dad may have lulled himself into a fantasyland where our family was perfectly fine, but here was the spreadsheet-backed, insomnia-inducing truth: "There's Reid's college tuition, too, and two households now. . . ."

"You're right. That's why your mom's going to have to go back to work," Dad said.

"What happened to giving Mom half your salary into perpetuity?" I asked quietly.

He didn't answer. Dad's reneging on his promise hung over me like toxic volcanic air, corrosive even in its silence. Grandpa had been right; Dad had never intended to honor that blurted generosity.

"She's planning to work," I told him hotly, without thinking. "In fact, we've been talking about creating a treehouse sanctuary together."

Before I finished, I knew I had made a strategic blunder.

"Really?" Dad said, and I could hear him shift into the naysaying business-manager mode with me, since Mom had relinquished that role. "What about the capital outlay? A venture like that will cost millions of dollars. And what does either of you know about managing a project that size? Or running a hotel, for that matter? And what about insurance?"

I grimaced, feeling stupid and interrogated. All I wanted to do was hang up and run away. Mom held out her hand for the phone. Glad to relieve myself of it, I still intended to eavesdrop unabashedly on my parents' conversation. But Reid was spread out on his stomach on the lanai, catatonic. My brother looked dead on the wood slats. I sat beside him and stroked his back.

"Reidster, you okay?" I asked.

He didn't move.

"Reid," I said, rubbing my brother's shoulder. He remained motionless. I looked up at Mom for help, but she was pressing her temples with her index fingers, trembling. Grandma held my mother, murmuring, "You're going to be fine, better than fine."

From deep within, I knew Mom was being nurtured. I turned back to Reid. What did he need to hear? My vision was so clear, so true: Reid shoving open a rusting gate, tall, broad-shouldered, grown up. I bit my lip because I hated seeing his childhood end, but reassurance poured out of me, the truth uncorked: "I am so proud of you."

While I didn't see any movement, I swear I could feel Reid paying keen attention to my words. And where this came from, I don't know—whether from my grandparents or wisdom from all the women before me—but I simply said, "One of the hardest things to do is to speak up. And you spoke up to Dad. You protected yourself, and you were protecting Mom. You are growing up to be such a good man, Reid."

Even as I gifted him with the words he needed, I felt better myself. And behind me, his chorus of support agreed: "You are," and from the steps, as Grandpa sidled over to us, "That's right." Strongest of all was my mother's voice: "So proud."

Chapter Thirty-One

For a full ten minutes, none of us spoke on the lanai, all of us busy with our own thoughts. If I ever needed a sign that I was on the right path with my treehouse sanctuary, now was the time. A sign, give me a sign.

Nothing.

I tightened my arms around my knees where I sat, leaning against one of the sleek wood columns. Dad was right. Given my family's ever-dwindling finances, that sanctuary idea? Utterly dumb as dirt. If we didn't have money for college or Mom's graduate degree, how the hell were we going to fund an entire sanctuary? And what if Dad was right about a gap year being tantamount to dropping out? What if graduate programs for architecture frowned on my decision and this came back to haunt me when I applied in four years?

Interrupting my lengthy list of anxieties, a FedEx

deliveryman lumbered up the driveway toward the lanai, toting a package under his beefy arm. He called, "Hey, I have a package for Rebel Muir. . . ."

With a start, I answered to my nickname for the first time in public. "That's me," I said, self-consciously holding my hands out for the box. My cheeks flushed at the way Mom and Grandma stared at me, dumbfounded. "What?" I asked them, shrugging. "It's what Jackson calls me."

"Rebel?" Mom repeated with a frown.

An enigmatic smile that would have made Mona Lisa proud graced Grandma Stesha's face. She nudged my mother. "Isn't that the name you wanted to give to Reb when she was born?" She cleared her throat. "Ahem, the name I thought she should have?"

"Really?" I asked, stunned, looking from one to the other.

"Your father thought Rebecca sounded more normal," Mom explained. Unconsciously, she ran her fingers through the wild disarray of her hair. Had I unwittingly suppressed my inner Rebel to become a whatever-you-say Rebecca, just as Mom had ironed herself into a trailing spouse who would follow, no matter the personal cost?

With one sentence, Mom showed me how well she knew my truest self, the one who felt called home by a single Rebel, the one who drew villages of fairy dwellings: "We have an hour before we need to leave for the airport."

My leave of absence granted, I sped off for the treehouse where, alone, I ran my finger across the name on the mailing label that I should have been given: *Rebel*. That strange synchronicity was the sign I had been yearning to receive: Welcome home to your life.

Heartened, I pried the package open. Inside was a small box, wrapped in comic paper. This was so classically reduce-reuse-recycle Jackson that I had to smile.

With my breath held, I lifted the box lid and found a round stone, translucent brown quartz, mounted on a leather bracelet, tough yet feminine.

An index card fell from the box, fluttered into my lap. On it, a single quote:

> I deliberately keep a tiny studio.
> I don't want to be an architectural firm.
> I want to remain an artist.
> —Maya Lin

Reading that card, those words, I held my breath, as though listening hard for the Truth. It didn't ring but was silent. Because. What more sign did I need that I had been wrong about Jackson? What more sign did I need that he understood me?

And then I saw his parting wishes, because that was what his words were: *Call me when and if you want. I've never wanted to be anything but good in your life. Be well. Jackson*

Here was a boy who texted me every evening to wish me good night, and first thing in the morning to let me know he was thinking of me. Who messaged me throughout the day with wry postings of all the inane things his dad's clients had said, the ridiculous forms he had to fill out at work—because he wanted to share his life with me. Who only went incommunicado when I asked for space.

Jackson's words, his actions, his gifts: They added up to one succinct message. His was a love beating with life because he knew me. He truly knew me.

I started crying then—for me, for Reid, for Mom. For what we had lost. For what I had given up so easily.

I thought about my list of angels on earth, people who would stand at my side, whether in crisis or in celebration: Ginny and Shana. And Jackson. I could ask any of them: Lend me your strength and wisdom and power. It was what I would do for them, as each of us forged our way in the world, Ginny and Shana unabashedly pursuing baking and photography, and Jackson, who knew the contours of the life he wanted, but not the details. Jackson who was letting me go, but with a last parting gift.

The sobbing intensified, increasing in pitch and volume. Panicked breaths gasped out of me. I couldn't breathe. I couldn't breathe. And then—

I was wrong, so wrong. It wasn't my mom I had heard in my visions. I wept, curled on my side on the slats of old-growth fir I had seen before. It was me, panting, a deer caught in the jagged teeth of a hunter's trap called Truth.

My father ran from Mom instead of facing whatever problems they had, whatever ugliness their perfect veneer of corporate coupledom hid.

I had been no different with Jackson.

The stairs creaked as footsteps thudded up to me. I couldn't lift my head off the hardwood floor that had been worn smooth.

When had I balled up on the ground? Even with my eyes screwed closed, I knew who it was. Who had always come whenever I cried, whether I woke sweat-sodden from a nightmare or was lake-soaked from a near drowning? Who was always at my side, divining when I needed support—when I contemplated sleeping with Jackson because I thought that was what I needed to do to keep him? I knew who was wrapping me in her arms, clicking her tongue sympathetically, breathing out a long "ohhhh" of shared sorrow.

"I hate him. I hate him," I said, not even knowing what words I was uttering.

Mom tightened her strong arms around my shoulders and rocked me. "He's just a man."

"No," I said, wiping at my tears. "Reid's more of a man than Dad."

Mom didn't deny it, not with outright words anyway. Instead, she remained silent, holding me as if she was giving me what strength she had left. Finally, smoothing my hair away from my face, she said, "Your father's only human."

How could I have not known my mother? She wasn't all angry harpy, harsh and strident, able to castrate with a single comment. Nor was she just an overbearing taskmaster of details and to-do lists, managing the minutiae of our lives. How could I have painted her always the villain?

I was weeping so hard, my tears themselves hurt.

"Reb," Mom said softly. "Rebel."

"I broke up with Jackson."

"I know."

I no longer questioned how Mom knew any more than I questioned how I knew that her dreams of Dad were even more troubling than mine. Weary resignation may have tinted the circles under her eyes, but her eyes themselves glowed, undiminished.

"I was scared," I admitted.

"Relationships are scary. Making yourself vulnerable is scary. Letting yourself be known . . . that's the ultimate scary." Mom laughed wryly even as she stroked my hair, comforting me. "I wasn't so good about doing that myself with your father. So, you know, Dad wasn't the only guilty party in our breakup. But, Reb, no matter how scared you are, you can't turn yourself off from love."

I startled at that, and Mom placed her hand on mine as if to tell me to sit still. It was time for both of us to stop winging away. Our hands looked so similar—the same long fingers better suited for women a half foot taller than we were, the same deep life line that curved to our wrists, the same two love lines notching the sides of our hands, beneath our pinkies.

"You can't shut off love just because you're scared some man is going to do to you what your father did to me. Because here's the thing." Mom traced her thumbs gently along the heart line, draining me of my panic. "After all of this, I still believe in love. I do."

"Mom, how can you even say that?" I pulled back but didn't draw away from her touch. "How can you even trust another guy?"

"How can I not? I don't want to go through the rest of my life bitter because of what happened. All shut down because I might be hurt again. I think about how lucky I am that this happened now instead of when I'm sixty."

Silently, I digested what Mom was telling me as a breeze

scuttled inside the treehouse, bringing with it the cleansing scent of hope. I said, "When did Grandma predict this?"

Mom smiled wryly. "Before I married your dad, she asked me if I was really sure of him. She said being pregnant with you wasn't good enough reason to get married at twenty-four. He was so hurt when I told him that."

"You told him?"

"I didn't want any secrets between us. I had seen what happened to my parents when they kept stuff from each other. Your grandma stopped telling Grandpa about the premonitions she had of him, until they stopped talking altogether. She stopped telling him that he was jeopardizing their future by spinning randomly from one pursuit to another. Instead, she started stockpiling savings for herself and me, working as a teacher just for the steady paycheck and benefits. You can't even imagine how silent the house was."

"And then they got divorced," I said, tracing the stitching on the orange pillow.

"Yeah, when I left for college, as if that would make it easier on me. So I didn't want a broken home for the two of you." She laughed ruefully, smoothing down the appliquéd flowers of her own pillow, petal by petal. "The best-laid plans . . . Look where they got me."

As I rubbed the quartz on my new bracelet, I thought about how hurt I had been that Jackson hadn't confided in me about his father's affair. But not once had I considered whether my own omission about my sixth sense would hurt him. After all, that was a huge part of me that I concealed from him.

Mom pulled her knees to her chest, hugging them close. "But then when I got pregnant with Reid, your grandma started freaking out, calling me every day—sometimes up to three times a day—to see if I was okay. Looking at your father with so much . . . distaste. At some point . . ."

"What?"

"She told me that your dad was going to really hurt me."

"Wait, I thought she left because she blamed Dad for me almost drowning? Letting me jump into the lake?"

"That was part of it."

Closely, I watched her. "And you told Dad what she said about him hurting you?"

"No, she did." Another rueful smile. "'Avenging angel' doesn't quite describe what your grandmother looked like."

"Oh . . ."

Outside, the wind chimes sang softly from the eaves. It didn't take a whole lot of imagination to picture Grandma marching up to Dad, eyes crackling fire because she knew that he would uproot and dump Mom, Reid, and me someday. The time line clicked. "Was this around when I almost drowned?"

"Exactly then." Mom kept her eye on the smoky brown quartz, tracing its rounded edge with her finger as though following a path to her past. "She knew she was putting a strain on our marriage."

"And the ironic thing is, Dad basically used Grandma's prediction to excuse what he did. Why didn't you tell me all this before?" But I knew. If it had been hard enough to choose between Columbia and Jackson, how could Mom have chosen between believing her mother's vision and wishing desperately for a solid marriage with Dad? "Mom, it's hard to be an adult."

"No, being an adult is easy; that's biological. It's being emotionally mature that's hard. Some of us never grow up." Mom stood up now, adjusted her skirt that had twisted askew from sitting beside me. "But you? You're doing a fine job of growing into a woman." Her hand lingered on my shoulder. "Just remember two things that I wish someone had told me a long time ago. First, there's a huge difference between being alone and being single. I'll never be alone, not when I have you and Reid, my family, my Booksters. And second, don't ever run from something just because you're afraid. It doesn't matter if it's a boss or a boyfriend."

"But you're the one who kept warning me that Jackson might not be The One."

"No." Mom crouched down beside me to stare into my eyes. "No, that wasn't my intention at all. Or not entirely. In some way this has almost nothing to do with Jackson and everything to do with your being too young to be in such a committed relationship. You've never dated anyone else seriously."

"We've been dating for almost five months!"

Mom laughed at that. "That's a nanosecond compared to a lifetime . . . and even then, you might find out that you hardly know a person. Or yourself."

Like the way we didn't know that Dad was capable of being so duplicitous. Or so miserable.

Mom twined her fingers in my hair. "Frankly, you're too young to know. And you're way too young to get pregnant."

"Mom! Geez."

She shrugged. "That's what I was warning you about all along, you know. We were such babies when we had you. I was just two years out of college. What did we know about raising kids when we hadn't even raised ourselves?"

"We're not you and Dad."

"No," she agreed, and settled back down next to me. "No, you're not, but I believe that at this time in your life, your job is to be selfish."

"Selfish?"

"What I mean is that you go out there and figure out what you're capable of doing. There's so much power in living your life intentionally, knowing what you want, and then pursuing it with all your passion."

"Passion and power. That's exactly what Grandma was telling me," I said softly, thinking about what I could do if pushed to full throttle. What were all of us capable of doing if we used our skills and knowledge and directed our passion and power to a singular path? The image of a grove of treehouses began to shimmer enticingly again.

"But I believe this," Mom said, shifting on her throw pillow. "Jackson is in your life for a reason . . . and there are lessons you're supposed to learn from being with him. No different from your father coming into my life."

"Don't you wish he hadn't?"

"Are you kidding me?" Mom looked me hard in the eye. "That's like saying I wish you hadn't come into my life. Your dad was here to give me you and Reid. Even now, knowing what he'd do to me, even knowing how much I would hurt and how much he would hurt all of us, I would never run from that. Never."

At some point, I must have let go of Jackson's bracelet. Before Mom left, she placed the soft leather in my open hand.

"That's beautiful," she said, smiling down at me.

"It's from Jackson."

"I know." Mom quirked her head to the side, studied the stone, and said, "Smoky quartz. It's a protection stone for endurance and clearing negative energy."

"Really?"

"You know," she said, laughing lightly, "this is an igneous rock—fired from volcano. How perfect is that?"

"Perfect," I agreed.

Alone but not lonely in the treehouse, I felt my family throughout Grandpa's inn, scattered in different buildings but bound together. This was the solace of space that I wanted to create for people who were aching, their lives upended, their hearts shattered.

I flew down the steps and walked into the sun. Basking in the warmth, I turned toward Grandpa's house, only then noticing the red flowering tree by the front porch, its vivid blossom the same one that Mom had given me on our visit to Volcanoes National Park. Wanting to remember the shape of the hardscrabbled tree, I began to sketch it, when Grandpa appeared from the forest, lugging Mom's baggage in one hand, mine in the other.

He smiled at me. "Ready to go?"

I nodded, grinned back at him, and pointed to the tree with my pencil. "What's this tree?"

"The namesake and mascot for this inn," Grandpa answered. He set the luggage down to kneel next to the plant, removing one of its blossoms carefully. "Ohia lehua." Gently, he placed the blossom in my open hand, and as I lifted it to study the unusual spiny flower, Grandpa said, "Hawaiians say their goddess of fire fell in love with a warrior, and when he wouldn't reciprocate her feelings because he loved someone else, she turned him into this tree. The gods felt so sorry for him, they gave him back his true love in the form of this flower."

"So they could be reunited," I said, staring at Grandpa, the fountainhead of the everlasting hope that ran strong in my family. Two decades after their divorce, my grandparents had reunited. What better example of forgiveness could I ask for? Or of enduring love?

Thousands of miles and an ocean may have separated Jackson from me, but I knew he was still connected, parting gift or not. We were in each other's hearts, after all.

My own armor slipped off, shedding like an exoskeleton I had outgrown.

For the first time in what felt like eons, I didn't wait for Jackson to contact me. Instead, I initiated the text: *I'm coming home today. Bracelet is badass. Would love to see you soon . . .*

Part Four

Architecture is about touching a lot
of different parts of our soul.
—*Tom Kundig, architect*

Chapter Thirty-Two

Our plane may not have landed on sun-hot tarmac as it had in Hawaii, but the moment the Bookster mothers encircled Mom, Reid, and me at Sea-Tac Airport, I knew we had reached safety. Here, right here in the port of these warm smiles and welcoming arms, we found another place of refuge.

I had yet to hear back from Jackson, despite checking my phone no fewer than ten times since deplaning. Accompanying my fretting, though, was real peace, because whatever happened, I knew I had held out an olive branch and told him what I wanted.

As our entourage escorted us to the parking garage, I whispered to my mom, "I think we need to repaint our entry." Even though it was admittedly odd, I needed to reclaim our cottage, forcefully and immediately. That urgency had thrummed in me during our entire flight home. What more efficient and budget-happy way to revitalize a space than a fresh color? Besides, I had a feeling on the plane that we might bump into Peter, our architect, at the paint store, too. Who was I to deny the siren call of a premonition?

In any case, I was relieved that Mom didn't question my suggestion as Ginny's mom drove us out of the parking garage. Instead, Mom said, "We have to select new colors for our home. Is that okay with you guys?"

So it was a sign of true friendship that the Bookster moms humored us with a pit stop at our favorite paint store in Seattle before catching the ferry to Lewis Island. Not wanting to rush us, they brought Reid to a coffee shop with a few good-natured comments: "You two are going to have to referee your own color wars!"

Five minutes in the store, and Mom and I had already amassed a wad of paint swatches as thick as any textbook. And still we stood mesmerized before a wall of swatches stamped with blocks of colors, laddered by increasing intensity. While we dithered in front of the paint swatches and I awaited Peter's arrival, I invoked his name: "Well, let's do a Peter."

"What do you mean?" Mom asked, lifting her gaze off the paint chips.

"He'd ask, 'So, how do you want to feel when you walk through the front door?' " I modulated my tone, trying to sound more patient than I was feeling. Personally, I was getting a smidge antsy because Mom, usually decisive, couldn't make up her mind. This was the side effect of a more relaxed mother that I had to accept.

"I'm not sure," Mom answered.

"Energized? Peaceful?"

She blinked fast, bewildered. But then what Mom said next raised a red flag of alarm: "This is your house, Reb."

That admission held an entire world of fear that Dad's abandonment had knocked loose: to be homeless. I knew the words my mom ached to hear, even if she didn't know it: "Mom, this will always be your home, too. Besides, you and Reid are going to live in it by yourselves while I'm in college. It so doesn't make sense to have to repaint it in a year. So you choose."

She nodded, pressed her fingers to her eyes.

"Take your time, Mom," I said, gently. "There's no need to rush. How about I go get the supplies?"

Just as I selected a few aluminum pans, paintbrushes, and roller sponges, I heard my name in the laughter-lush voice I had been expecting: "Reb?" Even so, I wrenched around so fast, I could have left skid marks on the linoleum floor.

Grandma says there are no coincidences in life, only synchronicity. That life presents us with moments and openings that line up in logic-defying ways, and it is our job to be aware of these opportunities and poised to accept them. Pity the list-checker who is so heads-down focused on the what-must-be-done that he misses the what-could-be-now, a twinkling jewel of an unexpected moment.

Like standing with a world-class, hugely respected architect who had turned me on to sustainable building and intimate spaces in the first place.

"Peter!" I cried as I threw my arms around him. He smelled like charcoal pencil and wood shavings the way I remembered.

"You remember Cameron?" Peter said, gesturing to the broad-shouldered young man standing next to him once I let go.

"Cameron?" The last time I saw Peter's nephew, I was ten and he was a scrawny, pimply high school senior. Our remodel project was stuttering to an end because, as Peter had warned Mom, men were better at demolition than at reconstruction. Having none of that, Mom threw an impromptu barbecue for the crew, partly to thank them but mostly to prod them to complete the last fit-and-finish items. The beer was held hostage until the punch list was done. Cameron had joined the job for the final week and was mingling with the men, although they were swigging beer and he was drinking root beer, like me.

Right in front of all those manly men, Mom asked Cameron point-blank, "Are you popular with girls?"

As expected, his face reddened, which only heightened the angry splotchiness of his acne. Even if he wanted to melt in embarrassment, Cameron gave a halfhearted shrug—gracious, considering I wanted to incinerate Mom on the spot.

But Mom's gaze was steady, and her voice was clear with conviction: "High school girls are way too young for you. When you're twenty-four, maybe twenty-five, you won't know what to do with all the women who are after you. Trust me."

A brilliant blush cascaded from Cameron's cheeks to his neck. To my astonishment, his eyes stayed riveted on Mom as if she were an oracle: "Really?"

"I promise."

After that exchange, I was ready to scurry away, embarrassed, when I overheard the foreman say, "Can you imagine if a woman told you that when you were seventeen? Do you know what a difference that could have made?"

"That was a gift," Peter had agreed.

Eight years later, Peter was grayer at the temples but still crinkly-eyed, as though he'd spent the last few years of his life smiling, and Cameron . . . My gosh, was Mom's prediction spot on or what? At twenty-five, Cameron was gorgeous, not because he had a model's chiseled physique but because his stance was so confident and his eyes glittered with humor. I was the gawky one, fidgeting under his scrutiny. When I fumbled my hold on the painting supplies, Cameron caught them with an athlete's grace.

Fortunately, neither Peter nor Cameron did the awkward "Whoa, just look at you—I remember you in pigtails" routine. Instead, Peter asked, "What are you working on these days?" Again, I was struck by how he treated me as though I were one of his contemporaries, so different from Sam Stone.

"I've been sketching," I said.

"Treehouses?"

"You remember?"

"I don't forget special clients." And then, as if there was one special client he wanted to remember in particular, Peter asked even as he scanned the store, "Is your mom here?"

Before I could nod, he'd located Mom. I knew she was as aware of Peter because she was dithering before a panel of lifeless tans that would never, ever disgrace a single millimeter on any wall inside her home.

"Elizabeth," Peter said softly.

Mom's answering grin was one hundred percent heartfelt.

They fell into the hug-or-shake-hands dance, with Mom extending her right hand just as Peter widened his arms. Peter won. He wove his arms over Mom, and she sank into his embrace . . . as though she belonged right there, tucked under his chin.

Shocked, I stood there, watching them even as part of me wanted to turn away. Their undeniable attraction felt so wrong. Would I ever get used to my parents being with other people? But as Mom burst into easy laughter, glowing up at Peter, I finally understood what Jackson had been trying to tell me: Perhaps the affair had been the best thing for Mom and Dad. Perhaps they had married way too young—after all, even if they denied it publicly, they hadn't gotten engaged until Mom was pregnant with me. Who knows what path they would have taken—whether independently or jointly—if that condom on that particular night hadn't broken?

Perhaps now that my parents had grown up, they were better suited to other people.

Perhaps Dad had found his soul mate, and Mom was free to find hers.

Perhaps . . .

"Weird, we were just talking about your mom this morning," Cameron said, his voice deeper than his uncle's. Despite being flustered by the appreciative way Cameron looked at me, I knew all too well what the next dance step was, because Shana had spoken of flirting so often. All I had to do to engage Cameron was angle my head just so, gaze slant-eyed up at him, drop a sentence that was at once witty, to make him laugh, and provocative, to gain his interest.

But there was Jackson.

My Jackson.

Unlike Dad, I didn't want to start anything new, no matter how tempting, no matter how exciting, because I valued what I had—and what I had given up. I intended to fight to win Jackson back, even if it meant possible rejection. Even if everyone was right and we were too young. Even if there was no guarantee that Jackson would forgive me for my abrupt breakup and equally abrupt silence. No matter how many *even if*s my fears and insecurities could manufacture, I would dare to try because Jackson was worth the risk of heartbreak.

"My dad wants a divorce." More than a way to distance myself from flirting with Cameron, these words had to be said. The situation marked clearly. This was fact. "My boyfriend thinks he's crazy."

"For what it's worth, your boyfriend's right. Your dad's crazy." Cameron strode to Mom then, as if to show her exactly how highly he thought of her. She was dwarfed in his tight embrace. And as loudly as Mom had declared way back at that summertime barbecue, he pronounced, "You were right."

Mom knew exactly what he meant, because with unabashed smugness, she poked him in his broad chest and crowed, "I knew it. Women can't keep their hands off you, can they?"

Cameron flushed, but an electric, satisfied grin lit his face.

"I knew it, I knew it." Mom raised her arms in victory and shimmied in the aisle, a public display that would have mortified Dad. She and the Bookster moms danced in the dark, laughed until they wet their pants, but never once had I seen Mom behave this freely with Dad. Maybe Dad had truly loved my mother to Bits, grinding her down in a million ways I had never noticed, smoothing the rough edges of her humble upbringing, but leaving her less than she was. And maybe Mom had been so enamored with the idea of being the upwardly mobile all-American family—the family she didn't have when she was growing up—that she had sacrificed who she was to keep our family together.

Maybe.

Peter grabbed my mother's hand to twirl her to a song no one but they heard. They danced in complete time with each other, anticipating each other's steps. "Elizabeth," he said as if he, for one, saw her whole and cherished every last bit of her, "you knew it."

The moment Mom and Peter's impromptu dance ended, awkwardness rekindled between them. She looked at me meaningfully: Do something. So I gathered all the gumption I could from generations on my maternal side—my grandmother who was afraid of water but led tours around the world, and my mother who was derailed from her life plan but was authoring a new one—and asked, "Peter, would you be able to give me some career advice?"

"I will if I can," he said automatically.

"I need to take a gap year," I said, alert with keen interest. "I'd love your advice about what I should do."

Peter checked his watch, then asked, "Do you have time for coffee now?"

Mom took a half step closer to my side in silent encouragement: *Seize this opportunity.* But the time wasn't right: Reid was exhausted, and the Bookster moms were waiting. More importantly, I knew I wasn't prepared, not for what I had in mind.

So I said, "Actually, we have to run home, but would you have some time this week?"

"I'll make time," Peter promised.

"I'll e-mail you tomorrow morning, then," I said, closing the deal.

Once back at our cottage, Mom fumbled with the house key, her hand shaking so badly we could have been entering Bluebeard's bloody lair haunted with specters of Dad and memories of when we were whole. I thought it would be hard, if not surreal, to walk into our denuded house, stripped of our furniture and family photographs. After all, what we'd left behind were objects that made the house rentable in an impersonal, Pottery Barn–catalog kind of way.

But I was wrong.

One quick scan, and I knew that the Bookster moms hadn't only cleaned, but they'd emptied their own homes to fill ours. New immigrants to our living room included the butter-yellow couch from Ginny's rec room and a heavy coffee table from Shana's family room. And on the mantel was a new framed photograph, the last picture Shana took of Jackson, Reid, Ginny, and me on the back porch, before we left for the airport.

So when we all gathered inside the kitchen, our homecoming felt more like a victory parade than an advance party scouting hostile territory. That, more than anything, convinced me I could never emulate Sam Stone's austere creations, his vast buildings that orphaned their inhabitants. However many awards he won, however lauded he was by peers and panels, he didn't create Home.

"What did you all do?" Mom wondered aloud, tears in her eyes, before the Bookster moms led her into the living room. And as they did, I heard a voice, so beloved to me, from the front door that was still open: "Hey."

"Jackson," I said, and drank him in, grateful that his velvety green eyes looked at me with lambent tenderness.

Where before we would have thrown our arms around each other, kissing hungrily, now he scratched the side of his nose, then his jaw. The moment was awkward, both of us uncertain of our standing: Were we or weren't we? From the living room came the welcome call of Mom's laughter, followed by the answering hoot of her girlfriends' even louder cackles. I peeked around the corner to catch Ginny's mom wriggling suggestively before the fireplace, whipping a pair of lacy undies like a lasso over her head. Mom covered her eyes with her hand.

"Girlfriend, meet your new wardrobe." Shana's mom snickered. "But I like what you're wearing now. So much better than your androgynous, pseudo-guy uniform. So. Much. Better. You know what I always said about Thom. . . ."

"Ack," I muttered, backing up into Jackson's broad chest. Instead of sidling away as a platonic friend might, I stayed in this intimate province of a girlfriend. "You know, there are some things you should never see. Let's go."

Only then did I hold out my hand to him. When his fingers twined with mine, relief and pleasure mingled inside me. Together, we walked down the familiar stone-studded footpath in silence, as though we both knew that our discussion could wait.

Every step toward my treehouse reminded me of the girl I had been, and the woman I wanted to be. It wasn't so much that I threw Mom's caution about the tender age of my heart to the wind. Rather, I leaned into that wind, and trusted what I felt, and relished this second chance. I knew love for what it was: a miracle.

"We're back," I whispered, almost in disbelief, when I pushed the door to my treehouse open and inhaled the scent of fir.

"You doing okay?" Jackson asked as he brushed my hair gently off my face. He hadn't yet kissed me, but now he pulled me into a tight embrace, our bodies touching, chest, hips, thighs. Over his shoulder I noticed my clock, the one that had broken in transit from Lewis Island to New Jersey. Its hands now ticked a steady heartbeat as familiar and comforting as Jackson's voice. The last numbed particle of me melted.

I tilted my face up to his. There, in our kiss, I arrived home.

"We should talk," I said when we finally untangled from each other. Where before those three words felt like the ominous prologue to ending a relationship, now I knew they were precious seeds for a relationship transforming. What better way to deepen love than by talking through molten issues and scorching doubts?

I cleared my throat and kept my preamble short, because the truth never needs embellishment: "So I was thinking . . ."

"Yeah?" Jackson said, his voice such a deep timbre, I could practically feel the reverberations, reminding me of how much I loved that voice. For my next birthday, I made a mental note to ask him to read my favorite children's book, *The Phantom Tollbooth*, aloud to me.

"You, Jackson," I said, "are one good guy."

"Now, that's what I like to hear."

"I think I totally misjudged you."

"Well, I could have told you that."

"It's so nice to hear that you haven't changed," I said, smirking, before continuing: "Whether I want to admit it or not, you have cracked my heart open."

"Is that bad?"

"No, it's good in all the right ways, and don't you get all he-man proud about it. Because I'll tell you . . ." My voice lowered to a whisper, and I pressed closer to him as I stared up, up, up into his rain-forest eyes. "I'm scared that you're going to break my heart."

"You could break mine."

"That's another thing I'm worried about! Everybody says we're too young to know."

Jackson tightened his arms around me as though he were

preventing my free fall into despair. In my mind, I could hear my friends, horrified that I would reveal my heart to a guy in such an open way, make myself this vulnerable. Ginny would say, "You're going to scare him off. Guys can't take depth. You have to keep it light." But Ginny was so afraid that a guy would abandon her unexpectedly, the way her father died without warning, she didn't let a single boy get close. And then there was Shana, who'd already become so jaded from guy after guy collecting her as a blonde trophy that she'd become a player herself, churning through boyfriends the way fashionistas cycled through trends. As much as I loved my friends, it was time to dam their voices and listen to mine.

If I wanted a relationship—a real relationship anchored in knowing each other—then I needed Jackson to understand the entire inventory of my fears. So I forged forward: "And besides, this whole thing with my dad . . . If he can do this—my dad!— it's just hard to put myself out there. I feel like an archery target: Hit me here."

The remarkable thing is, Jackson met me more than half-way. What he said was this: "You hurt me. You didn't even give me a chance. You just ran. And I felt completely powerless. Can I tell you how much I hate that?"

"I'm sorry."

"It's the truth. Everyone hurts each other. Even un-intentionally."

Ignoring nagging questions only made them fester. Look at Dad and his secret misery. So I found myself asking, "Who did you watch the Pleiades with?"

"A buddy of mine from Iowa. Grant." Silence before Jackson surmised: "Is that what it was about? Did you think I was cheating on you?"

No longer did I hedge or prevaricate. I simply admitted, "Yes."

"I wouldn't be with you unless I wanted to be."

"But there's your whole 'Ask for forgiveness, not permission.'"

"Yeah, but I also have a code. And that's to live by my word, which is something my dad doesn't do. And I gave you my word. I want to be with you."

"Oh."

"And only if you want to be with me."

We were quiet then, our silence bridging us rather than distancing us. I swear, I could feel Jackson's explanation nestle in my heart, his words soothing my emotion-raw skin. He pulled me into his arms. I shut my eyes, and there was only Jackson.

"So we'll screw up, and we'll learn," I said softly into his chest.

"That's all we can do, right?" he reminded me.

Even my grandmother would never say that she could predict the future with one hundred percent accuracy. She could only see what might be if we were brave enough to correct our course.

"True." For too long, everyone's voice—Mom's, Ginny's, Shana's, Grandma's, Grandpa's, Dad's, and even Jackson's—had been a roaring current of *Stop dreaming and start believing*, of *Break up because you're too young*, and *Work at a relationship because it's worth it*. However well-intentioned everyone had been, I was drowning in their expectations.

When I focused on what I wanted in my life, it was this: I wanted to build both a treehouse sanctuary and a relationship. Just as much as I wanted a career that could bring to life what I envisioned, I also wanted a guy who treasured who I was, and celebrated what I wanted to do in life, and was proud of what I was capable of doing. And I would commit to the same for him. I wanted both of us to be fully known, wholly accepted, and completely loved.

Despite my nervousness, I told Jackson: "You know, I had a feeling that something awful was going to happen when we moved." Then, staring him in the eye, I told him the entire truth: "I kept hearing crying in my head. Sobbing like you never want to hear in your life."

In the pause that followed, I waited for Jackson's scoff, waited to hear the skeptical *hmmm*. But as he had reminded me, he wasn't my father. Instead, Jackson simply asked, "When did it start?"

So I told him about the moving day from Lewis Island and how a primal weeping had frightened me. But in an odd, indefinable way, I felt I had heard the wailing before, it was that familiar.

"It's so weird," I mulled over with Jackson. "It was kind of like remembering a tune but not the lyrics. But then . . ." I hesitated, uncertain whether he needed to know that it was me who was weeping. But I forced myself to reveal even this because, as

Grandma said, only when we share ourselves, especially at our most vulnerable, can we be fully known: "I broke down on the Big Island, thinking about Mom and Dad. And Grandma and Grandpa, who lost more than twenty years together. Twenty! And us . . . So my vision was about me. Isn't that totally weird?"

There wasn't even a moment of silence before Jackson said, "I believe you."

"Doesn't it creep you out?"

"Nah. Didn't I ever tell you about when I was a baby? How Mom found me in my nursery with a blanket tucked around me, the cradle rocking by itself?"

"By itself? Really?"

"Mom thinks that house was haunted by the world's most protective ghost: Uncle Henry. But she had a little talk with Uncle Henry and told him it was our house. So he left."

"And you believe that? Really believe that?" I asked.

"Why not?"

I had to laugh because my intuition was a secret I had clasped to myself, hiding it as though it were shameful. And here he was, Jackson, with his own ghost story.

"Let's just say, I don't *not* believe it," said Jackson. "What'll creep me out is if you don't tell me where we stand. So, you re-upping for season two, or what?"

Again, I laughed at his apt choice of words. A second chance, another season in this show called Life. I was no prisoner breaking out of jail, no girl imprisoned by a family curse, but a woman who was opening her heart. Warmth filled me, and I felt the final vestige of my armor hit the ground. Jackson knew me. And he wasn't sprinting from me but staying at my side.

"The contract's already in the mail," I told him.

By the time we stopped kissing, the stars glittered high above. They were brighter here, I swore, even than in Volcano, Big Island, population: not many. Perhaps it was *this* island air, perfumed with fresh evergreen trees, that made the stars sparkle with breath-catching exuberance. Or perhaps it was simply the alchemy of a miracle called joy.

Chapter Thirty-Three

O kay, Jackson, time to share Reb!"

As embarrassing as it is to admit, more than Ginny's voice pulled me off Jackson the next morning in the treehouse, where we had been hanging out again. The scent of her baked goods worked its magnetic attraction: Smell brownie, eat brownie.

"Ginny!" I squealed as she swept into the treehouse, decked out in a frilly pink apron and hefting a platter of golden-brown croissants, at least three types of cookies (all appealingly plump), a half dozen brownies, and a miniature red velvet cake. Time apart hadn't diminished the measure of Ginny's love, which came in heaping cups and generous tablespoons in all things delicious. "What are you doing here? I thought school started!"

"Surprise! It starts in two days. Mom changed the flight. We'll leave tomorrow." She set the tray on my window seat and thrust two cookies like olive branches at Jackson before announcing, "But now it's girlfriend time. No boys allowed."

"Ginny!" I protested, but Jackson squeezed my shoulder before he fortified himself with an additional croissant and jogged down the treehouse steps.

"Yo, Reidster!" I heard him call. From my window seat, I made out Reid, scribbling in his journal by himself on the patio. Jackson held a Frisbee overhead, struck a Greek god pose, one hand behind his head, the other outstretched toward the blinding sun.

Without a word, Reid jumped to his feet and assumed the exact same pose. Boys.

"Oh yeah?" Jackson threw the Frisbee lightly at Reid so that it landed on top of his journal.

"Hey, how'd you do that?" Reid demanded.

Ginny drew back from the window and said thoughtfully, "Shana's parents had an emergency. So she had to hold down the office for them; otherwise she'd be here. But she gave me a message."

I had kept both my besties apprised about Jackson and how he had stuck by me all this time. Exasperated, I wondered what Shana might possibly object to now. "What?"

Tossing her hair and jutting one hip out, Ginny mimicked Shana: "Okay, okay, I might have been a little wrong about Jackson."

We laughed at that even as I lingered on the window seat, staring out to the welcoming waters of the Puget Sound. I thought now of Mom's unbridled laughter, her freed curls, her relaxation. If I had been wrong about Mom, did Dad even have an inkling about who Mom really was? Outside, Reid's loud cackle of satisfaction made me smile again. Our father had given up on more than his marriage. He was missing out on this moment, and Mom was right. Life is made of these small moments of togetherness. My anger at my father, to my surprise, had mellowed into pity. I felt sorry for him.

"All I have to say is this: I better get extra credit at school for this spread," said Ginny as she fanned cookies over the hole left by Jackson's excavation of croissants.

"Who do you think is going to eat all this?" I asked.

"Sheesh, with everyone dropping by in the next couple of days, you're going to wish I'd baked even more."

"Like a wake?" I asked sharply, wondering whether moving back home was the wisest decision. After all, Mom and I cherished our privacy. Case in point: treehouse hideaway. "No one died."

"Like a welcoming."

My eyes teared up. Did it really matter whether neighbors and strangers would gossip about us, when the ones who loved us knew the truth?

Ginny plucked a dark-chocolate chunk cookie from the platter and handed it to me. "Try. I added crystallized ginger." Then, like my personal shopper of desserts, she also selected a lemon bar for me. "Or here. Because when life hands you lemons, you make lemon bars. Honestly! As if lemonade is soul food."

"I wish I could cook like you," I said.

"It's just practice."

"Um . . . no. I could practice eight hours every day and never bake like this."

"But you don't want to be a pastry chef." Preparing for a long girl talk, Ginny plunked down on the hardwood floor and patted the spot beside her. "What did your mom say when you told her you aren't going to school this year?"

Before answering, I took a delicate nibble. The sweet heat of the candied ginger enhanced the bittersweet dark chocolate. "Ginny! This is beyond wow! Mom was pretty supportive once she got used to the idea."

"And your dad?"

I shrugged. "Weird, he was the one who said I was basically dropping out and grad schools would look badly on the year."

"So . . . you're changing your mind?"

"Not yet. I've got some ideas about what I want to do."

"Like what?"

No different from needing Jackson to accept me, I didn't want to hide myself from Ginny anymore, either. So I said, "I might help my grandmother with her tours."

"Her woo-woo tours?" An amused smile danced across Ginny's lips. "Really?"

Cookie crumbs littered my lap. I brushed them into my palm. "There might be something to those places she visits. I mean, being on top of the volcano, I definitely felt some energy."

"That would be called molten lava."

At another time I might have laughed it off, agreed with Ginny that "feeling energy" was as ludicrous as hanging out with space aliens. With the cookie crumbs still cupped in my hand, I studied these culinary inventions and asked her, "How do you know what taste combinations work?"

Ginny shrugged. "I just know."

"That's how my intuition works. I just know certain things might happen. Might happen, not will." I lifted my eyes to Ginny, who had crossed her arms. "There's nothing to be scared of by me knowing things."

"Maybe."

"Maybe" was a first, stumbling baby step to accepting me, all of me. I'd take that, but I had to finish saying my piece, too. "I don't need you to believe in my intuition, but I do need you to stop dismissing it in front of me."

Ginny got to her feet then, and I thought she'd leave me in a huff, the way she'd always stormed out when I predicted her future. I worried that she'd stay silent for another three months.

"Where are you going?" I asked her gently.

"To pull out the pies."

"How do you know they're done?" I asked, knowing that she rarely used the oven timer but relied on some inner baker's instinct.

With her back to me, Ginny said, "Okay, I get it. Look, I know you didn't have anything to do with my dad dying, but what you said was so . . . connected. So I still don't want to hear anything that has to do with me, okay?"

"You have my word," I said, because she did.

Chapter Thirty-Four

My hero who listened attentively to my childhood ideas for a treehouse now heard me out again. Peter and I sat across from each other at the long, battered table in his simple but comfortable office in Capitol Hill, a gritty neighborhood in transition in Seattle. Exposed brick walls, floorboards made from recycled gym benches—these materials warmed the space, making it feel authentic and original. What I loved most were the corkboards at each workstation, covered with photographs and paint swatches. I felt at home.

"Tell me what you're thinking," Peter urged, then leaned forward, hands on top of each other.

To prepare for this meeting, I had listed all the ideas I had collected for my gap year. More than that, I had even practiced my preamble.

"After doing some massive soul-searching and brainstorming with my mom and grandma, I know what I'd love to do. I want to create a healing sanctuary of treehouses for people. After what happened to us, we needed a place to retreat and to think clearly. And that's what Grandpa's place on the Big Island provided for us."

At that, Peter nodded in understanding. "But that's not big enough for what you have in mind."

"There are tons of people who could really benefit from a treehouse retreat," I said, my voice becoming impassioned the way Mom's did whenever she discovered an obscure new plant for the garden. I didn't need my notes any longer. My rehearsals—first with Mom, then with Grandpa over the phone—had prepared me well. Besides, in my gut, I knew Peter wouldn't scoff. His first inclination wouldn't be to throw up obstacles, citing finances and insurance and lack of experience.

As I suspected, Peter simply leaned in, nodding. "I know a couple of people who could use it now."

"So for my gap year, I could help my grandmother on her tours to sacred spots for inspiration about what makes a place special. But she wants to wind that part of her business down, so I don't know how many opportunities there'll really be," I said, cupping the heavy handmade teacup Peter had filled with a coconut-infused black tea. "One of her last trips is to Machu Picchu this spring, and possibly Scotland in the summer. What do you think?"

Peter set his glasses on the table. "Traveling is one of the best ways to broaden your creative palette, and if you're looking for spaces that heal people's souls, there's no better way to find them than traveling. You have to experience those places first-hand, stand in their space, breathe in their air. You can't do that through the Internet or a book. Actually, I took a gap year myself between getting my undergraduate and graduate degrees. I traveled around Asia, sketching."

"Sketching what?" I asked, entranced, and leaned closer toward him across the table.

"Like"—he frowned, remembering—"the layers of paint and paper on these ancient walls in China, thousands of years old. And the gorgeous carvings on temple columns in Thailand. And the amazing latticework in Japan. Believe it or not, I still flip through those journals for inspiration. So if you can travel, even in the U.S., that's always a good thing."

The idea of traveling right here in the States sparked a thought. "Grandma said she wanted to start a series of spirituality tours in Santa Fe. Or Sedona. Or right here."

"Oh, sure. There are a bunch of houses in town, Mount Baker, Leschi, and out in Port Townsend and Port Gamble that are haunted. A couple of restaurants in Belltown and Pioneer Square, too. And there's a guy, a tribal elder, who's a ghost whisperer and does exorcism for real estate agents. The newspaper did an article about him a couple of years ago."

"That's what Grandma was saying!"

Peter pulled out his iPhone, not to check his messages but to jot a few notes from our conversation. "Let me send you a list of those places to scout out. And the guy's name. But there are definitely things you could do that are more directly related to

297

architecture, if you wanted. You know, one of my buddies is one of the world's best treehouse builders. Pete did a project for two of my clients."

"Pete? As in Pete Nelson? You know him?" I squealed and set my coffee on the gnarled table so hard, it sloshed. Pete is the I. M. Pei of treehouses, a superstar who builds custom ones for clients around the world. "You really know him?"

"Yeah." Peter laughed. "He lives in Issaquah. I can introduce you to him."

"I might freak him out. I'm, like, his biggest fangirl!" I said. Then, more cautiously, "Do you think he might take on an intern?"

"You'll never know unless you ask." Peter sipped his tiny cup of tea. "One other thing that you could do to prepare yourself is to work on job sites. You know, Cameron paid for college by working for a painting contractor every summer. It's a hard job, super messy, but it pays well."

"I like painting. I can paint!"

"And the best thing would be, you'd get to know how job sites are run. And how to work with a bunch of guys. That's good, practical knowledge for an architect. Are you afraid of heights?"

"What do you mean?"

"You'd have to be okay getting on stilts."

"Stilts?"

"To reach high places. And those industrial-size paint cans are pretty heavy."

I thought about Mom, not much older than I was now, striding into boardrooms with men decades older than herself. She had demoed products, negotiated deals, answered tough questions, whether she was nervous or not. So I swallowed my fear and answered, "I can do it."

"Cool, then, I can give Jerry a call for you," Peter offered. He drummed his fingers on the table. "And then there's always interning with an architect so you know how to run the back office. I could use someone who can do computer work and help write grant proposals."

"What kinds of grants?"

Peter blew out his breath. "Well, we just finished a proposal for an expo in 2015. Living Oceans, so that visitors can learn more about living symbiotically with the sea. And then there was the City 2045 Building Challenge, where architects and city planners were asked to imagine what a city might look like in the future."

"That's so cool," I said, scooting to the edge of my seat. "I would love to work on projects like that! What do you get if you win?"

"Grant money. A lot of architecture work is speculative."

I sat back in my chair, literally rendered speechless by this bounty of opportunities, each sparkling appealingly. How could one conversation open up my life so powerfully?

"There's so much you could do in a year off," Peter said gently, as though he sensed how overwhelmed I felt. "You don't have to know exactly what you're going to do this very second. Sometimes you can just let life unfold."

"Who knew?" I asked, awed.

"And the best part is that you're only beginning. The more people you talk with, the more opportunities you'll have. And the more doors will open to that sanctuary of yours. You'll see."

"But how do I choose? They all sound so amazing."

Peter said, "You'll just know."

There it was again, intuition. I cocked my head to the side. "Come on, really? Leave my whole life up to my gut?"

"The entire creative process—whether you're talking art or writing or scientific research—is based on gut instinct working in tandem with know-how. It's no different from knowing when a space works." Peter shrugged like that was entirely normal, perfectly reasonable, one hundred percent fact. Then his eyes narrowed thoughtfully. I could see the idea coalescing in his mind, gaining traction. "I think you should talk with my friend Sybille. She's the most senior woman in construction in the Northwest. I have a feeling you could learn a lot from her."

I had an image of myself, toes at the edge of a diving platform, the pool far, far below. Even though I trembled, in my mind, my arms spread wide and I made up my mind to jump.

"I have a good feeling about this, too." Warmth and confidence stood alongside my nervousness, sistering me. I told Peter with heartfelt gratitude, "Thank you."

Chapter Thirty-Five

Two short days later—count them, two—I found myself sitting in a corner office on the thirty-fifth floor of a downtown skyscraper, overlooking Elliott Bay. Such was Peter's power to unlock the pearly-white doors of what my research had found to be the premier developer in the Northwest.

While the view was undeniably picturesque, with white ferries trolling the sparkling waters, what caught my eye were all the building materials layered like an archaeological site around me. Piles of seafoam-green glass tiles leaned against tablets of granite and slate. Beside the door, dusty gray-blue stones the size of bricks were roped together with rough jute.

Before I saw Sybille, I heard her footfalls, a purposeful stride as though she had no time to cover all the ground she wanted. Then her question: "Is Reb here?" Suddenly, every one of my insecurities came crashing over me. What was I thinking, borrowing Ginny's frilly black skirt and Shana's crisp white shirt, since all my interview-appropriate clothes were back in New Jersey? I rubbed my sweaty palms frantically down my thighs. Did I look matronly with Mom's red scarf tied around my neck? And what if Sybille was anything like Sam Stone?

As soon as she burst into her office, the warmth of her smile dispelled some of my anxiety. "Excellent, you're on time," she said, and stuck her work-roughened hand out for a firm handshake. "Peter has very good things to say about you."

Though she was dressed nondescriptly in an oversize black fleece jacket over high-waisted mom jeans, there was nothing plain about Sybille's startling green eyes, which peered keenly at me from under her graying bangs. Whatever answer she expected, my nod to polite conversation was decidedly—and almost rudely—short. I couldn't help but blurt, "What's the story behind those?" as I gestured at the stones on the floor.

"Now, that's the kind of question I like," Sybille said, motioning me to kneel beside her. She placed a sturdy hand on the stones. "These were recovered from a village in China. Remember the Three Gorges Dam? How all those villages in China were flooded to build it? Well, there's a guy in town who excavated these footstones before they were lost underwater."

"I love that," I said, and stroked the stones, worn smooth through thousands of years of people treading over them. Where I once might have been content with that nibble of information, I decided to channel my mom and ask for more: "There's so much history here. What are you using them for?"

"A foundation that supports environmental causes is building a new campus here in Seattle. We're putting these in the front courtyard."

"That's the perfect place. Are they going anywhere else?"

"Yeah!" Her eyes glittered with a fervor I understood. "My favorite installation is going to be the walkway to one of the meeting rooms on the campus. We're siting it in this ancient oak tree."

"A treehouse? You're making them a treehouse meeting room?" In my excitement, my voice went cartoon-squeaky. Instead of wallowing in embarrassment, I cleared my throat and took a deep, calming breath. Sybille simply stood near the door, expectantly. Mom would never have allowed a conversation to falter in this silence, nor would Grandma have allowed an opportunity to wither at this critical point in the conversation. Instead, they both would have steered the discussion in a new direction to deepen it, spark new life. And I had prepared for exactly this opening, practicing with Mom all the different ways I could integrate my passion into the interview. "I love treehouses! They're why I want to build a treehouse sanctuary one day for people who need a special place to heal. What do you think?"

"A treehouse sanctuary. Now, that's interesting," Sybille said, beckoning me to the couch at the opposite end of her office. She sat beside me. "Tell me more."

So I sketched my vision: a plot of land sited in quiet woods, location to be determined, peacefulness required, beauty essential. The sanctuary would be filled with treehouses, each unique, ideally ten, but no more than fifteen. Here, people could retreat and rejuvenate, the same way my family had found solace at my grandfather's place on the Big Island. Then I bridged the conversation back to Sybille: "Have you built a lot of treehouses?"

"We've worked with a specialist before and are bringing him back in for this project."

"Pete Nelson?"

Sybille cocked her head, eyebrows lifted as though she was impressed. When she nodded, I practically fell over. There was no way I could contain or secret away my enthusiasm. "I love Pete Nelson's work! Especially his Trillium treehouse—it's like a double-decker bus in the forest! What does the one you're building look like? Do you have plans? Can I see?"

When Sybille stood, laughing, I followed her to her mammoth desk before the wall of windows. I knew it would seem odd, but I had to touch the desk, hewn from a single, massive plank of wood, its edges left raw and natural.

No sooner did Sybille take her seat than she asked, as though proctoring a test, "What do you like about this piece?"

I flushed, surprised I wasn't all that abashed at being caught caressing the wood. Something told me that Sybille herself had done the same when she first met her desk. "I love that it looks real. Like you went to the forest and took a slice out of a fallen tree. Elm, right?"

Nodding, Sybille considered me for a long moment, then swiveled to grab a file from her drawers. As she set the file on the whorled desk, she said, "So, Peter tells me you have questions for your year off from school."

After running through the list of options I'd come up with for my gap year, some with Peter, others with my family, the rest by myself, I admitted my fear: "What if I make a mistake and choose the wrong thing to do?"

"Personally, I've found that even the experiences where you wonder what the hell you're doing eventually help. Actually, especially those hurt-like-hell experiences. You know, I started here as a secretary, but I decided to track down every single doorknob, every single door, every single window used in fifteen job sites. I saved the company a quarter million dollars, even though people thought I should have focused on serving them better coffee."

"That would be challenging."

"Do a job, and do it better than anyone expects: That's my motto. So why choose?" Sybille gestured broadly, as though taking stock of her own life. "Do you have to choose?"

I frowned, blown away by this concept. Her question, simple as it was, opened a new, untraveled path I had never considered. Why choose? Wasn't that what Grandpa had been saying all along—and look at the beautiful mosaic of a life he was crafting. Bits and pieces of experiences spanning construction to art had gone into creating his inn.

A solution began to materialize. I asked, "Do you think I could do a couple of two-month internships? My grandma asked me to help with her business. So I could do some research for her, work for a painter, write grants for Peter, and . . . maybe . . . possibly shadow you?"

"Let me give you some more unsolicited advice." Sybille gave me a meaningful look. "Make it easy for me to hire you."

I swallowed, feeling stupid for being so presumptuous. Why did I suggest working for her? A sheen of sweat began to form on my forehead, and I twisted my hands together. What would Mom do? Or my grandparents? Or Jackson? None of them would back down. Then, I knew. Like Sybille, they would never ask for permission. They would propose.

Refusing to give up what I dearly wanted because I was afraid of rejection or feeling silly, I straightened my back and declared, "I would love to work for you in whatever capacity you needed on a project or two. I work hard and learn fast. So if it's the treehouse or the stone installation or anything else, I am game. My end goal is to learn as much as I can about construction so that I can be the kind of architect who designs the kinds of things you build."

"You know, Peter told me that you'd remind me of myself," Sybille said seriously, leaning back in her chair. "And I think we'll be able to work something out." Pulling open her desk drawer, Sybille grabbed a business card and handed it to me. "Make sure to e-mail me tomorrow first thing. Word to the wise: Do your homework. Tell me what project you want to work on and why."

Grandma Stesha had assured me that opportunities would spring up almost magically when I was on the right track, that there would be an alignment of what I needed and what I was offered. That had sounded too New Age-y for a reformed skeptic like me. Until now. Suddenly, I laughed. I couldn't help it.

"What?" Sybille asked, smiling as though she could read my thoughts.

"I would never have believed this would happen," I said, holding her business card like a lottery ticket. In a way, it was: The riches I'd been given were incalculable. "That I'd be happy to have a gap year."

"I'm one of those people who believe that everything happens for a reason. And that everything works out, but in ways you'd never predict." Sybille leaned toward me. "Peter didn't reveal much about your circumstances, but I can tell you that I couldn't go to college right after high school, either. My family didn't have the money."

"And look at you."

"Yeah," Sybille said, and she scanned her office before resting her gaze on the expansive water view outside. "Life is good, and I would never have believed that I would be sitting here." She smiled at me. "Something tells me that your treehouse sanctuary is going to be very special."

The immensity of how far I'd come, too, struck me hard then. Here I was, stardusted with opportunities just weeks after despairing over my college-less future. Everything—every decision, every heartbreak, every action—had led me to this moment. Not only because of Dad and his affair but because I had listened to my grandparents, learned from my mother, and leaned into the future I wanted.

Laughing again, I shook my head. Even if I were given the chance for a complete redo of the last few weeks, I wouldn't change a thing. The slightest smidge of hesitation, a single retracted choice—all of that would have altered this landscape of opportunities. The sun warmed my face as I stood to shake Sybille's hand, rough and strong. Outside, the sun greeted me even brighter when I pushed through the brushed-steel door of the construction company and strode to the street corner.

Not caring who was staring at me from their office windows, shrugging off the amused smirks of strangers in their cars, I twirled in the middle of the crossroads because here was the beauty of the moment: I got to choose the path I would take.

Back at home, Reid was sprawled on our borrowed couch, writing in his journal as usual. From the kitchen, Ginny's mom exclaimed, "Dis-gust-ing!" Whatever commentary she was providing about my dad—what else would provoke that gut-deep response?—her obvious repulsion was fueling Reid's frenzied writing. He frowned, hunched over his journal, writing in all caps. He wasn't just telling himself a story, I realized. He was escaping our reality. At eleven, where else could he go but in his imagination?

"Reid," I said, but his fingers tightened painfully around his pen, and he refused to look up from his page to acknowledge me.

Our furniture was once again in transit, being trucked back from New Jersey, since Dad had decided to stay in the Manhattan apartment rather than the house. The deep indentations in our carpet here could have been made from the weight of invisible memories pressing down on us. Why was Reid here among the ghost images of our living room instead of upstairs in his bedroom? But then, had I spent much time in my own bedroom since our homecoming? Hadn't I felt shrouded with our old life there? Instead, I found peace in my sanctuary—my treehouse.

A clean start—that's what I wished for Reid and Mom, for all of us. So I marched across the living room, flung the bay windows open, and invited the early-autumn wind inside to cleanse our home. As I gazed out at the unobstructed view of the Puget Sound, I noticed for the first time a birch tree, limbed back brutally. Two years ago, Dad had groused about losing the view because of that damned tree, and on a weekend when Mom was out of town, he had hired an arborist to prune it.

"Hey, Reidster," I said now, shaking his feet lightly. He refused to respond. So, bad big sister, I tickled his soles. He growled. I said, "Come on, let's go to my treehouse."

That unprecedented invitation got his attention. "Really?" He leaped off the couch in his excitement, and guiltily I knew that I could count the number of times he had been inside my treehouse. Reid had been a toddler, barely walking, when my parents remodeled the house. Carving out a private space for him hadn't even been a consideration back then.

We raced down the path to the treehouse, Reid reaching its spiral staircase first. He looked over his shoulder for my permission to continue. When I grinned at him, he walked carefully up the treads, as though I'd retract my invitation, and paused for me at the locked door. I dug the key out of my pocket and handed it to him. His look of pleasure was my reward.

Because I had left the windows cracked open overnight, the treehouse smelled like the surrounding forest, mysterious and verdant. Though empty of furnishings or decorations, my treehouse felt so welcoming, Reid settled himself on the hardwood floor with his journal. He was that eager to escape into the world he was creating. I hurt for him because I didn't want him to flee his life, to write himself into a happier ending. I wanted him to embrace his new life and the promise of all the good things to come. What he needed was the same reassurance Mom had given once upon a time to an insecure boy who grew into his name: Cameron.

"Wait," I said.

Once, a few weeks ago, my brother had nearly begged me to reassure him that everything would be all right. I couldn't provide that comfort to him then, too afraid to tap into my sixth sense, too afraid to step out of the circle of our dad's approval.

For the first time I could remember, I openly courted a vision. Sitting cross-legged with my eyes shut, I slowed my breathing. It felt odd, disconcerting, doing this when I had forcibly and physically stopped myself from seeing anything for a decade. Instead of the aching sensation that hurt me whenever I halted any dreaming, my body lightened and floated.

My breathing eased, and I relaxed even further.

I saw: a young man, his eyes hidden behind highly reflective sunglasses. Gregorian chanting, deep and pensive, gives way to wild cheering. Then, a voice: "In the midnight still, the Oracle of Delphi has been stolen. . . ."

"Sunglasses onstage. Not a good look," I told Reid, who listened to my every word with rapt attention.

"Comic-Con," he whispered, eyes shining. "It's got to be."

"Comic-Con?"

Reid frowned as though I were the biggest idiot on earth. Um, excuse me, who just read one potential future for him? But I kept my mouth shut so that he could enjoy his superior knowledge this once.

"Only the biggest comic-book convention of all time," he said. "Was it a novel I was launching? Or a game?" His eyes widened. "Or a movie?"

"I don't know. It was more of a feeling and just that one image of you."

"Well, look again!"

"I'm not a Magic Eight Ball that you can shake on command."

"Oh," Reid said as his eyes unfocused and he stared off into the space of his vast imagination. I could tell he was writing in his head, spinning some new idea that my vision might have uncorked in him.

For the first time, I could understand why Grandma Stesha's tours to sacred spaces were so oversubscribed that some people waited more than a year to snag a spot. Who wouldn't want a little comfort when every decision we make, every friendship we foster, the relationship we commit to alters our life in some unforeseen way? Even the colleges we choose—and don't choose—change our fate.

The knowledge that I had helped Reid felt more than good, but powerful. No wonder Grandma Stesha said her calling was to heal people. How could I ever question my calling to create sanctuaries for people when I got so much joy from watching

Reid jot a note as though whatever unformed idea he had was so good, so luscious, he had to plant its kernel before he forgot?

That space to create—Virginia Woolf had written about how women needed a room of their own. Grandpa George had created an entire retreat for Grandma Stesha. In the same way, Reid needed a greenhouse for his ideas. He deserved much more than the tiny hobbit house we had left behind, unfinished, in New Jersey. I glanced around this life-size treehouse and knew I could provide a true nesting place for my brother. Now.

Whether I ended up at Columbia or the University of Washington or another college next year, I would be embarking on my own adventure away from home. And afterward there would be graduate school and global travels, where I'd collect ideas for new sanctuaries.

So as Reid threw himself back into his story, I quietly worked the key to the treehouse off my key ring. Despite my stealth when I slid the key beside his hand for him to find later, Reid glanced up at me. "What?"

"You are the keeper of the treehouse now, Reidster," I declared as majestically as any oracle could. Just as I had promised my mother that she would always have a home here, I wanted Reid to know he would always have a private space of his own here, too. "And forever."

"Really?"

"Really. Just remember, I want to be super tall in your book or game or whatever you're creating. And I want to wear motorcycle boots. Because I am the Oracle of Delphi."

Awed, he asked, "How did you know?"

"I just did."

That night, I woke at three, knowing precisely that I had to write to Sam Stone and tell him that his one question had transformed my life.

"Do you always do what everyone tells you to do?" he had asked me in his ice cavern of a corner office, hawk eyes probing me.

The truth was: I had.

Sitting up on my air mattress, my blanket falling to my side, I thought about how I had repressed my own dream of building treehouses. In my heart I had always yearned to design skyscapes, not skyscrapers. Now I leaned over to grab my computer from the floor and powered it on. For a moment I sat before the blank screen, fingers poised over my keyboard. I closed my eyes and welcomed the rush of my lifelong love for small spaces to fill me.

Then I wrote.

Dear Mr. Stone,

If a moment can change a life, then the fifteen minutes with you rearranged me.

You were right.

I have been a "me too—yes, sir—whatever you want" girl my entire life. My decision to go to Columbia was made to please my dad. So was my so-called career aspiration to create corporate offices.

I love intimate spaces, whether treehouses or urban fills or small rooms within large homes. You said in your book that your mission is to create buildings that fill people's spirits. I share that, but in a different way. Creating sanctuaries where people can refuel and recharge—that is my architectural vision and mission.

And that is why I've decided to do something radical because it is time for me to do more than think for myself, but to develop my own creative palette. I am taking a gap year to define what I like in architecture and what, specifically, I want to build. I intend to be as precise and intentional as you are with the buildings you choose to create.

Fired with passion, I wrote about how I believed tiny homes were the answer to conserving resources and creating community. Based on my interviews with Sybille and Peter, I was committed to custom-designing more than treehouses, but an entire sanctuary of them. My fingers flew as I typed, putting words to my vision. Each treehouse would be highly crafted, completely unique. And every last one of them would exude the safety of home and the healing power of sacred space.

Done, I set my computer back on the floor and walked to my window to ponder my words one last time before I sent them. Sam wasn't the only person I had to tell. There was my father. And, in the future, the skeptics. Not everyone would love or respect what I created. Not everyone would approve of my small scope. My father had made his opinion about my tiny aperture quite clear. But these treasure-box spaces, these love nests, would be world-significant to the ones who needed them.

All I had to do was remember Reid's delight as he clutched the key to his adopted treehouse.

Wouldn't my clients' pleasure be what truly mattered?

And wasn't it my personal responsibility to craft a life where my passion merged with my power?

The Oracle of my life had spoken, the words wise and true.

I would tell Dad soon.

Maybe that was all we had to do: listen to our inner voice, the one that warns us when we're on the verge of a bad decision, the one that encourages us to jump even when we're shaking, the one that says open your lips and let the truth soar where it will.

I made my way back to my computer, settled it on my lap, and added one final note to Sam Stone direct from my heart: *Thank you for prodding me past my fears.*

Chapter Thirty-Six

B ouquets of cheery balloons festooned the white columns flanking my uncle's house, where Dad was spending the weekend with us, his first in Seattle since we'd been back. It was Labor Day weekend, and Dad was determined to celebrate my uncle Adam's birthday with overly bright fanfare, as if to signal to Reid and me that we were still his family despite the impending divorce. I appreciated that gesture. Most of all, I appreciated Dad's committing to visit us at least once a month while he resided on the East Coast. So did Reid. As soon as Mom parked in the long driveway, my brother flew out of the car, leaving his overnight bag in the backseat with me.

"Reid!" Mom called, but he was already ringing the doorbell. Slumping back in the driver's seat, she sighed. "I didn't even get to say good-bye."

"It's better for him to feel comfortable here, Babycakes,"

Grandma Stesha said. She had insisted on accompanying us, even though it was a three-hour round-trip commute from the island to Seattle and back. I was glad for that. It hurt to imagine Mom making the trek home by herself.

The massive front door opened, and Dad was there on the wide porch, hugging Reid close to him. Another barnacle of resentment sheared off me; I could see and feel Dad's love for us.

"Okay," Mom said. She nodded resolutely at me in the rear-view mirror. "Good luck talking to your father. Are you sure you don't want me with you?"

"I'm sure," I said. I didn't need Mom to be my messenger or my henchman. What Dad needed to know, I would tell him myself.

Despite her death grip on the steering wheel, as if she were physically restraining herself from following me, Mom nodded. I noticed she didn't drive away, though, but waited in the drive-way. I appreciated the safety net of her presence, too, because as I walked toward Dad, my emotions clustered in a messy knot of anger, disillusionment, resignation, and gladness. Where before I might have drowned in these conflicting emotions, now I knew them for what they were: the mile markers to healing and forgiveness.

Unlike Dad, who had preemptively ended his marriage without giving Mom a second chance, I planned to remain through the weekend and all the other ones when he was in town, despite any confusion I felt. I would stay not just because he was my father. Not just because I didn't want to become one of those bitter people who were desiccated with blame. Not just because I refused to drown in the pain of his past actions. I would stay because I loved him. So Dad was right in a way he had never intended: Some relationships truly are worth the effort, regardless of how difficult they are.

"Guess what? I figured out how to pay for your college," Dad said, beaming at me. So thrilled to share his solution, we stayed on the front porch. "You'll be able to go to Columbia, where you want, no worries at all."

"How?" I asked, as excited as Dad, lulled for a moment back to his vision for my life.

"You can work at Muir and Sons." He looked at me expectantly when I stared at him, speechless. Unable to continue meeting his eyes, I slid my gaze to the Ionic columns with their opulent scrolls flanking the front door. Our gargantuan Grecian temple in New Jersey dwarfed my uncle's. Dad continued, "My brother said you could work as an office assistant every summer, Christmas vacation, and spring break, and then our mother will cover the cost of college."

How easy would it be to capitulate with that succulent carrot of full college tuition dangling before me? Just work at the family business, the very business that Dad had done everything he could to escape—moving us first to Lewis Island, then to Manhattan—so he wouldn't be under the thumb of his mother, wouldn't be compared to his rock star of an older brother.

What would be the price of that?

318

My body answered for me as I listened to the Columbia-to-career lullaby Dad had crooned to me since I was little. My lungs collapsed the way they had the one time I stepped into Stone Architects, starved of oxygen and life and creative force. My heart felt dehydrated. And my legs? They refused to move.

Just a few weeks ago, fear had immobilized me—fear that Mom, Reid, and I would have nothing, fear that we'd never be loved again. And most of all, fear that I would lose Dad forever. But consider all that we had gained: a new life filled with grandparents, a relationship with Jackson that I cherished, and a purpose that resonated with my soul.

My fingers closed over the quartz of enduring love laced to the leather bracelet, the one from Jackson to remind me that I was tough and soulful, strong and feminine, analytical and intuitive all at once. I was neither my father's buttoned-up Rebecca nor my mother's little-girl Reb.

Instead, I was Rebel with a cause. And my cause was to nurture my vision, to architect my life, to create a sanctuary that would provide solace for others.

No way was I giving up my gap year, not when I had five pallets of history-enriched stones to install in a week. And travels to a Peruvian medicine man in April and a Scottish fairy castle in June with my grandmother. Then I had grant proposals to research and write for Peter. A pitch I was delivering tomorrow to shadow the treehouse builder on my weekends. A business plan for the treehouse sanctuary Mom and I were committed to develop together by New Year's Day. And a couple of astronomy courses Jackson and I were looking forward to listen to on road trips to forage for dilapidated barns. And all throughout this year, I had biweekly lunches scheduled with my new mentor and friend, Sybille.

This is what women do when they defend their dream.

They pick their way through their own sharp-edged doubts and swim through the sea of skepticism. They remember that nothing and no one can turn them into powerless victims—not reneged vows, not betrayals that have ricocheted them from one end of the country to the other.

This is what women do.

They speak.

"Dad," I said firmly, "we need to talk."

Startled, Dad stared at me before dropping his eyes. With a hot flash of intuition, I realized that my father might be as scared that I would abandon him as I was of him leaving me forever. Cut off all ties—no more treehouse campouts over the summer, no more holidays, no more conversations.

I empathized. Wasn't that what had worried me all along?

But as Sybille had said, why choose? Why did abandonment have to be the only path to get what we wanted?

"Dad, I appreciate that you want me to go to Columbia, and I appreciate that you're working hard to figure out how to pay for college." Echoing my brother when he advocated for himself, I said, "But Columbia is your dream, not mine."

"Your mother—"

"No, Dad," I said, refusing to let him blame Mom yet again. I stepped away from my role as his accomplice, pitting us, the dynamic duo of fun and games, against Mom, the dour disciplinarian. "Columbia is your alma mater, not hers. But I'm not going to Columbia." I stared Dad down, daring any further challenge on that point. I received none. "And second, I know what I'm doing with my gap year. I'm traveling with Grandma for part of the time, and—"

"This is what you're doing instead of going to college? Skipping off to fairy circles?" His eyes darted to Mom, who was sitting in the car, sending her a silent, urgent look I had seen a thousand times before but had never translated correctly. This was Mom's cue to turn his unspoken wishes into family law. To be the iron fist who doled out decrees and punishment.

Mom didn't budge, nor did I.

Instead, I straightened to my full height and told him, "I'm taking some time to figure out which college will help me build what I want. One day I'm going to create a retreat where people can heal."

Again, Dad's eyes flew to Mom: *Handle this.*

"I thought this through carefully, Dad. While I'm figuring out which college is best for me now that I know what I want to do with my life, I'm going to do a bunch of internships to learn as much as I can. I'd love to talk with Uncle Adam to see if we can work something out that makes sense with what I've already arranged." Then, with the authority of a woman who owned boardroom negotiations and a septuagenarian woman who could still rock motorcycle boots, I declared, "I know one hundred percent that this is what I'm supposed to do."

Silence, and then Dad said, "You sound like your mother."

There was nothing damning about Dad's tone; the words were spoken with his usual mildness, no inflection of accusation. But now I heard the insidious suggestion. Once, the faintest comparison to Mom made me cringe and align myself with rational, logical Dad. I closed my eyes to regain my balance, and the voice I heard was my mother's, strong and true. Her voice that promised Reid and me that she would never abandon us. That we were the foundation and walls that shaped her life. That she still believed in capital *L* Love.

I heard my grandmother: knowing. And my grandfather: believing. And my brother: becoming.

What were those voices if not the sound of unwavering optimism and loyalty, strong and evergreen? And who was I, if not the daughter of my mother, who could envision the future, and my father, who was the visionary CEO?

"Thanks, but actually, Dad . . ." I said, looking with admiration at my mother and grandmother, who were smiling proudly at me from the car. My voice rang with passion and power when I introduced myself to my father: "I sound like me."

Chapter Thirty-Seven

With an expert roll, a wide swath of sunshine streamed across the last wall in the entry until there were no seams separating my brushstrokes from Jackson's. My arms, despite being toned from painting and hauling around heavy cans for a subcontractor over the last month, still ached from reaching overhead for so long. I took a step back to inspect our paint job and nodded, satisfied.

Within the span of two days, our bland white walls, marred with fingerprints and nail holes from our old life, had undergone a colorless-cocoon-to-colorful-butterfly transformation. Mom had chosen well: sunflower yellow to greet us in the entry, Tuscany orange to warm our living room, fern green to encourage new growth in what had been Dad's man cave and was recast as her crafting room. Our home didn't just look different; it had never felt more like us: wild and creative and lush with life.

"What do you think?" Jackson asked as he placed his paint-brush next to mine in the aluminum tray. He stood at my side, arm draped easily around my shoulders.

"I wouldn't want to be anyplace else," I said, and leaned back into him. "Or with anyone else."

He tickled me under my rib cage, and I squealed, laughing as I reared back. Even with paint splotched on my hands and spotting my hair, Jackson looked at me with a warmth that made me snuggle at his side.

"Who would have thought that Dad's leaving us would open all these things of mucho amazingness?" I asked.

"It's syzygy," said Jackson.

"What?"

"When the sun, moon, and earth align. It's happening in your life now."

I loved that image—the celestial bodies of my grandmother returning, my mother healing, my opportunities blooming.

"You know what?" I slipped my hand into Jackson's as easily as we had slipped into each other's lives, ourselves aligning heart, body, soul since the moment we met. The twenty-some years of silent reproach separating Grandpa George and Grandma Stesha could have been healed with words. What was the point of hoarding our appreciation, as if those words were secrets worth keeping? I bumped his hip with mine. "You know what I love about you?"

"You mean, aside from my brawny muscles? And astonishing good looks?"

"Your humility."

Jackson threw back his head then and laughed. Trust me, I appreciated the way his brawny arms pulled me close and his astonishingly good-looking eyes gleamed at me.

"But seriously," I said, "I love how you speak geek. Like, how you can pull bits of random info out of nowhere, and it's . . . perfect."

Jackson tucked me even closer into his side, the way he had that first time in Tuscany, like there was no such thing as too close for comfort, only comfort in closeness. He kissed the top of my head. "Baby, I'll speak geek whenever you want."

"Sweet syzygy, I think he's got it."

"But you . . ." His voice lowered, softened the way it does when he's about to be serious. "What's great about you is how you haven't let all this crap take you down."

Raucous laughter rang from upstairs, where the Bookster moms were repainting Mom's bedroom, accompanied by an intermittent "Stop! Now *I'm* going to pee in my pants!" I peered up at Jackson with a rueful shrug. "Dude, I'm afraid eternal optimism is genetic."

"What do you want to do?" Jackson asked.

"Head for the beach."

Both of us shivered from the cold as we made our way to the water. On the bulkhead of piled boulders, we sat with our shoulders pressed together while we listened to the lapping of seawater.

"My dad still wants me to go to the Naval Academy next year," Jackson said. He fixed me with a piercing gaze. "What do you think I should do?"

I stared out at the vast horizon, pondering the question. Figuring out our calling was something only each of us could do, which might explain why oracles spoke in riddles. It forces those who question their lives to think and imagine and answer for themselves. So instead of telling Jackson what to do, I asked, "What do you want to do? You, not your parents? You, if you could do anything you wanted?"

That, really, was the only series of questions that mattered. And the only answer that counted was knowing our power and following our passion, no matter how crazy and quixotic and impractical it might seem to others, even parents.

Like Grandma Stesha, who could wait all night, all month, even twenty-two years for the right answer, I stayed silent. While I gave Jackson time to reflect, I spiraled back to the Place of Refuge on the Big Island where even the worst traitors were washed clean of their crimes. Whether we hurt the people we loved or careened off course in our lives, there was always the possibility of redemption and forgiveness.

That's what I held on to with my father. That one day I would reach a point of equanimity, achieve true peace with his breaking our family, and forgive him fully. But for now I accepted the détente my father and I had struck: respect. He had stopped questioning my gap year, even though I could still feel his skepticism about my expanding plans for a treehouse sanctuary. (Why stop at one sanctuary? Why not build a series of them, located throughout the world, each with a different cultural bent but with the common thread of healing?)

Jackson said finally, "I don't want to explore what's underwater. I want to know what's up there. I want to study astronomy."

"Of course you do."

"Even if space exploration budgets are being cut."

"For now."

He grinned at me. "You're right. For now."

As the sun dipped beyond the horizon, I brought Jackson's hand to my lips and kissed the middle of his palm. My crimson lipstick left an imprint. Folding his fingers over that kiss, I held his fist tight in my hands, that Ohia bud of love, and reminded him, "Ask for forgiveness, not permission."

We grinned at each other. Then, together, we walked up the stone-paved path that Mom had dug into the dirt one summer and lined with tufts of baby plants that had matured into lush, beautiful ground cover.

Epilogue

A great architect is not made by way of a
brain nearly so much as he is made by
way of a cultivated, enriched heart.
—*Frank Lloyd Wright, architect*

Seven years later...

Even after its grand opening, Toda Vida is a sacred space-in-progress, no different from the clients who've been flocking from around the world to our alpine sanctuary of treehouses for the last three years. Beaten down by breast cancer or broken marriages or a myriad of other woes when they arrive, most have remembered their best selves by the time they leave. Despite the positive reviews Toda Vida has been garnering—which Mom insists on reading verbatim to me over the phone, even if I'm in a studio class or trying to capture some much-needed sleep after my final exams—we'd never claim to heal anyone. Just awaken them to live everything.

"Reb! You up yet?" Mom calls through the closed door of my private treehouse at Toda Vida.

"Hurry!" chimes Grandma Stesha, knocking hard. "It's already ten!"

"Some of us need our beauty sleep," I groan, rolling onto my back to stare out the skylight at the bright morning, flocked with a few clouds. I had insisted that every treehouse in the sanctuary have a skylight for stargazing in bed, one of the most healing and soothing activities, if I say so myself.

Healing is a long, circuitous process. But if my experience over these last seven years means anything at all, what I know is this: Reaching joy is worth slogging through the volcanic terrain of hate, and the badlands of blame, and the deserted island of self-inspection.

"You've got two minutes before we use the master key and pull you out of bed," threatens Mom, but I hear the chuckle in her tone. "So make it easy on everyone and meet us at the Jeep fast."

"You won't need any makeup," Grandma says slyly. "Just your bikini."

As I get out of bed, I hear their footsteps racing down the spiral stairs. What do they have up their sleeves? I make time for one quick yoga sun salutation before I pull on a bathing suit and top it with a T-shirt and a short skirt that flares when I turn. I open the door and behold what we created together, from our imaginations into reality.

Who would have known that Sam Stone, Scary Architect, would like my thank-you-slash-apology letter so much that he would e-mail me throughout my gap year to keep tabs on me? Or that he'd be the one to write a glowing letter of recommendation to Cooper Union, a school in New York that provided me with a full scholarship to its architecture program? Would any of that have happened if life hadn't unfolded the way it did?

So while many of my classmates are celebrating graduation day by traveling the world, I am in the sunlit mountains of New Mexico. In this untamed land of the purest light I have ever seen, I am Home. I hurried to the Jeep, where the women in my tribe are waiting. They smile their secret oracles' smile at me, mysterious and knowing, and Mom drives us toward the Rio Grande. The wild river rages so fiercely, I can hear its operatic rapids from the opened roof of our Jeep.

"What are we doing?" I ask suspiciously as I pull my long hair into a ponytail.

"Something I believe you asked us to do the first time you came out to Ohia," says Grandma Stesha. "I think you insisted."

"But I wanted to stay in Vida for a day, at least . . ."

"Oh, you just want to revel in—what did the *New York Times* say?" Mom gestures like she's waving the memory back into being. "Oh, right. 'Each treehouse, as exquisitely conceived by Rebel Architects, is a unique treasure box, perfect in its simplicity.'"

"My favorite line," adds Grandma, turning from the front passenger seat to wink at me. "'Here, you will reconnect with your inner playfulness, remember what it was like when childhood was simple, and life was only about joy.'"

"They said a lot about the gardens and programs, too," I say because, of course, the article went on to rave about Mom's healing garden filled with medicinal herbs (organic, naturally) and soothing scents. And Grandma's eclectic roster of teachers, from energy readers to nutritionists to soothsayers, curated from years of travels around the world. But our secret, unsung heroes for opening the sanctuary on time and under budget? Grandpa George, who project-managed its creation; Reid, who buffed himself up with manual labor; my father's family business, which built the structures; and my mentor, Peter, who always tells me we're equal partners.

"Let's face it. You just want to get started on phase three of the construction," guesses Mom playfully as she meets my eyes in the rearview mirror. The years since her divorce have been kind to Mom, which isn't to say she hasn't aged. Though her hair may be graying now, and laugh lines may bracket her mouth, I have never seen her look so fit or so free. And a great part of Mom's radiance is thanks to Peter, who's managed to wrangle an engagement ring onto her hand.

"Workaholic." Grandma Stesha sighs. "Obviously, she hasn't taken enough of our life-balance yoga classes."

"Workaholism runs in our family," I tell them.

Which is a good thing, because we still have a ton of work to do—new structures to build, since demand for our facility has outpaced the room space. New gardens to dream up. New programs to offer. New ideas to implement from my backpacking trip through Costa Rica, where architects are testing cutting-edge eco-designs for entire villages. And doesn't a Costa Rican rain forest sound like the perfect location for the next treehouse sanctuary? *Toda Vida: Costa Rica* has a nice ring to it.

As we pull into a graveled driveway, I'm reminded of my grandparents' property on the Big Island, Ohia, sold to fund our desert sanctuary. Saying good-bye to that magical spot nearly broke my heart but, as Grandpa said, "Some things in our lives need to be pruned back, and some things must die."

Grandma had chimed in then, as we closed the front door to the Nookery for the last time: "How else do you clear space for new opportunities? And we just have to have faith that something better is in store for us."

As far as I'm concerned, that's true. Look at my life that's flourished after an unexpected, unwanted pruning.

Like Jackson.

When we both headed our separate ways to different graduate schools three years ago, we had let each other go. It wasn't because our love for each other had faded or that we'd drifted apart. Far from it. When life presented Jackson with the opportunity to work in the Canary Islands, where one of the world's largest telescopes is located, I insisted that he take it. He had to. Meanwhile, I was being pulled around the world for research trips during my breaks.

For people who claim that platonic relationships are impossible or that people can't remain friends with their exes, I have one thing to say: Puh-lease. Look at Mom. While she and Dad aren't exactly BFFs, he and his wife number three have taken Mom and me up on our invitation to visit Toda Vida this summer. After two years of boycotting my treehouse campouts with Dad because they were too bittersweet, I proposed that we change instead to a yearly adventure: rock climbing in the Gunks one summer, canyoneering in Bryce Canyon another. Dad actually accompanied me on a trip to Rwanda. There, we visited a church where two thousand parishioners had been slaughtered, every last one of them. He surprised himself and me by admitting that he could feel the residual horror and sorrow in the ocher building. After we stumbled back into the sunlight, he held me tight and whispered, "I'm sorry." So while people may not make one-eighty changes, transforming dramatically from cynic to believer, for instance, it's completely possible and infinitely probable that we are all able to make small shifts in understanding, small steps toward forgiveness.

Just yesterday Jackson called me, telling me that he wanted to spend a few days here this summer, timed so that we can finally watch the Pleiades meteor shower together. He followed up that conversation with a texted factoid that the star cluster is also known as the Seven Sisters, a perfect symbol for Mom, Grandma, the Bookster moms, Ginny, Shana, and me. That startling fact made my heart bloom in ways that Grandma might call True Love. So you never know. That is the wonderful weirdness of life. The twisting of fate can happen at any given moment and hand-deliver a second chance.

Like now.

Mom speeds past a wooden sign with an etching of a large wave: RIVER RUNS THROUGH IT.

"You are kidding me," I say, whipping around to make sure I had read the sign correctly. "Did that really say 'river-rafting outfitter'?"

My mom and grandmother cackle. To be accurate, they guf-faw, which deteriorates into gasped snorts at the sight of the inflated river rafts tied on top of a fleet of vans. I join in with my own high-pitched hysteria because, really, who would have imagined us—us!?—white-water rafting?

"Our people drown," I finally manage to mumble.

"That's why we've been taking swim lessons for the last seven summers, remember?" says Grandma Stesha smartly before she waves at Grandpa George, Reid, and Peter, who are milling in front of a raft, wet suits on.

"Come on, honey," Mom says, holding my door open for me.

"Hey, isn't that my denim jacket? When did you comman-deer it?" I ask as I check out Mom's outfit, a flirty short skirt and a T-shirt silk-screened with a compass, topped with my favorite, long-lost denim jacket that I haven't seen since the summer our lives were upended.

"I literally just dug it out of a box that must have gotten mis-placed between all the moves."

"Uh-huh."

"And you've got to see this." She unbuttons the front pocket and draws out a river rock, my wishing rock that she had plucked from the shores of our island home so long ago. "Here. For you, again."

"Come on already!" yells Reid, his voice at eighteen deeper now. What I never tell him is that sometimes I miss his boy voice. Every once in a while, I catch a fleeting expression that reminds me of him at ten, which, oddly, makes me love my brother even more. He tips back his baseball cap, embroidered with the title of the novel he's been busy revising: *Delphi*. Mom had those hats made for all of us over Thanksgiving, after Reid snagged one of the best agents in publishing.

Before long, dressed in our wet suits, we join the guys. And let it be known: Armor, whether neoprene or metal, is never a good look.

As brave as I fancy myself, my courage flees when we are deposited at the put-in spot for our raft. Now every warning from our five-minute training session about how the Taos Box is the "most exciting rafting trip" and "*not* for the timid" comes rushing back at me as I stand before the merciless river. My breathing quickens. If anyone so much as brushes against my hand, they'll gag at its clamminess.

How could I have forgotten that the river isn't a swimming pool, still and calm, the only way I like my water? The river is churning with life, its breath the current, its emotions the rapids. This is no docile pony ride at a petting zoo.

"What's the worst that can happen?" the guide asks as he beholds me staring at the raft bobbing madly in the river.

"Drowning!"

"You won't drown. The worst that would most likely happen is you falling in." As if he could picture that scenario all too well, he double-checks my helmet and tightens the chin strap. It's a good thing he hadn't chosen medicine as his vocation; his clinical bedside manner has left me more worried than before. "So just lean back. Don't fight the water."

The last time I had been in open water, nobody noticed that

I was drifting down to the lake's bottom until Dad jumped in to rescue me.

And now it's Mom who hands me an oar.

"You first," she says, gesturing to the raft.

"But you're the wise mother," I retort, gripping the oar tightly. "Aren't you supposed to show me the way?"

"You're young; you'll heal faster."

"You're older and more experienced."

"Watch and learn, then." Mom shoots a cheeky grin at me. Peter holds his hand out to help her board. *Serious. Directed. Goal-oriented.* Those were the words I had heard applied to Mom before the divorce. But now? How would people describe her? Describe any of us?

As if he hears my question, the guide answers, "I've never taught three generations of newbies before. Adventuring must run in your blood."

"It does," Grandma Stesha, Mom, and I say in unison.

Upriver, a raft launches into the water. A woman screams. I shiver, alarmed, until I hear the encore performance: her peal of laughter, a sound that sings of life and fun and adventure.

I close my eyes and consult my heart. My inner voice whispers: *Yes.*

Maybe that's just it. We all have a choice after being hurt by people we love, pummeled by life circumstances we cannot control. We can choose to cower at the river's edge, watching as life sails past us, always the bystander, never the participant. We can shade our eyes and fret about all the untold dangers below the surface. We can play and replay all the warnings we've ever heard.

Or.

Or we can equip ourselves with what we need to survive: wet suit, helmet, a good guide. And our own oar. We can quiet our fears and shore ourselves up: *Enough. This is enough. I have all I need.*

I board.

"See?" says the guide loudly above our exuberant cries after our raft drops precipitously and we are airborne for the first of many long, frightening, exhilarating moments. "Nothing to be scared about."

Yeah, right, I want to correct him, but I'm too busy oaring and clinging and laughing and screaming.

An hour into the rafting trip, the guide tells us that we're all way too dry. So he steers us over to a cliff, some twenty feet high, and asks in half challenge, "Who wants to jump in?"

Grandma, Mom, and I glance at each other swiftly, and our answer can be read in our actions. We clamber out of the raft, one after another, and ascend the narrow trail cut into the hill. Twenty feet seemed a whole lot shorter from the raft than it does standing on the edge of the cliff.

"Who's going in first?" the guide calls from the raft.

"Wait! I need to do something first," I say, and I unzip my wet suit enough to remove the smooth wishing rock from inside my bikini top. I hold that skin-warmed stone to my heart, close my eyes, and lift my head toward the sun. And then, and only then, do I throw my wishing rock, which has journeyed so long and come so far, into the river.

What I wish for, I already have.

I hold my hands out now to my mother on one side and my grandmother on the other. You would think from the matching silhouettes of our shadows that we are sisters.

"Ready?" I ask them.

I don't know if I squeeze their hands or they squeeze mine. Sistered together, side by side, we fly.

Acknowledgments

The last few years have convinced me that I am the luckiest woman to have the friends and family I do . . .

My thanks to Mama and Baba: my parents, who are Love and Strength.

Pete Higgins, Robbie Bach, John "JB" Williams, Craig Beilinson, Mike Wagner, and John Launceford: my guardian angels whose wingbeats sound of beginnings and yes. Lorie Ann Grover, Dia Calhoun, and Sue Lim: my beloved sanctuaries on two continents, always. Sherilyn Anderson, Lauren Stolzman, Molly Goudy, and Ardeth Hollo: my guides, wise and beautiful. Janet Lee Carey and Martha Brockenbrough: my muses, who kindled this book with walks and retreats. And Peter and Jill Rinearson: my innkeepers, who opened their haven to me so I could finish this story.

Deep gratitude to Blaise Goudy, Cindy Edens, Jim Graham,

Lisa Chun, and Josh Brevoort: the creative spirits who shared their love for all things architecture. Pardon any mistakes and creative liberties I took, especially with Columbia University.

Jerre Learned, Michelle Morgan, and Sophia Everett: gorgeous women in the know.

Steven Malk: my champion and warrior whose unrelenting belief in me is oxygen. Alvina Ling, Bethany Strout, Connie Hsu, Megan Tingley, Tracy Shaw, Victoria Stapleton, Zoe Luderitz, Barbara Bakowski, and the entire Little, Brown team: My goodness, how I adore you.

Derek Dohn: my great adventurer of a friend. You are so spy! And Sofia and Tyler: you are my every word. Always.

Discussion Guide

1. At the start of the novel, Reb is a self-proclaimed "Thom girl," conspiring with her father against her mother. Describe how Reb views Elizabeth, including how she is physically characterized. To what extent has Reb's father shaped her view of her mom? Identify several significant moments in the novel where Reb's perception of her mother shifts. How does their relationship change as a result?

2. Jackson's personal motto is "Ask for forgiveness, not permission." How do you interpret this saying? Why does it upset Reb? Describe how her feelings about forgiveness change over the course of the novel. How does Grandpa George's explanation of Hawaii's ancient Places of Refuge influence this change? Do you think it's wise to live by Jackson's motto? Why or why not?

3. The dissolution of her parents' marriage is told from Reb's point of view; however, these events greatly impact her brother, Reid, as well. If Reid were the narrator, how would his age and gender affect the tone of the story? Considering his imaginative prowess, what additional story elements might you expect?

4. "If you cut a part of yourself off—especially to please someone else—do you think that you're really being celebrated for who you are?" Grandma Stesha asks her granddaughter (page 206, chapter 24), called alternately Rebecca, Reb, and Rebel. Describe how each name makes Reb feel and how each variation plays a role in her attempt to please others. How does the

name she ultimately embraces reflect her process of becoming "authentically [her]self" (page 206, chapter 24)?

5. The theme of coming home is prominent as the novel moves from the Muirs' home on Lewis Island to their new home in New Jersey and then to their grandfather's home on the Big Island. Compare and contrast how each setting affects Reb, who has a keen "ability to feel space" (page 45, chapter 5). How does the novel demonstrate that homecoming can be experienced in people as well as places?

6. How does her father's behavior in relationships affect Reb's view of her relationship with Jackson? Are her ensuing actions justified, and to what extent do they mirror her father's? What does this tell you about human nature in the wake of hurt and betrayal?

7. Compare and contrast the characterizations of Peter Nakamura and Sam Stone. How do the architects' differing philosophies represent both sides of Reb's internal conflict? How does each philosophy shape the career path on which Reb ultimately finds herself?

8. Reb struggles to accept her gift of intuition. What prompts her to begin to trust it? How does "heeding [her] inner voice" (page 241, chapter 28) affect the story? Would you consider Reb's inner voice a supernatural power? Have you had moments of intuition similar to Reb's, and if so what do you make of them?

9. "Everywhere I looked, verdant green bloomed in lavish defiance of the very real, very persistent volcanic threat underneath us" (page 188, chapter 21). Explain the symbolic significance of

the landscape on the Big Island. What does it teach Reb about the aftermaths of devastation in her own life?

10. Reread the epigraphs that introduce the book's four parts. How does each architectural quotation speak to the section it precedes? Do you believe that architecture—the art of designing and building structures—is an apt metaphor for life? Explain your thinking.

11. Keeping in mind the relationship Reb and the women in her family have with water, study the cover of Return to Me. What mood does the image evoke? What is the significance of this image to the meaning of the novel as a whole?

12. What was your initial interpretation of the title Return to Me? After finishing the novel, what additional meaning does the title have for you?

13. Return to Me is largely about discovering your calling: "when what you love intersects with what you're good at" (page 240, chapter 28). Take some time to ponder this question: Where do your passion and power collide?

Turn the page for a sneak peek
of Shana's story!

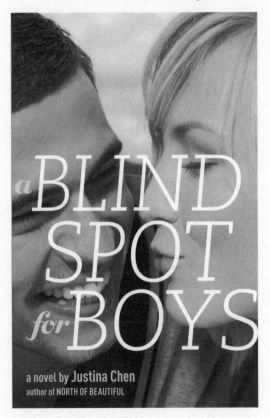

Available August 2014

Chapter One

I f you want to see the world with fresh eyes, haul yourself off to the Gum Wall in Pike Place Market. At least that's what Dad said twelve years ago when he brought me to the brick wall studded with spat-out, stretched-thin, and air-hardened wads of gum. Thousands of pieces. Hundreds of thousands. Both of us were armed with cameras for my first photo safari. His was a heavy Leica with a powerful telephoto lens, mine a red point-and-shoot I'd inherited from him, not some chubby plastic toy.

Back for what must have been my thirty-sixth trip to this weirdly mesmerizing wall, I still felt vaguely nauseous as I looked at all that petrified gum. I sighed, restless from fifteen minutes of positioning my tripod and another five waiting around for the perfect light. Last night, Dad had suggested the wall might make the perfect addition to my college application portfolio. He was right. After all, what's more unique and memorable than the Gum Wall? But then Dad begged off this morning—yet another panicked SOS call to our family business, Paradise Pest Control—leaving me to face the gum alone.

The morning sun had yet to trace its way over the alley. I shifted my weight and fiddled with my camera some more. Patience has never been my virtue, which could be a slight problem. My favorite photographers talk about being on constant alert for that split second when the ordinary transforms into the extraordinary. Until my portfolio review a few months ago, I thought I'd captured plenty of those moments: my grandparents holding hands, gnarled fingers interlaced, during their fifty-sixth and final anniversary together. The sunburst of disbelief on my mother's face a moment after her only game-winning goal in her adult soccer league. The first grin from the guy who stole my heart...

Stop, I told myself whenever my thoughts slid back to the boy who ruined me for love: Dominick Adler, Crew Boy, Mr. Yesterday. *Stop*.

As if my thought had conjured Dom himself, my heart lurched as it had done for the past year whenever I glimpsed a black Gore-Tex jacket. Always thinking, hoping, believing it might be—

I lifted my camera, tripod and all, and zoomed in on disappointment.

Not Dom.

Just a balding middle-aged man venturing down to the market for first dibs on fresh fish and flowers. Of course. Dom, a.k.a. Mr. Wrong—wrong boy, wrong time, wrong place—was in California, interrupting the best years of his post-college life, not to mention my love life, to create some rescue-the-rat cell phone game. A game, excuse me, I had inspired after telling him about an impossibly huge alpha rat that had outwitted Dad's traps and bait for months. A drop of rain hit my head as if I needed a reminder that Crew Boy had washed himself of me seven months ago. And that was precisely what I should do with this inscrutable Sphinx of a Gum Wall, all come hither but never revealing its secrets.

But I couldn't bail on the wall, not when I needed an iconic shot. The associate director of admissions at Cornish College had said as much with my portfolio laid flat in front of her. "Your photos of street fashion are really good, and good makes you pause," she had said after a close look at nine of what I thought were my best shots. "But a great photo knocks your heart open. So give some thought to that. What knocks your heart open?"

I didn't have to think; I knew. But it wasn't like I could exactly call Dom up and ask to take a series of portraits of him, not when he'd been black-ops incommunicado for more than half a year.

The Gum Wall, I figured, at least forced a reaction. So I spent another couple of minutes fussing with my tripod. The sky, though, remained stubbornly dark.

Time to face facts: This scouting trip, like every other boy after Dom, was a total bust. I was about to lean down to unscrew my camera off the tripod when the clouds parted. Through the cracked gray sky came a luminous ray of sunlight. The Gum Wall glowed with an otherworldly translucence. Right then, I could almost believe in miracles.

The decisive moment, that's what Henri Cartier-Bresson, who pioneered street photography, called it. The fractional instant when a moment's significance comes into sharp focus. And there it was at last: my decisive moment.

I crouched down to my tripod, perfectly and painstakingly positioned, already savoring my photograph.

"Whoa! Behind you!" a voice called above the whirring of bicycle wheels that turned to a squeal of mad braking.

Startled, I lost my balance, jostled the tripod, and only at the last second caught one of its legs before my camera could smash onto the asphalt. I wasn't so lucky. My elbows broke my fall. I gasped in pain. Not that I cared, because a cloud scuttled across the sky. The fleeting light vanished. The colors of the Gum Wall muted. My knock-your-heart-open moment was gone.

—⚡—

"Are you kidding me?" I wailed in earsplitting frustration as I scrambled off the ground and checked my camera—thankfully, fine. My elbows, not so much. They burned. Even worse, the fall had ripped a hole in my favorite sweater, cashmere and scavenged for three bucks at a rummage sale.

"You okay?" asked the moment destroyer.

Only then did I lift my glare to a dark-haired boy with Mount Everest for a nose, jagged as if the bridge had been broken and haphazardly reset. Twice. I pointed the tripod accusingly at him. Everest was about to see some volcanic action. "You ruined my shot. Didn't you see me?"

"I thought I had enough clearance, but then you...and your..." said the guy, waving at the general vicinity of my bottom.

"My what?"

"Well"—he cleared his throat and shifted on his mountain bike—"you got in my way."

My eyebrows lifted. *I got in his way?*

He rubbed the side of his nose. "Can you take it now?"

I jabbed the tripod toward the cloud-filled sky. "The sun's gone."

"It'll be back."

"You're not from around here, are you?"

"Not yet. I'm Quattro."

Quattro, what kind of name was that? Then, I guessed, "Oh, the fourth."

A startled look crossed his face as though he wasn't used to girls with healthy gray matter. I smiled sweetly back at him. *Hello, yes, welcome to my brain.* With slightly narrowed eyes, Quattro inspected me as though he was recalibrating his first impression of me. I stared back at him. Mistake. He swung one leg over the bike, propping up the kickstand as if he'd been invited to stay.

I sighed. Here we go again. Why does the right trifecta of hair, height, and hamstrings give me the illusion of being more attractive than I am? It was more than a little annoying, especially after last night, when Brian Winston—senior at a rival high school and latest post-Dom conquest—lunged at me as if three dates qualified him for a free pass to my paradise. Sorry, despite my everchanging stable of guys, I am virginal as fresh snow. Shocking, isn't it? It was to Brian. And to Dom. And all the boys in between.

I quickly unscrewed my camera off the tripod, which should have been universal sign language for *Sorry, but this chicky babe isn't interested.* But did Quattro catch the hint? No. He said, "I'm visiting UW. What do you think about it?"

This guy was harder to lose than a case of lice. But thanks to hot summers toiling at my family business, deploying pest control techniques on rats, wasps, bedbugs, and other vermin alongside my twin brothers and Dad, I knew exactly how to handle this situation.

I assessed Quattro with an expert and clinical eye: nearly my height, at just over five seven. Brown hair streaked with gold. The poor guy must have been color-blind. What other possible explanation could there have been for pairing purple shorts with red sneakers from Japan and an orange Polarfleece pullover? It was almost tragic how much he clashed. My eyes widened. The pullover hugged the lines of his V-shaped torso closely. Much too closely for an off-the-rack purchase.

"You didn't actually have that *tailored*, did you?" I couldn't help asking him, as I gestured at his chest. His barrel-shaped chest.

Quattro had the grace to flush as he plucked at the fabric. "Oh, this? Let's just say my kid sister's life goal is to be on *Project Runway.* She raids my closet for"—he made quote marks with his fingers—" 'practice.' You should see what she's done to some of my jeans."

In spite of myself, I laughed and watched his eyes slide down to my mouth as I knew they would. I could practically hear my best friend, Reb, teasing me: *Man magnet!* Quattro was more appealing than I had first thought. Just as I was trying to decide whether to retort or retreat, the sun reappeared.

"Lo and behold," said Quattro, his eyes gleaming with a

decidedly self-satisfied look. The light illuminated his cheek-bones, so chiseled Michelangelo might have used him as a model. I blinked, stunned.

Lo and behold, indeed.

Lifting the camera before the quirk in his lips could vanish, I zoomed in on hazel eyes that tilted at a beguiling angle that I hadn't noticed either. Hazel eyes framed in criminally long lashes. Hazel eyes that were rapidly narrowing at me.

I snapped a few shots in quick succession.

"Hey, who said you could take my picture?" Quattro demanded before he wrenched around to face the wall.

But he *owed* me. I moved in to capture his profile. He was the one who'd ruined my perfect shot, gone in a flash of an instant.

"I hate having my picture taken," he confessed, his steady gaze meeting mine through the viewfinder.

Damn it if I didn't see a hairline crack of vulnerability when he self-consciously rubbed his nose. His beakish nose. A flush of embarrassment colored his cheeks. Guilt flushed mine. I lowered my camera. I could empathize. When I was in second grade, my feet sprouted to women's size eights, which was traumatic enough since I kept tripping over them. I didn't need my older brothers to call me Bigfoot or joke that I had mistakenly swallowed one of Jack's magic beans to make me more self-conscious than I already was.

"I wasn't taking a picture of *you*," I said before adding guiltily, "per se."

"Really."

I held my camera in front of my chest. "It's for my blog."

"A blog? Don't you need some kind of a release form? Or my consent?"

"I've never needed—"

"What blog?"

"*TurnStyle*."

His expression began at startled and skidded toward fascinated. A girl could float away from an admiring look like that. The set of his lips softened. "No kidding."

Him? A follower of street fashion? Not a chance. He was obviously about to feed me a line. Even though I'd pretty much heard them all, I leaned my weight back on one foot and waited. Impress me, O Color-Challenged One.

But then Quattro said unexpectedly, "My sister reads you. Religiously."

"Really?" I frowned.

"Seriously. Kylie's going to think I met a rock star. But I wouldn't have guessed you'd be into fashion."

I crossed my arms over my chest, now acutely aware of the hole in my oversize sweater and the messy ponytail I'd tucked into a faded black baseball cap. While this was my uniform as a photographer, nothing flashy to draw attention to me, Quattro with his precious watch and designer sneakers would never understand that I had to go thrifting for my wardrobe. Trolling Goodwill and garage sales for clothes is much cooler when it's a choice, not a necessity. So I've made it my personal mission to help girls see that style has nothing to do with the shopping mall. Not quite a save-the-world ambition, but it was mine. I tightened my grip on the camera.

Lifting my chin, I clarified, "Street fashion."

"Okay."

I appreciated that he didn't ply me with a lame compliment, especially the one usually dropped on me: *You should be in front of the camera, not behind it.*

Instead, Quattro said, "Bacon maple bars."

"What?"

"My modeling fee." His expression was dead serious. "They've got to be on the menu wherever you're taking me."

"I don't pay modeling fees. And gross, you don't actually eat those, do you?"

"Well, yeah. Bacon. Maple syrup. Deep-fried dough. You know you want one. So . . . ?"

"I'm not hunting for doughnuts with you."

"Nothing to hunt. Voodoo Doughnut in Portland."

Voodoo. A small smile played on my lips as I recognized the name. More accurately, I recognized their most infamous offering, shaped like a certain male appendage. Luckily, before I could point that out, Quattro jabbed his thumb southward and asked, "Want to go?"

"It's a three-hour drive each way. Seriously?"

He looked stricken. "It's not a drive. It's a pilgrimage."

Despite my best intentions, his words made me laugh again. Then I scrutinized him, really scrutinized him: His fashion taste was questionable, but he was funny, smart, and buff—his-muscles-had-muscles kind of buff. A sly whisper insinuated itself into my head: *And best of all, he's from out of town.* Which meant there'd be no possibility of a relationship, no drama, no trauma. I was officially between boys. So what was wrong with a little harmless flirting?

"Afraid?" he challenged me, lifting his eyebrows.

That did it. No boy was calling me a boot-quaker. So I said, "You're on. Voodoo Doughnut. Tomorrow."